CAMBODIA NOIR

A NOVEL

NICK SEELEY

SCRIBNER

NEW YORK   LONDON   TORONTO   SYDNEY   NEW DELHI

Scribner
An Imprint of Simon & Schuster, Inc.
1230 Avenue of the Americas
New York, NY 10020

First Scribner hardcover edition March 2016

SCRIBNER and design are registered trademarks of The Gale Group, Inc., used under license by Simon & Schuster, Inc., the publisher of this work.

For information about special discounts for bulk purchases, please contact Simon & Schuster Special Sales at 1-866-506-1949 or business@simonandschuster.com.

The Simon & Schuster Speakers Bureau can bring authors to your live event. For more information or to book an event, contact the Simon & Schuster Speakers Bureau at 1-866-248-3049 or visit our website at www.simonspeakers.com.

Interior design by Maura Fadden Rosenthal

Manufactured in the United States of America

10 9 8 7 6 5 4 3 2 1

Library of Congress Control Number: 2015023691

ISBN 978-1-5011-0608-8
ISBN 978-1-5011-0610-1 (ebook)

For Kate, who made it possible.

D I A R Y

June 28, 2003

Airports kill me.

I need to stop thinking about Paris, which is close to impossible at the best of times. But in the farthest wing of Frankfurt terminal, a couple of hours before dawn, as I'm waiting for a plane to carry me away to a city whose name I cannot properly pronounce . . . well, it's a terrible place to be alone with one's thoughts. The lights went dim sometime after two, taking the incessant chatter of Sky News with them, so I have no way of knowing quite what time it is. It feels like the heat's gone, too, and I'm sitting wrapped like a bonbon in souvenir scarves, scribbling nonsense.

For the first hour or so I kept my eyes closed and tried to picture beautiful things: the quiet terraces of Machu Picchu at dawn, or the minarets of Istanbul from the window of a descending plane. But all I could see were the catacombs, with their walls of silent skulls and femurs. In the air-conditioned chill, I felt like I was still down there, rubbing elbows with six million Parisian dead. It was peaceful. No war or massacre filled these halls with bones: they were carted here at night to clear out the city's teeming cemeteries. In one spot, where the remains didn't quite reach the low ceiling, someone had installed electric lamps on a wire, so you could see how far back the charnel house went: row upon row upon row, under glowing bulbs that swept into the dark like the lights of the Vincent Thomas Bridge. . . .

That's when I smelled it: that perfume, like copper and roses, saturating the air around me, and my eyes snapped open. There was no one there, of course: just an airport, scented with nothing but industrial-strength cleanser and heartbreaking loneliness.

I have to think about something else!

Write something. Anything . . . eeny-meeny-miney-moe . . .

Keeping this journal is supposed to . . . I don't know, make me aware or mindful or something. These days I'm not certain that's such a good idea. A lot of my life would be better off forgotten. Perhaps I can find a certain ink that will fade, slowly, into the cream of the paper, taking all my history with it. Or just a marker: I can be like the post office girls in the war, inking out indiscretions from soldiers' mash notes and love letters. My diary will read like the NSA's Greatest Hits: page after page of neat black lines.

I've written things here I've never said out loud, things I've barely dared to think. Surely I could put down why I had to leave Paris?

But you would just think I was being ridiculous. Someday you'll read this, laughing, shaking your head at the silly girl you used to be. You'll wrack your brain, totally unable to imagine where you were when you wrote it, or what you might have been thinking.

Isn't that what I'm hoping for, really, as I fill these blank pages? They hold the promise of that day: when I will be long gone, and you will have forgotten what it's like to be haunted.

WILL

I used to be good at this goddamn job.

Most guys act like there's some big secret to shooting news, but that's bullshit: 90 percent of everything is just being there. I was always there. I don't buy the superstitions, the prayers or the signs and portents crap, but I had something: luck, a nose for it—whatever. Blood hit the street, I was the first one with a camera out.

Now I'm stumbling downstairs at 5:00 a.m., wondering how much I've missed. I should have known something was going down tonight, should have smelled it on the wind—

Instead I was fucking dreaming. Can't remember what, but it felt important. Violent. Then the phone, and I was fighting, kicking, clawing my way back through last night's whiskey and cigarette tar and dirty sheets, until I found the fucker under a pillow. Khieu's voice on the line: that meant police stuff, probably drugs. Still, I almost went back to sleep. Fucked if I was getting out of bed to watch Cambodian cops score a few baggies of Captagon and yaba, and I told him so.

"This different," Khieu said, voice calm as a telemarketer's. "Police make raid on army."

That got me up. Fortunately, I was still dressed.

I bounce off the wall at the bottom of the stairs and shove through the door into the garage. It's packed with the low-grade touristic paintings and fake temple carvings my landlord sells on the street, and I try not to fall on my face as I squeeze past them. Fumble through the three padlocks on the security grate, morning air damp on my face.

The street outside is empty, silent. Mist hovers over the lawn of the National Museum across the road. On the corner, the motodops are sleeping on the seats of their bikes, knees in the air. They're the hungry ones: nowhere else to go. As I hit the sidewalk, one of them wakes, pushes off his kickstand and starts nosing toward me. I shove past him—bad manners, but he drives too slow.

Prik's still snoring. I swear, the Khmer guys call him Prik: means "hot stuff." He's got the most crapped-out two-stroke scooter I've ever seen, but he drives like he's found a way off this rock. I shake him awake.

"Street 602—hurry!" He pivots into the seat like a gymnast. I jump on back and we're off, spraying gravel over the dirt road.

Maybe we'll make it.

I shut my eyes and feel the morning glide over me. As soon as I do, the dream comes back—like it was waiting. There's a river, wide and dark and slow. Towers on fire in the night. And again that feeling it means something, that the world's about to change—

The smell of rotting vegetables drags me back to the present. We're passing the traffic circle where the neighborhood brings its garbage. This city hasn't had regular services in decades, but the Khmers cling to some crazy sense of order, piling their trash in neat mounds on curbs and medians, sometimes seven or eight feet high before some-one finally hauls it away.

Buildings flow by—shadows in the dark. French-colonial apartments from the fifties and sixties, peeling plaster, wrought iron dripping rust. I check my cameras as Prik slaloms around mud and potholes. At the corner a chunk of road is missing, and we have to slow to a crawl in the uneven dirt. Light a cigarette.

Khieu said the cops were going after the army. That's messed up, even for Cambo. It's no secret the army controls most of the drug trade—the stuff going overseas, anyway. The police have their own rackets going, and they leave the army alone. If this bust is for real, it's a message—but who knows what it means? Maybe some general overreached, and this is a slap on the wrist from on high? Or a dumb show for the foreign governments that pump money into the war on drugs? The cops have been talking tough about trafficking lately. Good for business, with the government the way it is: roust a few pill factories, show the world Cambo hasn't totally fallen apart.

But it could be something else completely. Since the election went bad, everyone's a little wild. The PM didn't get his majority, can't form a government, so the state looks weak. All the old deals are breaking down. Hun Sen won't fall—he's been prime minister for twenty-five years, no one's laying a glove on him. But who's in his corner, who's out in the cold? It's all up for grabs, and the dogs are circling.

A little action would be nice: I gotta sell something.

Try to remember the last time I sold a picture that was actually *news*.

There is no news from Cambodia. These days everyone's jazzed on Iraq, Bush's war starting to go bad. I wanted real work, I'd go there, get embedded. Should be good for some bang-bang.

If anyone'd take you. Nine years out here, what are you?

Not much better than those empty fuckers hanging around the riverside, calling themselves journos as they shoot portraits of their hooker-girlfriends and blag for gear. Another ghost, whose luck ran out a long time ago—

Stop.

There's stuff I'm not allowed to think about.

Lean forward so my mouth is by Prik's ear. "Faster," I say, in Khmer.

No more war zones. I can die here just as easy, and it's more fun.

The address Khieu gave is in the middle of Phnom Penh, off a main road near the university. The streets are still dirt, but there's more road than pothole. New apartments, villas with lawns for well-off business-men and foreigners. Not the place you'd expect a drug bust. I lean for-ward again as we turn onto the side street:

"Slow down."

Prik nods and eases off the gas. For a minute we're coasting as I scan the silent houses: uneasy. It's more than the square-john neigh-borhood, something else is making me nervous—a hint of warning in the air? In the distance I hear the crackle of a megaphone; shouted orders I can't make out.

We turn the corner, still cruising slow, and I see the scene up ahead: beat-up cop cars lining the street, headlights picking out a house in the middle of the next block. More shouting from that bullhorn.

Now the feeling hits me full on: danger. I can almost smell it, coming from that lit-up house and blowing down the street, drifting over the cops huddled behind their cars and making the hair on their arms stand on end, slamming windows all along the block until it reaches me, setting the blood rushing to my hands and pricking like needles in my fingers—

It's the smell of nerves on edge, of tempers frayed; of drawn knives, and fear, and things about to go very bad.

Prik feels nothing, doesn't even tense, and I start to tell him to pull up, to wait, but as I open my mouth I see the nearest police car flash white—

For a second, everything stops. Then the air splits and shivers around us, and we're spinning, unstuck from the pavement and skidding sideways off the road—

Crashing takes forever: Prik struggling with the handlebars, sparks flying as the chassis hits the ground. Numbness as we start to slide, in my leg and up my arm. I'm still hanging on to Prik, weightless as the bike drifts away from us, finally coming to a stop against a wall, and over and over in my head I see that car turning to fire. My ears are ringing—eventually I realize it's the explosion, grenade probably, nothing big, but if we'd been closer—

Grenade.

The word snaps the world back into focus: *You are in shock.*

Sound comes back first: deafening spatters of gunfire. Screaming. Then pain, racing up my side where I've slid through the dirt. Prik's a few feet away, up on one elbow, staring at the flaming wreckage of the police car. I grab his arm.

"Move! Now!"

We drag ourselves off the street, behind the corner of the villa we've crashed into. I run my hands over him, checking for wounds, for bones out of joint—his left side is a mess of scratches and blood, but I don't see anything permanent.

There's blood all over.

"Now feel me," I shout to him, in Khmer. His lips move, but I'm having trouble hearing him. "See if I'm hit." I could be bleeding to death and not even know it. Prik looks puzzled, so I reach out and put his hands on my chest, and he gets the idea. Pain shoots through me as he touches my left arm, and his hand comes away red and shiny. He grabs again, harder, and the world goes dark at the edges—

"You okay," he shouts. "Just skin."

My arm is a raw, red thing, but the camera looks all right. I take a test shot: there's no light back here, but I hear the shutter snap and the screen comes on. I gesture to Prik to stay put, and I crawl to the edge of the house. Put the camera out first, watch what's happening on the screen:

Car headlights, muzzle flashes. Fire and smoke. Hard to see anything clear. Glimpses of the cops running, sometimes shooting—they look focused on the house. I step out onto the street, camera held high over my head. I'm still a block away, well behind the firing line, but I can see it now: uniformed figures crouching, moving, guns out, hide—shoot—hide. That officer still shouting, but I can't hear him. No one even looks my way.

Take a few steps forward: line up my shot. Crank the ISO. I'll get heavy grain, but I can't use my film camera—it's loaded for flash and I can't risk it, not until they know I'm there.

Through the lens, shadowed figures. About a third of the guys are in helmets and tac vests, the rest are just uniforms. I hold the shutter: long bursts, *clickclickclickclickclick,* hoping to catch faces lit by the shooting. Get one huddled behind a car, gun over his head, firing at random—he looks about sixteen. Just a kid: the older guys know a car won't stop a bullet.

Another step closer. The air stinks of melting upholstery and CS gas.

Zoom in on the wreckage of the car. Men on the ground—three at least; one is screaming, one maybe unconscious. Blood on the pavement. Uniforms rushing to pull them clear, put pressure on wounds. Lucky: A grenade against a whole line of cops? Could have been a lot worse.

The officer's voice, louder now he's got his bullhorn back:

"Stop, stop, stop!"

A last few gunshots in the direction of the house, then quiet.

I walk right up to the cops—careful, deliberate steps. Focus on the guy with the megaphone: small, wiry, a captain by his stripes. Snap. Pan my lens down the line: tired faces, puffy eyes, lips tight with tension.

Snap.

Men rushing to help the wounded.

Snap.

The kid who was firing his AK over the car sees me. He waves to the captain, shouts something I can't catch. The officer makes a dismissive gesture.

The kid comes over. "Off-limits."

"I'm with the paper." Hold out my press badge.

He looks at it, frowns. "Off-limits."

I slide out the $20 bill I keep tucked behind the ID card. The kid takes both. After a second, he gives the badge back with a shrug: *Your funeral.* Turns away, already bored.

With the guns quiet a moment, I switch to the real camera: better resolution. The tactical guys are lining up, ready to bust down the front door, and I shoot a few as they get ready. No one stops me. Then they're up the steps, battering through the lock and tossing in a couple more tear-gas canisters. I get as close as I can, clicking away as the armored figures vanish in the smoke.

Then it's quiet.

People are coming out of their houses. Motos buzz by on the nearby streets, and a few stop at the ends of the block to stare. The jerk from the AP shows up, parking his big dirt bike with a flourish, tossing back his hair and looking around to see who's watching. He glares at me for being here already, then makes a big show of passing his papers around to the cops, who don't exactly care.

Somewhere in here, my knees start feeling wobbly. I'm covered in blood. The whole left side of me is torn up. Ripped jeans, leaking red. Thoughts held down by shock and adrenaline start bubbling over. It occurs to me I almost got shot for a picture no one wants. Light a cigarette and wait for the jitters to pass.

In the house, shouting. Footsteps. One of the tac guys comes out and waves to the captain, who follows him inside with another officer, and the street goes still again: everyone's watching. After a while, they get tired of it. People are just starting to mutter and turn away when the brass come back out. Behind them, the tac guys are frog-marching two middle-aged men down the steps: loafers, shirts with alligators on them, hands cuffed behind their backs. They look about as unmilitary as it gets. Was Khieu way off base?

The cops hustle the men into the back of a waiting van, and I move in quick with the digital. They wince and turn away from the flash: haggard faces, unreadable under fresh bruises. One has blood coming from his eye. I'm about to ask who they are, but the captain steps in, face clear as day: *That's enough.* I back off, hands up, but he's already moved on, barking orders.

The van drives off.

More journos are showing up now, crowding around the wreckage, pestering the cops as they go through the long, boring business of searching the house. One more guy gets hustled out—a young thug, bleeding pretty bad. From the scraps of chitchat I hear, there's more won't be coming out standing.

I've smoked through my whole pack by the time Khieu shows up. Even at this hour, his trousers are perfectly creased, his hair pomaded into a curl. If they put five-foot-three Cambodian guys on the cover of *GQ,* he'd be it. I can see my reflection in his shoes—it's not pretty.

"Nice of you to come," I say.

"I'm all the way across town."

"You just didn't wanna get shot at."

He gives me an enigmatic little smile. I pull out the camera, show him the guys in the van, but he shakes his head: doesn't know them. "I be back." He wanders off before I think to ask him for a cigarette.

Hell.

But I'm not waiting long. After a minute I see him pushing back through the crowd, with Bunny from Radio Ranariddh limping behind him, grinning like a maniac. I can't help grinning back.

Bunny is probably four foot six, with squat, uneven legs, a hump on his left shoulder, and dangling arms that end in stubby, shortened fingers. His real name is Bunly, but he simplified it for the foreigners. He doesn't mind not being taken seriously. The radio station he works for is the mouthpiece for Prince Norodom Ranariddh's FUNCIN-PEC party: they're the strongest opposition to Prime Minister Hun Sen—not that that's very strong. Prince Ranariddh spends a lot of time at posh embassy parties, and half of Bunny's job is to go along and soak up the gossip. His looks make people uncomfortable, but they also make him harmless. He smiles and wisecracks, and folks tell him where all sorts of bodies are buried.

"Keller," he crows in his strange accent, a mix of Khmer and Oxford. "Glad there's someone still trying to be a pain in everyone's ass."

"I hear you're keeping up," I say. "You got told by the man himself."

He laughs. "You know, now he doesn't have a government, he's not really prime minister, is he? So it's no harm to the national interest if I point out a few little things."

"Doubt he'd agree with you."

"He's too big." Bunny laughs again. "A pest like me? Not worth the candle." He wiggles his eyebrows. "I'll keep my head down a bit, it'll blow over."

"Good luck with that."

"I'm a lucky guy."

"Better than smart."

"You'd know, Keller. Now give us a look-see, eh?" He's excited: his sources haven't told him who was in the house yet.

I hold out the camera, screen zoomed in on that beat-up face.

Bunny lets out a low whistle. "That is *General* Peng Lin. Four stars, head of international cooperation at the defense ministry." Shit: Khieu was right, after all. Big rank to get stuck in the back of a police van. In chinos and a polo shirt, he looks like he should be running a laundry.

"Why's he here?"

"Police say this drug house," Khieu says, trying to keep up with the English.

"Sure," I say. "But that could be a cover. Maybe someone just wanted Peng out of the way." I look at Bunny, who shrugs.

"Drugs wouldn't be a shock. I've heard rumors about a crew in ICD calling the shots."

"Yeah?"

"The army's basically a cartel, eh? Someone's gotta run it. Not the guys at the very top, the political figures: they don't want to be too close to anything. The bottom ranks just do as they're told. Somewhere in the middle are the guys who actually make the decisions."

"And you think Peng's on the list?"

Bunny grins. "Could be. At his level, he'd be number one, maybe number two in terms of operational control of the drug traffic for the whole damn country."

"Maybe not for long. The political guys won't like this."

"We'll see. We still don't know why the police would move on him. Now if you'll excuse me, I'm going to try to find out." Bunny lurches off to talk to the brass, still grinning, with Khieu trailing after.

I am drained, empty. Still out of cigarettes. Thinking about leaving, but something stops me. A change in the air? I push back toward the house—see the guy from AP watching me funny, like he wonders what I know. More cops have arrived now and staked out a perimeter. Just inside, the captain and his officers huddle together, talking low. Now and then one of them throws a glance up at the door of the house, face hard and tight. I get them in frame and take a shot—waiting for what's next.

They head up the steps, standing on one side in a line. A uniform comes out; on his shoulder, a flat, brown bundle the size of a cinder block. I hit the shutter and freeze him in the flash, carrying what looks like eight, ten kilos of junk.

My mouth starts to water.

This town has been dry since I got back, and now here's the fuzz with an exact metric shitload of the stuff. It's still wrapped in that waxy yellow plastic, dark red stamps on the side: a dragon in a triangle, laced with twining script—Burmese or Thai, can't be sure. Straight from the factory, barely cut. I'm snapping frantically, my palms tingling like they're scalded.

Slow down.

Think about the shot, not about the junk.

The uniform starts down the steps, and behind him comes another, with another bundle. Then another. They just keep coming. The cops around me are statues, staring. Half these guys probably deal on the side, but they've never seen shit like this.

The shutter clicks, recording stony faces, frozen eyes, and nervous fingers. Everyone thinking the same thing. This isn't some scrap over territory, or a put-on for the foreign donors.

This is a goddamn war.

DIARY

The world can surprise you: it is so very big. Fly far and fast enough, and when you stop you can actually feel it curving away beneath your feet. A new country always feels like a fresh start.

Here's what it's like:

A tiny plane, smelling of cigarettes.

Heavyset men in suits—Chinese, Vietnamese, Thai—squeezed into the seats like overstuffed toys. What are they traveling for? Shiny hotels and business lunches? Or unspeakable appointments in Phnom Penh's dancehalls and massage parlors?

Seat pockets stuffed with newspapers in a dozen scripts, none of them Latin.

Purple velvet outside the windows. We fly low.

And then landing, tumbling out of the sky in jerks and stalls, through clouds of evening rain.

No one respects the fasten seatbelt sign . . . bodies tangle in the aisles and soak me in their tarry smell. . . .

When the door opens, the heat slams into me like a fist, a physical blow—then gives way, suffocating and wet. I have stepped into the maw of something, I am breathing its air.

Metal steps down to the tarmac, still glistening from the monsoon. The runway is a narrow ribbon of black; beyond, darkness and wet grass. In the distance, hot wind whips a row of palms against a sky of looming violet cloud. Lightning in the distance flashes red, like a scar.

Cambodia.

WILL

OCTOBER 3

The new scum are swarming the office when I arrive. A fresh batch, but they're always the same: greedy fucking American twentysomethings, sniffing around a newsroom for the stink of human tragedy. They're huddled under the AC now, scrubbed pink and shiny with sweat, pretending to listen to Ray as he goes on about ethics or something, but they don't give a shit: it's blood they want. They fly halfway across the world for it; now it's in the air.

I'm in no mood for interns, and I fix my eyes on the carpet, hoping to slip past before they see me. No chance, the newsroom barely holds ten people, and they're on me like fat, white leeches:

"Mr. Keller—"

"Was it Hun Sen?"

"Are you all right? We heard—"

"What happened?"

Never look at the eyes, they'll go into a frenzy. I'm trying to push past, face to the floor, following the twisted vine of computer cables over frayed carpet—

"What happened?"

Flashback: that stretcher getting shoved down the steps. For drug dealers, the cops don't always bother with a sheet, and there was my eating money: the only shots the local tabs will actually pay for.

Snap, snap.

By the time it was done, the city was turning hot and brown. It took me ages to get out of there: rush hour, sweating, gridlocked between the aid agencies' giant Land Cruisers and the swarms of motos buzzing around them. My bang-bang high had gone south, and all I could think about was how to get another. The paper wasn't open yet, so I hit the twenty-four-hour Internet shop, bought a six-pack of Beerlao, and spent the next hours uploading the digital shots. An act of contrition, mostly: it may be war now, but it's not a war anyone cares about.

I should have called the office at some point, but I just sat there smoking, staring at the little gray bars as they ticked across the screen and wondering what I just saw. It wasn't until the pictures were mostly done that I noticed I was still covered in blood. Decided a shower was in my best interest—to prevent exactly the kind of scene I'm in now, surrounded by cutthroat children looking for war stories.

"What do you think this says about Cambodia's political stability?" one of the little monsters asks.

What the fuck is he talking about?

Ray saves me. He leaps in and starts screaming at them, some stuff about integrity and restraint. He's got his voice cranked up to fever pitch and the bloodsuckers scatter, cowering back into the shadows and crawling under desks, and then Ray's shoving me into the back hall—

"Hey, man, hey, where you been? Gus is eatin' the fucking walls, man, says he's gonna break your goddamn fingers."

Not necessarily an idle threat. On top of running the paper, Gus is now the informal manager of a Khmer kickboxing club. I piss him off, he'll be rattling my cage at dawn, dragging me out to the club's shed by the lake for some concussion therapy. I've got reach on him, but he's still two hundred pounds of angry Argentine, and he goes down hard. Worse is when he makes me fight Khmers: fast little fuckers, love a go at a big guy. After sparring with them you're lucky if you can stand, never mind walk away.

"What time is it?"

"Man, it's, like, two thirty already," Ray says.

Shit. I think back through the hours; can't account for them. What happened to today? "Here." I shove my memory card into his hand. "Get a layout from that, then tell Gus I'm in the darkroom."

Turn to go, trip over another bunch of cables. Sparks; shouts from the newsroom as computers go black. "Christ. Somebody's gonna die in here someday."

"No shit, man." Ray stares at me. "We got a pool goin'."

The art is good. Digital's all right for flash and bang, but you want the real thing, you need film. For some reason I loaded color this morning, which is pointless for the paper, but I'm not regretting it.

Here's the captain, haggard and red-lit by dawn, looking down at the charred pavement, glinting gold with spent casings. Behind him, smoke from the burning car obscures the sky. He's got a face like one of Rodin's burghers: satisfaction barely registering in his eyes, in the set of his mouth. But there's disgust, as well, with what he's had to do and what it cost him.

Here's the ambulance man, a cigarette dangling from his lips as he wraps gauze around a cop who took shrapnel in the side. He's smiling, making a joke, but you can see the hollowness in his eyes.

Here are the uniforms, pushing down the stairs with those great bricks of heroin on their shoulders: faces blank, eyes glazed and terrified. Actors who've forgotten their lines. They don't even know what the play is anymore.

Been a while since I did anything this good.

Shame no one will buy them.

Behind me, I hear something like a gorilla try to tear the door off its hinges. Then there's Gus, shoving himself into the tiny room, breathing in my ear as he stares at the luscious brown bundles.

"Khieu says that's ninety ki's prime Burmese heroin," he whispers. "Pulled it out of the fuckin' walls. That's millions by the time it hits Sydney or Hong Kong. Someone fucked up big."

There's no space to turn around, but I can feel him looking: he thinks I'm up to something. It was drug shit this morning, so he's been waiting, wondering what story I'll tell. He doesn't actually care what I do, he just gets his kicks giving me a hard time. You make your own fun in Phnom Penh.

"This isn't a fuckup," I say. "You don't catch the head of the army's drug business in a house with half the country's product just 'cause someone was careless. Those cops didn't know what they were gonna find, but someone did."

"You think Hok Lundy's trying to push out the competition?"

I mull it over. The cops mostly deal internal, small-time stuff, but the head of the police has his own outfit. One of the few who can: his daughter's married to the prime minister's son. Over time, Hok Lundy's built himself up into a major player. He's strong in Phnom Penh—maybe he thinks he's got strong enough to tell the generals to get off his turf.

"Could be," I say.

"He's a brave guy."

"Brave has a short shelf life."

"He could take it quite far, though."

If he tries a coup, we'll have blood in the gutters by nightfall.

We're both quiet a minute. Finally, Gus: "These are good shots."

"Fuck off. You're gonna use the shit I gave Ray, the guy shooting over the car."

He doesn't bother denying it. "It sells papers. These are better." Unspoken accusation in his voice: *Why don't you get out of the sticks, Will, go do something real? Go to Iraq like everyone else—*

"Fuck you," I say too loud. "And your war. I'm fine here." Now I do turn around, forcing him back against the door. "You really gave a shit, you'd gimme a little time out of this fuckin' city."

For a second I think he looks surprised. "What do you want to do out in the provinces?" Suspicious bastard.

"Take pictures I can fuckin' sell. It's Phnom Penh no one cares about, fuckin' politics. They'll buy KR. They'll buy *landscapes*. Shit, I can take pictures of kids with big, hungry eyes and hawk 'em to Oxfam for brochures, but this—"

"So it's money." He's done being surprised. "I thought you went to Vientiane for money. A week back, you're broke already?"

"I was broke when I got back. Vientiane went bad."

"I don't want to know! And I can't pay you to fuck around in the trees when there's a war about to start."

"There's always a goddamn war."

I feel my jaw clench. See it in his eyes: *A good war is just what you need.*

I want to hit him in the face. Reach for a cigarette instead.

He grabs it out of my mouth. "*Hijo de puta,* what's wrong with you?"

Fucker went to Georgetown, speaks better English than me—he just swears in Spanish because he likes the sound.

"Don't be a baby. I won't burn the place down." Take another one from my pack, light it.

Gus's eyes are narrow, bloodshot. He runs a huge hand through three days of beard. "You just fogged everything that wasn't fixed."

"Who cares? No one'll use 'em, anyway."

"Do what you like," he says finally.

The scum are still floating around as I leave, excited looks on their pasty faces as they chew over all the things that could go wrong between now and tomorrow. I'm dizzy from hours in the dark and too much developer. Gus is off in graphics, so I stop at his desk and steal the cigarettes he keeps for emergencies. Then I'm back on the street, dazed by the afternoon sun. The Cambodia theme song starts playing:

"Moto? Moto?"

". . . need a ride?"

". . . want a girl?"

". . . come and eat—"

". . . anywhere you want—"

". . . where you go, handsome guy?"

". . . she very pretty—"

I pass by and they sink back to their perches, waiting for the next mark.

Trees line the block outside the office, curving overhead like a roof and splashing the ground with dappled light. Even in the shade it's hot, and my shirt is stuck to my back in seconds. Day workers sleep on the grass next to the snack carts. It's quiet: you wouldn't think a war was about to start.

I'm only going a few blocks, but the state I'm in, not sure I'll make it on foot.

I stop to buy a fried banana from an ancient woman with a table by the side of the road. It's the tiny, sweet kind—tastes of woodsmoke and honey, and I savor the rush of sugar.

It's not enough.

The country can go to hell without my attention. I need a beer.

"Moto, mister? Moto?"

"Sure. Take me to the river."

The Foreign Correspondents Club will be rammed: anytime a gun goes off, all the journos and aid workers get thirsty. I don't want to hear more people talking about how thrilling it all is, I just want a drink.

There's a new place just across the road—an open-air pub on the corner, looking out over the quay and the water. Posh, empty; the neon over the awning says THE RIVER'S EDGE. I go in. A hardwood bar carved with twining snakes, and a girl behind it: black eyes, face like a temple statue, busy doing nothing. She smiles as I step off the sidewalk and tells me I am very pretty. Then she says I look like I need a drink.

"Those things don't go together."

"I not see you yet," she says, whatever that means. "How long in Cambodia?"

"Nine years."

"Oh!" She grabs my hand in both hers, like I've just told her about Ma's tragic death in that threshing-machine accident. "You want a lot beer." She smells of cheap soap and whiskey. "I am Chantrea. You call me Channi. I work before at Ms. Pong bar, but I not see you there. I think you new, but you old."

"Don't flatter me."

She giggles. She's still hanging on to my hand, and I'm not minding it too much. Force the feeling down with a pint of cheap beer. Chasing girls in a place like this is a good way to get knifed: managers don't like it. I case the joint as I finish my drink. Shiny: fresh paint, wooden chairs—no plastic lawn furniture here. Someone had cash to play with.

A wiry thirtysomething with little scars all over his hands pops up next to me as Channi pours my second. He's the manager, he says. Terry. He asks if the girls are paying attention to me. "Lip service," he calls it, with a little *Mona Lisa* smile, "they giving you lip service?"

"Channi's keeping me in peanuts."

Terry used to work in steel in the Midlands, but there was no future in it; then he did travel for a while, but that didn't suit him either, so now he's moving into food and beverage—hey, everybody's gotta eat. He winks like we're in it together now. He's bringing some class to this place, there's a second floor, I must try the snooker table—

"If the beer runs out," I say.

He puzzles over that. I turn away and he dives for the sidewalk, and fresher-smelling punters.

I have a third, then a fifth. A truck roars by in the distance, ancient engine clanging. Outside, the streets are coming alive: blaring horns, slamming blinds, people finishing errands and scurrying for cover. Time to wrap up what you're doing; to get home, if you have one. Time to take shelter. A final door bangs shut and for a second there's perfect quiet—like someone's clicked a shutter and we've been caught, frozen in this moment forever.

Then the monsoon hits. Sheets of water rip across the world beyond the awning.

Terry doesn't seem to notice the rain. He's busy smiling his *Mona Lisa* smile at me over his shoulder. Channi's smiling, too, as she tops off my beer and slides over more peanuts. It's like I just won some fucking award.

Something's happened, but nobody else notices, they just keep grinning. The moment passes. Not even a snapshot: just a rumble in the distance, then the rain.

———————

Back at the house; unsteady on the narrow stairs. Almost night now. I rattle Gus's gate in the dark; no answer. Up to my floor, stumble over the suitcases on the landing. When I was in Vientiane, Gus put one of those American vampires in here. Girl left her shit while she went on some backpacking jaunt, and here it is, still in my hall, waiting to kill me. Consider trashing the stuff, but it's too much effort. I'll make Gus deal with it later.

I thought the beer would get me to sleep until it was time to go out, but I just lie there in my cage, listening to the rain. Pictures keep flashing in my mind: men in dark uniforms with plastic-wrapped bundles on their shoulders. The general and his aide crumpled into the back of a police van like yesterday's newspaper. The police and the army, facing off. Why now? The Eastern drug trade is peanuts these days. Ten years ago, maybe, it was big—four times as much dope coming out of the Triangle, all headed for the States. But times change: a few warlords crash and burn, supply declines. The US invades Afghanistan and a new supply appears, traveling west through Turkey and Europe. Cambo gets left with the scraps, again.

But out here, we're hungry. Even scraps are worth fighting over.

DIARY

Phnom Penh airport is tiny, made of cinder blocks and glowing with yellow sodium light. Border officials wear uniforms embroidered with pagodas and elephants. . . . Stamps, visas . . . and then waiting, and more waiting. I'm not sure if the men here make a fetish of blond girls the way they do in Japan, but I don't much want to find out. I wrap myself up and fade from view. It is one of life's little consolations: realizing I can choose whether or not to be seen.

It's a while before the boy comes, but I spot him at once. There aren't many foreigners here, waiting—or arriving, for that matter— and he's the only one who fits the type. He might be 25 or 26, actually, but there's still something boyish around him. He's got that phthisic look, with curling blond poet hair and a hawk nose, and, pinky swear, he is actually wearing round, gold-rimmed spectacles! He's like a cross between D'Artagnan and Sherlock Holmes. He's worrying about whatever made him late, and not sure who (or what) he's looking for, but still he moves with the thoughtless grace of someone who has always been beautiful.

Jealousy.

I let myself remain invisible for a while, just to watch him, until . . .

"Hello?"

"Oh! Um, hello?" Very proper English accent. Very posh!

"Are you looking for me?"

A pause. "You're Jun Saito?"

Even when I let them, they don't see me.

———————

It took some time for him to drag my stuff into this huge black monster of an SUV, but now it's done and we're off. The boy is up next to the driver, chatting to me over his shoulder as if he's some midnight DJ, talking us through the gray pre-dawn hours on the freeway. I know I should be listening, but I can't stop looking out the windows and writing it all down.

An airport road goes nowhere, connects to nothing. Its end is the edge of the real world, a border between us and the sky. We cross over and for a moment we touch the clouds—but we always end up in another airport, on another airport road.

Just past the soft shoulder, men and women sit in lawn chairs in little circles of light—not from streetlamps, but electric bulbs hanging on poles or swooping from billboards on ribbons of wire. Old women fan themselves next to carts stacked with juice, or food, or Fanta bottles that the boy says are full of gasoline. Old men play cards on folding tables and drink strange canned drinks. A few young girls sit alone, and I don't dare ask what they're there for. They watch the cars with the faces of stargazers watching comets, hurtling distantly by with a whispered promise of obliteration.

Then the city, glowing like a Catherine wheel. The boy sends the driver down Sisowat Quay, which he says is our neighborhood: It runs all down the Tonlé Sap river, and we drive through the wide lawns of the old colonial hotel district . . .

. . . along an acre of bars and cafés, tiny shops offering Internet from child-sized bamboo cubicles, restaurants serving seafood and pizzas laced with marijuana for the tourists . . .

. . . past wide green festival grounds around the royal palaces, gleaming gold pagoda tops in the background . . .

It's all brilliant-colored and strange and exciting. This place is so beautiful . . . I can't help but think that everything will be different.

––––––––––

The apartment is shatteringly empty. It's like a prison cell.

A long, rectangular room of cinder blocks . . . on one end, a door leads to a balcony; on the other, a second opens onto the landing, where a camp stove on a counter makes the kitchen, and a corner next to the stairs is walled off to form a tiny bathroom. The doors aren't even solid, they're grates of heavy steel without glass. The windows have these slats that only close to a 45 degree angle: this place barely counts as indoors.

They called it the cage, and so it is: I am a bird now.

There's no furniture but a bed with a single sheet and a bare wicker desk. Apple crates pretending to be shelves hold a few dog-eared airport crime novels, some colored filters and lens cases, and a stack of manuals for camera equipment. The photographer's room is a perfect reflection: he leaves nothing of himself behind.

When he returns, I wonder what he'll find of me?

It was practically a party when the boy and I arrived. The house sits on a dark side street near the river. The bottom floors are a Cambodian artist and his wife, the third is the paper's editor, Gus, and the fourth is the photographer (now me). They all met us outside as we pulled up. The artist had to welcome us with all sorts of complicated greetings, which the others stumbled over each other to translate. Gus is older, late 30s, I guess, but crazy and South American and built like a wrestler, wrestling me and the boy and my luggage out of the car as he kept up a patter about the paper and the elections and what all we'd see and we'd do, and the boy chiming in on the choruses . . . and in the background the photographer, just leaning against the building, smoking and watching. I don't know how to describe him: big, I guess. God knows how old he is. I think he's like me: when he wants to, he can make your eyes slide right past him. We all sat in Gus's room, and he poured us whiskeys and congratulated me on not dying in a fiery plane crash, at which the boy laughed. I did, too, as it seemed expected of me.

It was an odd night. On the one hand, oh God, the awkward . . . phony cheer and big smiles. There was something between the two men, I could tell by the way they danced around each other's words. I've taken the photographer's room because he's traveling, and at one point I asked him where . . .

"Laos," he said, "Vientiane."

"What for?"

"Work."

Then he lit another cigarette. He's like that. And I would totally have called him on it, but suddenly Gus was asking me about school, and the program that sent me here, and what my training had been like, and I had to think of the answers and so I forgot all about the photographer . . . just like I was supposed to. I want someone who protects me like that.

The boy wanted to be charming, but there was something on his mind as well: he kept getting dragged back into his thoughts when the conversation lulled.

But despite all that . . . it was kind of wonderful. The three of them, they would never admit it, but they were friends. They had that way about them: they'd been through things together, and often when they spoke it was in words that barely made sense to me, an inner language that might as well have been Cambodian. (The older two actually speak Cambodian—they call it Khmer—which only made things worse.) How long would I have to stay here, before I could understand what's going on?

But for a couple of hours, whatever it was they had, I felt like I was part of it.

And then, just like that, it was over. The photographer had to catch a plane. Gus and the boy had work in the morning, never mind Sunday. They told me to take the day and explore the city, and then suddenly they were all gone and I was back in this empty cell.

I know it's impossible, it's too dangerous, but I catch myself wondering—what would it be like to stay?

WILL

OCTOBER 3–4

Friday night, the river is a regular Chinatown fair. Under carnival lights, journos and aid workers argue and drink and dodge the foreign students, who act like sailors on shore leave. Bar girls shout from the sidelines; beggars and touts flog what they got to flog. I light a cigarette and breathe deep, trying to catch the pulse of the night. No one's sleeping: they're all here, looking to talk about where they were today, what they heard, who did what. *How long do we have, before the shooting starts?*

Something's still bothering me. I can't figure it out—but I'm starting to wonder if it's connected to this morning at all. What if the faint tingling in my fingers is a warning of something else? Something seen and forgotten, unnoticed—

Still coming.

My cigarette tastes stale. I toss it on the pavement. Fuck signs and portents. Half the city's out tonight, must be somebody I can bum a joint off.

The River's Edge is crowded. I see Channi working the tables out front, arms full of drinks, smiling pretty at the barbarians. She gives me a quiet wave. I'm about to head over when I hear Rockoff's voice from up the street: a wordless growl, like a stereo with the bass too high.

He's our local celebrity: made his name in '75, shooting the fall of Phnom Penh. Someone famous played him in the movie. He got evacuated in the embassy siege, then came back as soon as he could. The place had its hooks in him. He's outside Happy Happy now, sitting with Doyle from the *Daily,* and that bearded Welsh photographer whose name I can never remember. Gus, too. They're real gone already, the table covered with half-eaten pizza and roaches and beer cans, and Rockoff holding forth on who knows what.

I sit down.

"William," Gus shouts. "*Qué fiesta,* eh?"

"Hey, Gus. Hey," I say to the photog whose name I forget.

"Hey," he says. Doyle nods more or less in my direction—the other papers don't like us much. Rockoff just keeps talking: "Fuckers in editorial. Never been out here, don't understand how a revolution happens. Not just 'boom.' These places got a tolerance for chaos, they can limp along for ages—" Bland waitress, Beerlao. "Every time some asshole gets an itchy trigger finger, the fucking *Times* thinks the whole country's gonna collapse—"

"You saw the pictures, eh?" Doyle says. "That's a hell of an itch."

"That jerk Keller," Rockoff snorts. "Makes everything look like the end of the world."

I'm sitting right here. Not sure Rockoff has ever asked my name.

"Party's at Vy's," Gus says, handing me a spliff.

"Shit."

"*No pasa nada,* she's in Paris till next week. Someone has a key."

He looks wrecked. Something's up with him. Didn't show up at the house after work, must have been drinking all day. Odd.

My beer comes. I drink it, order another.

"It was just the same in '75," Rockoff is saying. "No one sees the shit coming, not until it's way too late."

I can't help staring. Rockoff was made for Cambodia. He'll never leave, he can't. When he dies—if he ever does—he'll still be right here.

———————

Vy has the best apartment in Phnom Penh. I haven't been in years. Banned for life—possibly after smashing up a Danish-modern dining room, but I'm not sure. Those memories are difficult to get to: reach out and they slip between my fingers.

From the street, I can see people crowding the terrace, a big wrought-iron job that curves around the third floor, over the river. Gus stops at the quicky-mart while I linger on the sidewalk, watching the rickshaw drivers doze in their contraptions. I had four more Beerlaos, listening to Rockoff and Doyle argue about whether Hun Sen is going to take back the government by force, and I've gone right through the day's strange anxiety and out the other side. Nothing I need now but more.

A Psychedelic Furs song drifts down from the balcony. I know it, I can see Butler pulling his shirt off on the record cover—first track, but can't remember the title. Gus comes out with two six-packs, and we head inside. Vy's paintings are the same, but the furniture's new: weird postmodern stuff in primary colors, Keith Haring on a ketamine binge. Someone's strung Christmas lights—Vy would think it's tacky, but she's not here. The Furs have been replaced by some southern hip-hop, and the room is packed with expats dancing like it's their last chance.

I head for the kitchen, start jimmying the cabinet where Vy hides the good wine. There's a decent-looking Chilean: I look for a glass, then think better of it and drink from the bottle. I'm not sharing with humanitarians. Four swigs and I'm brave enough to face the party.

I make it halfway to the balcony before I get cornered. She's about twenty-five, with a maroon tank top and a black clove cigarette. She looks like everyone else here.

"Malbec," she says. "Nice."

I hold out the bottle. She takes it and gazes up at me for a long time. I wonder if I could fuck her.

"I'm Andrea." She takes a long swallow.

"Will." Another pause. It goes on awhile. I could get her talking if I start on the day's violence, but I'm tired of it. I don't want to hear what any more children think about Cambodia's political stability. "What brings you here?" Safe question—you can take it any way you want.

"Ohmygod, I don't know, y'know?" She laughs. "This place is intense, and I'm just, like, 'How did I end up here?' I did poli-sci at school, but then, hey, guess what? I wound up working as a manager at an interior-design firm in Minneapolis, which wasn't really where I saw myself in twenty years, you know, so I just—"

Where will I be in twenty years? Will there be anything left, except the hunger and the fixes?

"—after that, I'd had it, y'know? So I volunteered with this NGO—"

I can't fuck anyone who talks this much.

"—now it's Worldwide Relief, we do this thing out in the villages, teaching kids to avoid land mines, but it's really, y'know, tough—"

I'm getting frantic. Her face is going blubbery with self-pity and I may not be able to control myself.

"—keep writing these letters home, trying to explain what I'm seeing, y'know, how important it is, but I think my friends don't even get what I'm talking about—"

I can see Gus: he's on the porch, deep in conversation with a very hot girl with multicolored dreadlocks. I will him to look my way. The girl next to me is still going:

"—do you think so?"

"Absolutely." She gives me a funny look: that must have been the wrong answer. I take another long swig of wine.

"What do you do?" she asks.

Not a safe question.

"I take pictures of dead people."

She laughs, but it's nervous. Without realizing, she takes a quarter step back.

I let the silence go on awhile.

"Just dead people?"

"If I can't find any dead ones, I'll do live ones. They don't sell as well."

Her left hand crosses over to hold her right elbow: shielding her body from me. I step a tiny bit closer, take another drink. Wait for her to speak.

"Doesn't that make you feel kinda . . . gross?"

Feign shock: "It's my job. You know what we say: 'If it bleeds, it leads!' " Give her a Walmart grin. She looks sick. "Let's talk about you. Land mines, wasn't it? I get a lotta work from land mines." Watch her face; wait. Any more, she'll cause a scene.

"Y'know, I'm not loving the wine," she says. "I think maybe I'll get a beer. I'll be right back."

I head for the porch. Gus is still there, wedged into a rattan armchair with the dreadlocked girl sitting on his lap. With them is some scar-faced local fixer whose name I have forgotten, and Number Two, who's got a huge bag of cocaine open on the table and is looking around for a razor blade.

"Sit down, Da," he says, when he sees me. "You look like you might lose your dinner."

"Aid workers."

"The horror, the horror."

Number Two does crime at the paper. He's got a way of making you check your wallet when he's around, but he's an okay guy to hang out with. Came as an intern last summer and just stayed, which indicates strength of character. He's skinny and British and went to Eton or something, but he's actually fucking smart. I'm fairly sure his name is Chris, but there's another Chris at the paper, so Two got stuck with digits.

Gus waves to me, still looking distracted, but the girl sticks out her hand.

"Meg."

"Will."

Number Two goes back to describing his trip to the Svay Pak brothels two days earlier. "—truly bloody vile. I mean, it's a dead duck in a shell."

"That's a delicacy for you," Meg says. She sounds Australian.

"A metaphor for the entire Svay Pak experience: Who wants to eat an abortion? But Barry had nine of the bloody things. He started getting it on with this girl, after five minutes he just lost control. Chuntered all over her."

"*Hijo de puta,*" Gus mutters. His eyes are about a million miles away, but Meg's looking at Two like he's the world's first dancing cockroach.

"Can he do that?" she asks.

"Well, we had to pay extra."

"I meant banging the women you're supposed to be writing about, Goldilocks—"

"Barry's econ desk, what does he care?"

"You telling me you went out there and didn't ride the ride?"

"Purely research." Number Two's guard is up now. His eyes are darting side to side, like he can't tell if he's being screwed with. "I mean, it's the trip, innit? The whole fucking wretched, vile ambience. The red lights, the little nightgowns, the bloody duck eggs. It's awful, it's like being in a novel, which is much more interesting than a screw."

I wonder. Two is hard to figure—the way he jumps on all the sex-crime stories. Svay Pak brothels may woo clients with delicacies like fertilized duck eggs, but they're also known among a certain class as the best places to find prepubescent girls in these trying times. What was our crime writer getting up to while Barry was being sick?

Not your business.

Meg's had her laugh, but before anyone can move things along, the Khmer fixer decides to get into the act, putting a hand out and fondling Number Two's blond curls. "Are you sure you are not secret woman?" Everyone goes quiet. Khmer humor: often not very funny.

Two takes it in stride. "You should see my pubes." He grins. "You could die choking on them." He finally tires of looking for a razor and pulls the key to his Vespa out of his pocket. "Trusty scooter," he says, dipping it in the bag and taking an enormous bump.

"Glad to see it's good for something," Gus says.

Two glares at him, hands me the keys. I take two bumps and the night snaps back into focus. Pass the bag to Gus.

"No, no, don't give that wanker any." Two grabs it out of my hand and gives it to Meg, who snorts off her fingernail.

"*Cabron, te cagas en las cinco heridas de Cristo—*" Gus says.

"Don't fuck with me, Argentina. You can mock my hair, but you cannot mock my bloody scooter. I'm bloody serious."

Gus stares at Two a second, then bursts out laughing. Now I'm laughing, too. I finish the bottle and let it drop on the tiles, thinking of Vy's naked thighs as I lie next to her in the dying sun, fat with smack and feeling nothing at all.

By four, we've burned through the whole bag. The fixer has wandered off to chase foreign tail, and Gus and Meg are looking very preoccupied with each other, so Two starts scheming about where we can get more gear.

"Sharky's," I say.

"All they'll have is yaba."

"Not gonna get much better at this hour."

A guy I don't recognize comes out on the balcony and tells us we have to go. The music has long since died, and the sound of boats and distant motorcycles drifts up from below.

"You get it, then," Number Two says. "That place is vile, I honestly cannot go in there. It's dark, mate." He drawls the word, *daaahk*. "I might have an adverse reaction."

"I'll go."

We wander down to the street, past the sleeping rickshaw drivers. The quicky-mart is the only thing still lit: windows glowing yellow in a city of silhouettes, shark logo blinking blue neon. I go in. Sharky's can be dangerous at the wrong time—scary people hang out in the bar upstairs. Now it's just sad and tired. A couple skinny guys in blue polo shirts sit by the front window, disconsolately smoking. Guess they're doing the laundry, and the counters and coolers are covered with piles of the same shirts. The smell of cheap speed fills the room.

"Hey, man," one of the guys says. "You wan' something?"

"What you got?"

"Girls, man."

He points to the front counter, and I realize there's a girl lying pillowed among the drifts of blue, wearing nothing but a shirt about four sizes too big for her. She looks twelve.

"No thanks."

"H, man?"

I feel my eyes light up. Glare at him. "There's no H in town. I'm not paying a heroin price for ground-up Norflex."

He frowns. "We got yaba."

I hand him a ten and walk out with a small bag of red pills. Number Two has walked his Vespa up to the door, and I wait while he stands astride it, tilting it sideways almost to the ground as he turns the ignition. After three or four tries, the motor catches and I get on behind him.

I look over as we pass the Edge, half hoping for a glimpse of Channi. Like all the bars, it's shuttered and dark. Phnom Penh is a late-night city, so it always surprises me to see it in the gray furrow of morning, wide streets faced with row on row of steel grates, locked tight against something. The junkies and gangsters are nodding out or asleep; maybe it's ghosts they're scared of.

My place. Work through the padlocks and the security grate in silence, and we slip into the garage, edging carefully around the bad art.

Up the narrow stairs. Sky starting to get light: a pale glow streams into the landing. Open the cupboard, looking for tinfoil.

"So do you think it was Hok Lundy?" Number Two asks. "That's what Gus says."

"Gus says all sorts of shit."

"I don't buy it. This has to go higher up. This place can't afford to be a shithole forever."

"Why not?" I'm half listening—finally, tinfoil. There's nothing here but a wok and two broken knives, so I'm not sure how I lost it. Drop a pill on the sheet, pull out a lighter.

"The guys at the top, right, they *want* the drugs out, so they can get rich off sweatshops," Two says. My lighter's dead. He goes for his. "So they set the dealers up to wipe each other out. Even the corruption here is corrupt—"

"No decency left."

"Least they're committed, eh?"

Laughter. Fire in the hole.

———————

Somehow I'm walking back down the river, watching the morning with high-contrast eyes. Even in full light, everything has the bright grain of a night photograph. Faint ghosts dance around the kids on bikes and the twisted silhouettes of rooftops. Number Two's gone back to his place, and I'm alone in the growing heat. A few of the riverfront bars are opening—I stop in the first one that'll let me. Looks like it used to be a garage, and they haven't redecorated much. A pretty girl with a rag wipes the motor oil off a plastic tablecloth; I sit and order an Angkor.

"You are welcome," she says.

The beer is icy, in a frosted mug. The first sips fill me up and I let myself drift. Here's the Cambodian educational system in three lessons: cocaine at night; yaba before dawn, sucked down in acrid curls of smoke; beer and blinding sunrise. I understand this place perfectly.

Then I see her: a silhouette in the glare off the water, growing solid as she comes toward me—like Venus out of the sea. Sun on black hair. Skin like antique ivory, unlined: she's fourteen or she's forty. Her Japanese eyes say nothing, but they're looking straight into mine.

I'm still floating—check my pulse to make sure it's not permanent.

She stops next to my table, watching me the way a Vermeer watches you. Her clothes are traveler chic: tan Mao coat in microfiber, matching slacks, running shoes. I can't place her perfume, but she's close enough I notice it. Guessing it's not cheap. Her style says LA, and something else. LA girls are all trying to be mysterious or exotic—this one doesn't have to try.

"You're William Keller?" she says, like she doesn't want to believe it.

Don't answer: clearly she knows who I am. Try for a smile instead. Gesture for two more beers and the waitress scurries. I can feel the perspiration on my brow and the wrinkles in my shirt. This woman doesn't look like she wants me to buy her a drink. She gazes down, lips pressed into a worried line. "I apologize for disturbing you, so"—she pauses—"so late into yesterday. But I'm told you can help me."

"Can't imagine how."

"I find it hard myself. But I need help." Now there's the tiniest crack in her voice, and I see it: the steely calm is her armor, but she's hanging on by her fingernails.

This is work, then. And this girl is money all over. Should be good news. So why am I feeling it again—that pricking in my fingers?

She takes her time sitting down, lighting a cigarette from a black lacquer case, but her hands are trembling. Her shirt is open just enough, and as she leans in, I see tiny beads of sweat slick the brown space between her breasts.

She sees me staring and holds out the cigarette case. I take one. She doesn't light it.

"I just . . . don't know where else to go." Beautiful, scared, alone.

"What's your name?"

"Karasu." A single word in Japanese makes her a different person. When she goes back to English I can still hear it, buried somewhere deep under Beverly Hills. "You can call me Kara. Kara Saito."

Saito. Something ticking in my head, but I can't place it. "How did you find me?"

"Gus Franco. He says you've been in Cambodia a long time. That you know how to get things done here."

The waitress brings the drinks, and I find myself pressing my hand hard to the cold glass. Be careful—I can feel the metal hook in my mouth. "I'm a photographer."

"Gus says you find people."

"Who've you lost?"

"My sister."

Hell. I expected traveling buddy, boyfriend, dealer maybe. Family is rough—but still, I hold back. "Have you gone to the police?"

"You know they won't help me." Her hands are clenched together, white knuckled. "I need someone on my side. Someone who will actually look for her, and"—she notices her hands and teases them apart; sets them flat on the table, so close her fingers almost touch mine—"quietly," she almost whispers.

For a moment there's nothing in the world but her hand, just millimeters away: I feel it there like a blazing coal. In my head, her voice, her *lips*—

Grab my beer and take a long swallow, trying to talk sense into myself, but it's too late. This is where I bite down. "And what happened to . . . your sister?"

"June," she says. At least I think that's it, there's that strange something in her voice again. She's looking at me like I just asked what color the sky was. There's something I should have figured out, but I have no clue what. "She never came home." Kara's still giving me that half-puzzled look. The silence drags on. After a minute she gives up and slides a wallet-sized photograph across the sticky plastic tablecloth: a soft-focus glamour shot of a sour-looking blond girl in a high school graduation gown. It hits me like I've stepped into a right cross.

I know this girl. I met her—

"Jun?"

"It's Japanese, whatever. . . . Everyone calls me June."

—in my own goddamn house. She's the American: Gus's fucking intern, the one whose suitcases I keep tripping over.

Fuck, fuck, fuck—

June fucking Saito. She's gone—and she's all over me. She's on my doorstep in a pile of mismatched luggage. The pricking in my hands is like fire, telling me this is bad. My pleasant morning buzz has vanished and I'm choking back nausea. The beer smells acid. I realize how much I'm sweating—I want Gus, or Number Two; I want Rockoff to wander over and tell this woman to fuck off, but of course he doesn't.

I go to push the photo back across the table, *No, thank you,* I don't want this job, and as I do, I look up at Kara—

It's the speed, Christ, I'm losing it, but—

When I was a teenager, backpacking across Asia taking pictures, I saw a tiger. Not a tired old thing in a zoo or safari park: a real tiger, so close it could have reached out and ripped me open. It was supposed to be a safe trail, a tourist track half a mile outside the little hill station where I was staying. I had a girl with me and I pulled her off into the brush—it felt like just a few feet—and there it was, half-sleeping on a rock. It opened its eyes a lazy sliver, and that was enough to turn my guts to water and set every hair on my body on end. The girl pissed herself.

I have done too many drugs.

I don't understand anything except that this is not a woman I can say no to. I cast a glance down the street, looking for the watchers I'm sure are lurking in the shadows. There's no one: just me and her. We're alone in the sunlit darkness an hour after dawn, and there are no doors, no exits.

The only way out is to go on.

Find words.

"I'm five hundred a day, plus expenses. And I'll need an advance."

DIARY

The night is hung in black velvet, torn through by bright neon and Chinese lanterns. Iron balconies cling to crumbling façades, and garages gape like shocked mouths. No one uses them for cars, they all have motorcycles, so most have been re-shaped into strange, cave-like rooms. A few are still lit:

A workshop crammed with broken machines, where a man strokes a greasy lathe under a naked bulb . . .

A sitting room where a family crowds together on a ragged couch, watching television in the flicker of fluorescent tubes . . .

The ground is muddy and full of holes. A big brown sedan crawls up beside me, and a fat-faced Cambodian man looks out the window.

"Taxi?" he says. "You want taxi? Anywhere, five dollar."

"Okay," I say, getting in.

I'm here to get lost.

W I L L

OCTOBER 4–5

Kara is gone, but it's too late: everything's got way too real. I'm trying to hold off the paranoia, but I've done way too much yaba and my nerves are like hangnails. I can feel the craving welling up, red and in my bones. Need something to get me through the day. Two more yaba to hold off the crash, and I flag down a moto.

Hang on tight.

Wind cools the sweat on my face, and I force the panic down. Try to think back: the night I met June Saito. No chance I'd forget, it was the night I left for Vientiane. I was hanging around Gus's apartment, drinking and waiting for my flight, when Number Two showed up with this girl in tow.

What was she like?

She got my attention. My first thought was she was sick, maybe dying. Couldn't say why: she was cancer-ward thin, but there was something else—some asymmetry to her features, maybe? Unwholesome. She had this baby face, where nothing seemed to go with anything else: tiny, flat nose, downturned mouth, almond eyes set too wide and blue like empty sky. Big cheeks, acne scars. No eyebrows, and silver-blond hair. My second thought was to go for my camera: I could have shot her all year. I guess I wondered if I could fuck her. Whatever she was, it wasn't boring.

But what was she *like*? I know we talked—I can see the way she held her wine glass next to her face as she spoke, the practiced cock of her eyebrow. What did she say? Was there something that could have warned me?

Beyond the image, nothing.

She's disappeared.

The bike turns off at the graffiti-tagged wall of pink cinder block that surrounds the mosque, and the road narrows. Walls of pressed tin and ragged wood crowd in on every side; graffiti in English. The shacks and shanties have grown along the lake for years, spreading into each other, merging and dividing until the neighborhood has become a living thing, unplanned and trackless. The back doors of little guest-houses open into the storerooms of tiny shops that share bathrooms with the neighboring cafés. Rough structures weave together through makeshift passages and temporary walls: a maze of back rooms, alleys, and nameless, interstitial spaces. Easy to get lost. Down in the guts of it are dark places, but the main street is safe enough. Foreign money grew it: a slice of exotic for the backpacking crowd, slums for tourists.

The driver pulls to a stop in the rutted dirt, and the touts close in.

"Pizza, happy pizza—"

"Girls!"

"Hash—"

"Pizza—"

"—very pretty!"

Elbowing to the front is a cheery, one-eyed pusher I've known for ages. "Wah you wan', man?" He grins. Never use a sullen dealer, you'll get catnip and coriander seeds. "You wan' happy?"

"Yeah, gimme happy."

I pass him a five, and he slaps a bag the size of a cigarette pack in my hand. I pocket it and walk down the track, past the pizza joints and the tattoo parlor and the secret things that live behind them. Stop for rollies at a window stocked with razor blades and cans of skin-lightening cream, and slide down an alley to the Green Dragon Excellent Traveler Hotel. A hall that's shoulder width, paste-wood doors leading to guest rooms. Most are shut, silent, but a few offer desolate snapshots of occupation: a black toilet bag spattered with toothpaste, dust-stained flip-flops on a dirty towel.

End of the hall, through the bead curtain: a sitting room full of tattered couches, and a deck over the lake, set with tables. Thankfully it's empty. Mama T is sitting at her counter in the corner, chewing peanuts and watching some Cambodian soap opera on the TV. She doesn't say hello, just looks me up and down and vanishes into the kitchen. I take a table next to the water, and a minute later her son, Sammy, comes back with beer and black coffee. Mama T always knows what you need. I start skinning up. You can't just get off a trip like this, your only choice is ride it out. Coffee versus beer, yaba versus pot: get the ratios right, you can work your way almost back to human.

"You all ri', Mr. K?" Sammy asks. He's in his thirties, but his moon face and wisp of mustache make him look like a kid.

"I'm okay, Sam."

"You not lookin' so good. You sick?"

"Nothing a little happy can't cure." He spies the joint rolling itself between my fingertips. "You want some?"

"Yah, okay." Lots of Khmers won't touch the stuff: it's a painkiller for old men, not a recreation. But years in the guesthouse have given Sammy *barang* habits. He sits, and we smoke the first one of the day together.

"You look like . . . not here," he says, after a while.

"It happens."

"Maybe you wan' go back to America?"

Anything but that.

The last toke. Watch the roach go spinning into the scummy water below.

———————

Another joint, three cups of coffee, and two more pints of beer, and I'm back where I need to be: far from missing interns and demanding relatives. In the Dragon, the phantoms vanish back into the sunlight. The red ache is fading, but I still want something.

I've watched a whole crew of chirping couples eat their pancake breakfasts by the time the girl comes out. Got America practically stamped on her: tank top from a party school in the Midwest, beige capris with cargo pockets. She's spilling out all over. She sits a table away and I see her notice me. I start to skin up again, taking my time so she can see what I'm doing. She looks interested, so I pull my chair over.

"Hate to smoke alone," I lie. "Care to join me?" She giggles without thinking, throwing furtive glances over her shoulder. "It's okay." I light up. "They're paid up with the right people."

I pass and she takes it, drawing down the heavy smoke without antics.

"I'm Will. Photographer. Been in Iraq awhile. A friend told me Cambodia was the place to unwind, and I'm starting to think he was right."

"I'm Claire. I just finished school, so I'm backpacking from India to Japan before doing my master's." Her little smile says, *I know that's cheesy, but what can I do?* She's exactly what I've been waiting for.

Getting laid in Cambo is risky: disease, jealous boyfriends, bosses, pimps. Locals are bad news. Foreign girls are safer and usually more athletic, but they'll run if they know you live here: all the guidebooks helpfully point out that half the foreign guys in this country have

AIDS. NGO girls won't even fuck plastic, but backpackers are some-times game—if they think you're one of them. The Dragon is the best place to find them: Mama T weeds out most of the junkies, and the brats look for someplace with sheets.

All Claire wants is a good time and a few weeks' escape from Der-rida. If I can keep from sweating and being obviously speedy, I should be all right.

"Are you staying here?" she asks, glancing around the deck.

"I'm staying with a friend." Sometimes they catch on if you go to a house, but it improves the venue a lot. "I found this place yesterday, and I like the view. I got three days here, three in Siem Reap, then on to Koh Phangan."

"Wow, you'll love it. I just came from there!"

"You'll have to give me some advice. I'm new."

Claire has no plans.

Four lines of yaba in the Green Dragon bathroom, then I take her to the National Museum—right across the street from my "bor-rowed" room. Getting her up the stairs is the toughest part, but not that tough. A joint and an OxyContin and a few drinks of sweet, imported wine and then she's in my bed, sweaty in the midday heat, and I'm licking the salt sheen off those big, American breasts.

She has a tattoo of a blue-and-yellow lizard on her right hip bone; its green eyes stare down into the reddish-dark patch between her legs. I lick it and she laughs, hips writhing their way into the creased white of the sheets, and the sun rays are bouncing around us, painting the walls with ripples like we're underwater and hiding the dark forms that grow in the shadows.

We fuck hard, fast; she pants and I push and she screams. Frantic kisses, like tiny bites—

Then the quiet, euphoric and dizzy and sick all at once, and she goes to the bathroom naked, sunset caressing her so she glows like an image on a lightbox, transparent, and she comes back and—

"You're not staying with a friend, are you?"

I just stare at her from the bed.

"There's only one toothbrush and the suitcases in the hall are a girl's suitcases and—"

Then I don't listen because I can't stop the room from spinning—

—did she say there was a girl in the suitcases?

"Jesus, fuck . . . lied to me . . ."

"I'm not, come with me to the temple—"

"Get lost! I can't believe I'm here—"

come with me, it's sunset

and she's dressing, throwing clothes left and right

and then she's leaning over me and saying something even now it doesn't make any sense but I just laugh because the thing in the suitcase has gotten out and I feel it creeping up behind—

"When you find her, she'll make you wish I'd torn you apart."

And then it's finally dark.

Head full of grenades: concussions pound me from sleep. Open my eyes, but everything stays black. For a moment I have no idea where I am, and I reach across the bed for a hand that isn't there, hear strange voices whisper my name—

Outside, a dog barks. Night wind comes warm through the windows.

My apartment. Phnom Penh.

Alone.

I get up and pad to the door. Legs feel weak, shaky—like the fever that took me once in Battambang. Stumble across the landing, go to the bathroom in the dark. My head still pounds. Splash some water on my face and stand at the sink, listening: no motors on the street. No bats, just the distant barking of that dog. Smell of night rain over wood smoke.

Back on the landing, I reach for the light switch—then think better of it. Tea lights are by the sink, for when the power goes, and I light a couple; even their dim glow burns my eyes.

I haven't eaten anything in two days except beer. Bread rolls in the freezer: I pull one out and halfheartedly heat it over the burner. Scorch the outside and give up, sucking on it frozen. For a moment, I feel better—then my knees buckle. Hang on to the countertop, let it hold me as I slide to the floor.

I'm shaking too bad to stand up, so I reach over to the fridge. Two more frozen bread rolls. On the shelf, a packet of Styrofoam cookies, three left. I stay where I am, back against the cupboard as I work my way through them. Sugar helps, and the fit subsides.

After a while, I realize what I'm looking at.

June's suitcases.

They've been waiting here for days, weeks—who knows? For a moment I feel it again, like on the river: something rushing at me out of the dark. Then it's gone.

There are two cases: a black sports duffel, carry-on size, and a black, soft-sided roll-on, much larger. Too large: How much stuff do you need for three months in Phnom Penh in mid-summer? I open it. Inside: clothes, carefully rolled to maximize space. Underwear on top in a mesh bag. Sundresses and summer-weight pants: the things she'd need most, easily accessible. Under them, more layers. Skirts and tops; a pair of sneakers and a pair of summer sandals, carefully wrapped in plastic grocery bags. Either this girl is used to living out of a suitcase, or she's a massive control freak. Likely a bit of both.

By the time I get to the bottom, it's clear she didn't pack just for Cambo. There are sweaters, long underwear, a worn pair of Doc Martens. A heavy leather biker jacket, good for cold and rain. I hold it up: it would have been huge on her. She dresses like some kind of hippie punk. Blue jeans with flowers embroidered on them, *salwar kameez* shirts, loads of scarves. She doesn't have any *gear*: no brand names, no microfiber or roll-up water bottles or any of the fancy crap the scum bring with them. This one isn't reading catalogs: she just puts her stuff in a bag and she goes.

No club wear, not even a little black dress: not a party girl, then.

No birth control. No tampons.

A few personal items are rolled up with the winter clothes: a carved figurine from one of the markets downtown, a small brass Eiffel Tower, a few strings of carnival beads. She wants mementos, but has no room for big things.

Most interesting: a bag with a few dozen rolls of unshot 35 mm film, various speeds and stocks, including a couple I don't recognize at all. Somewhere, there should be photos.

Once the case is empty, I make sure nothing's stuffed in hidden pockets or sewn into the lining. Check the clothes as I put them back in, especially the leather jacket. For a moment I can almost see her, wandering up St. Mark's in a peasant skirt and a moth-eaten sweater, with the leather thrown over the top, her pale fingers clinging to the sleeves as she chews on a lock of that strange platinum hair—

I turn to the second bag.

More scarves, a light jacket. A cloth sling bag, rolled into a tiny tube. A makeup kit—the contents barely touched. A soft leather pencil case, filled with pens and markers in a dozen colors. A battered Walkman, a few unlabeled cassette tapes. A Graham Greene novel, a *Lonely Planet Cambodia,* a book of what appear to be ghost stories in Japanese. A round hairbrush. Spare glasses, two pairs. A Samsung phone charger.

Four letter-sized, heavy-duty, spiral notebooks.

These aren't reporter's notes. The covers are garish with ink and

pictures pasted from magazines. No titles, no obvious dates. Inside—
it's hard to tell. Pages packed with colors and lines and glue and words.
Tiny, ragged letters, jammed together, covering every inch of space.
Drawings, photos, all overlapping. Part journal, part scrapbook, part
art project? I set them aside and finish with the case.

I'm thinking of what I don't see. No laptop, no power cords or
adapters. She could have taken all that stuff with her, but it'd be a
funny choice for backpacking: I'm guessing she didn't have a computer. No documents—medical records, insurance cards, all the stuff
you're supposed to have when you think your life is worth something.

Stuffed into an outside pocket are two bottles of Malarone. One
is empty, one has a couple pills left. Another puzzle: you don't worry
about malaria in Phnom Penh. Was she spending a lot of time out
in the woods? Did she take the pills with her? But then why not the
bottles?

No empty space.

These cases don't match the storyline, and an unpleasant thought
is forming in my head: Assume there's no laptop, and she doesn't carry
personal documents. Then the only things missing are the phone and
the camera.

Then it starts to look like June didn't expect to be leaving at all.

The duffel has a semi-concealed zip pocket; inside are two small
photo envelopes.

I get the tea lights from the counter and sit cross-legged, spreading
the pictures on the floor: squares of black and white on the tile. The
candles I've lit make them orange.

I sit there a long time, trying to push down the dizzy feeling I get
when I look at them. Everything else in her cases makes sense in some
way, but these don't:

A bit of a finger on a table, next to something white.

A blurred form that might be a bug on the edge of a sink.

A field of gray, white lines—light reflecting on water?

No parties. No friends. No architecture. Just these frames of nothing, out of focus. Most give no clue as to location. A couple seem to be from Europe: muddy shots of nameless heaths in half light. Others are clearly Cambodia. A shudder runs through me as I realize two were taken from my bedroom: the balcony rail in grainy black and white, the landscape beyond just a haze of reflections, but the silhouette of the museum roof is unmistakable.

A couple bits of riveted iron, part of some structure I can't make out.

A flat, gray body of water, dark specks that might be trees visible in the distance.

Who would take pictures like this?

Maybe she thinks she's an artist—but these just look like mistakes. Still. There's something about them—unsteady, unsettling in their painstaking carelessness. They make you wonder what she was really trying to shoot.

The image is a distraction: what you want to see is somewhere else.

Only two photos of her. They're different from the others—typical snapshots, taken by a friend or fellow tourist. In one, she's on a tour boat. I'm guessing Paris, though I can't make out any landmarks. She's standing too far away and staring out at the water, all you get is hair and glasses. In the other, she's on a street I've seen somewhere in the city, but I can't place it. Khmer writing around her, a neon halo. It's night, but she's lit by something behind the shooter that makes her features pop. She's making a face, a mock snarl at whoever's holding the camera, one hand held up like a claw.

It's a lucky shot, or a good one: an unfeigned moment in perfect light. The graduation photo Kara gave me made her ugly and mean. Here, she's charming: the innocent abroad.

Trying to imitate her care, I repack the second case—all except the photos and the journals, those I carry back to the desk in my room.

The floor by my bed is covered with shattered glass. My shaving mirror. What happened? Must have been the girl . . . Claire? I step cautiously around the pieces. Mrs. Mun will never ask when she cleans them up.

As I go through the pockets of my jeans, I realize the money is gone. Everything I had on me—including my advance. Bitch must have taken it: payback for lying to her. Shit. Doubt I can go back to Kara begging for more. I'll have to find another source of cash, at least for now.

The graduation photo is still there; I set it next to the other on my desk. Pick up one of the notebooks. The page I open to is so jammed with colored scrawl it's unreadable. A few words remain:

Once again I stay, when I should have disappeared . . .

> *. . . was I thinking? That they mean something?*
> *Who . . .*
> *. . . nothing to do for it . . .*
> *. . . ever escape . . . this?*
> *. . . told me, then . . . sorry, I said. I didn't mean to*
> *be, what . . .*
> *. . . like that again.*

I close the book. I don't want to read this. My head hurts. I need to piss.

When I have, I'm tired again. Lie on the bed and wait for dawn.

———————

Sun in my eyes. Traffic noise from the street, and a voice in my head saying something's wrong.

"Really?"

Not in my head: on the stairs, the landing below. Gus. He's on the phone, I heard it ringing, but it was his voice that woke me: a whisper loaded with anxiety . . . sadness?

"Fucking hell," he says. "Fucking hell . . . all right. All right . . . I'll find someone. . . . No, definitely not. No . . . *mierda*." Then silence.

My head still hurts. I dress without thinking and walk downstairs.

Woman's voice: "Should we tell—" Australian accent. The dread-locked girl from the party—I've already forgotten her name. Gus hushes her:

"I'll let Khieu sort it. Christ, I don't—"

They're in their landing-cum-kitchen, eating breakfast, and their faces look worse than the fry-up Gus is wolfing. He's leaning against the bathroom wall, eating with his fingers from a cracked plastic plate. She sits on the counter, staring at the floor.

"Who died?"

They look up like I've caught them screwing in church. "It's noth-ing," Gus says, grabbing a chunk of fried egg and sucking it down. Neon yolk stains his fingers.

"Don't take up poker."

He sees my face: knows he's busted. What's so bad he'd try to hide it from me?

"Journo got shot."

First thought: *I'm late again.* "Where?"

"In the face," the girl says, snagging a huge chunk of tomato off Gus's plate. Her nails bite its skin and it bleeds on her.

Gus glares: we'll dance on every other grave, but this is one of our own. "Outside his office. Two guys in helmets got off a moto and shot him. They grabbed his wallet, so officially it's a mugging gone bad."

"How does a mugging go good?" the girl asks.

Gus is still hiding something, I can see it all over him. He hasn't answered my question.

"Where?" I say again, louder.

It costs him something to answer, but he knows the alternative is violence. I think he considers it anyway, but the girl sitting there changes his mind.

"Radio Ranariddh," he says softly.

"Who is it?" They wince like I'm screaming—maybe I am.

"We don't have a name yet," Gus says, and it's another goddamn lie. I'm heading for the stairs, not listening to whatever else he's shouting after me.

I wish to hell I could say I ran for the door, but I didn't.

I ran for my cameras first.

Radio Ranariddh runs out of a converted house on a suburban side street. It's usually quiet: today it's something out of Breughel. Uniforms setting up sawhorse barriers, pushing against seething knots of angry FUNCINPEC sympathizers, gawking neighbors, restless kids. Private security swarming the station office, facing off with the cops. AP and the Welshman are here already, along with some of the local stringers, pointing their cameras at anyone who'll mug for them: stirring things up. It's not gunpowder-tense yet—but it could get there with a few bad moves.

I'm late, but not too late: Prik drives fast. My head is still screaming, and I have to force myself not to shove people out of the way. Keep my press badge and camera visible: don't want to get beat up today. Not that they'll help if something sets this thing off.

I reach the barrier and look out over a sea of red, mud and blood baking dry in the morning sun. The potholes in the road glisten scarlet. In the middle, there he is. Someone's thrown a tarp down, but no mistaking who's under it: I can see the shape of his hunch against the fabric. One stunted hand pokes out from under the edge, twisted in the dirt.

Bunny, you dumb asshole. You said you were safe. You said you were lucky.

It's the money shot, and I raise my camera. Find his hand in the frame, but all I see are his eyes laughing at me in the gray morning:

"A pest like me? Not worth the candle."

I can't push the button. Suddenly I'm shaking because this reminds me of something, it's happening again—that's the thought that keeps going through my mind: *It's happening again,* but I can't think *what,* and I just keep staring through the lens.

All that blood.

A slow gush, spreading over the road: It wasn't a clean shot. Caught him in the neck, maybe, and he'd have lived a minute or two, gasping in the dirt while his heart kept pumping, watching as the life poured out of him—

Just like—

Enough.

———————

The sun is murder, and people keep shoving me. For a second I'm disoriented: *What just happened?* Christ, I must be getting heatstroke. There's a crowd around me, pushing up to the barriers, shouting, shoving. An ugly scene, and getting uglier. Vans on the corners, pouring out more police, these in tac gear.

Check the camera: film counter at twenty. I've been shooting, then. I keep it up, trying to edge my way out of the press.

A man half-shouting at a cop over the barricade of an old wooden sawhorse; nervous eyes. Snap, snap.

A gaggle of women watching the investigators, wringing hands with guillotine fingers. Snap.

Through the lens, I see their frustration, their fear: It doesn't touch me. I seal it in silver nitrate, for others. I am a blank, a film cell. I am the thing that records.

The crowd surges and swells, and I breathe deep, forcing myself to go along. A young guy suddenly rises—he's balancing on two police barriers and chanting something, I'm having trouble making it out. My brain feels like it's made of cotton fuzz. Point the camera, wait until his head knocks the sun out of the frame. Snap, snap, snap. The police lieutenant, wondering how dangerous it will be to come over and knock him down. Snap.

The crowd shifts, a few start chanting along. I've got to get off this street.

There, on the corner opposite the station: an apartment under construction, five or six stories. That should do. I push my way through the last few feet of crowd.

No one's bothered with a fence, and as I duck into the ground floor, I see I'm in luck: the stairs are laid already, bare concrete with no railings. My heart's pounding as I take them up through the shell. Reach the roof and look down at the street. Yes, there's something there: the movement of the scene, the tension—onlookers straining against cops, security. It's not a riot, yet, but it'll do.

In the left of the frame, a cop's waving hand draws the eye to the dark red patch of earth where the body fell—

They've taken it away already, so no shot there. I'll give it ten more minutes here, see if a fight breaks out, then head for the morgue.

Zoom in: snap, snap. Maybe time for another angle, but—

A tickle in the back of my neck. Fingers pricking.

Turn around. Slow.

He's sitting a few feet away, tucked into that little Khmer crouch next to a pile of two-by-fours. I couldn't see him from the ground. Young guy, skinny, wearing a green tracksuit. Hard, flat eyes. I guess he was watching the street, but now he's watching me.

He is serene, expressionless. My stomach is doing backflips.

"Hey," I say in Khmer. "Just taking some pictures. For the paper." Flash my badge. "You working here?" He doesn't say anything. "Hope it's okay I'm on your roof?" Nothing. "I'll just go then. Sorry to bother you." I take a last shot—aimless, trying to be nonchalant. Then up, slowly, head for the door.

He moves so fast I barely see him, his leg swinging into my midsection like a baseball bat.

On the ground, blood in my mouth.

Cradle my camera—he grabs at it, I hang on. He launches two swift kicks at my fingers: cling tighter, so he plants his foot on my torn-up arm. My hands go numb—

He starts on my face.

Then he's at the edge of the roof, dropping my camera over with a grin.

I should get up—

Then nothing.

DIARY

July 2

There's this place the guys go . . . it doesn't have a name, it's not even really a bar, just some plastic tables and chairs a Cambodian couple has set up in the street outside their garage. The boy likes the curry they make, so he goes when he's been working late, and last night he dragged a bunch of us along. I was excited to be asked. (The other interns are big, jock-ish jerks from J-schools in the Midwest, and no one invited them.) The guys started us drinking early, never mind it was a school night, and then there was a better bar to go to, and another, and another until who knows when. . . .

So we were all ruined in the office this morning, of course. Everyone was trying not to let on, but Gus is not an idiot and obviously he knew, he was glaring and growling, just waiting for us to slip up. But we were in it together. Even Barry, the business guy, who can be pretty surly . . . we were in the kitchen trying to make coffee, and we were too messed up to get the filter to work, and just kept spilling things everywhere and watching each other trying not to crack up.

I didn't get into the drugs with them, of course. . . . There's something else I've never written down before!

Back in high school, the very rich and very bad girls would gather in the music-room closet and toke on little joints of Mexican grass, and a couple times I went in, too. They got high and giggled about menstrual blood and sex, but me the drug took, like some deep-sea creature come up beneath a swimmer in dark water. Three times I tried it, and always the same: a terrible sense that the world beneath my fingers was a dream. I could be dead, or lying in a hospital bed, eyes twitching away in a coma. . . . I could wake and discover I was someone else altogether.

So now I roll a spliff with the best of them, but I definitely don't inhale. Which, possibly, was why I was slightly less messed up than everyone else . . . so when the call came, there was Gus, waving the phone around and talking about "some NGO, claims they've been broken into and the government's behind it," and the crime writer could barely raise his head and the econ writer was asleep in his chair, so his eye fell on me . . . looking wrecked and wretched, I'm sure, but just conscious enough I might be able to turn around a story, and he stuck the phone in my hand:

"Get directions and go. Take Khieu, just in case."

"Just in case of what??"

As I was heading out, Barry woke up enough to catch my eye. "Khieu was with Gus in '98," he muttered. "Guy knows how to drive while being shot at."

Indeed, it turns out that Khieu, despite doing everything else at quite a leisurely pace, drives insanely fast. I tried to tell him that speed was actually irrelevant if you didn't reach your destination alive . . . but the wind whipped my words away, and there was nothing to do but keep my arms wrapped tight around him and hang on. He was worse than the moto drivers. We reached the main boulevard, packed with cars, and rather than wait he just swung left into the wrong lane, and for nearly two blocks we dodged oncoming traffic until *finally* he saw his chance to cut right and get back to our side of the road. I'd just started to breathe again when traffic seized up and he started squeezing between cars, still going as fast as he could. Right when I thought we were going to get out, a white Toyota behind us tried to pull out, too, knocking us off-kilter against some SUV. Khieu kept us upright and I thought I was fine, until I realized the cool wind on my leg was carrying away little drops of blood. I ruined my scarf for a makeshift bandage, but I didn't think it would do to show up at a crime scene bleeding.

The NGO office wasn't far from my house—a big grimy office block on the grassy swath near Independence Monument. The bottom floor was all glass windows, except the glass was all over the pavement and there were cops everywhere. Cops: I almost couldn't get off the bike my heart was pounding so hard—but I remembered myself. I am a fearless reporter. I'll take my notebook and stick my nose anywhere. The pain in my leg was actually kind of steadying. I just marched across the lawn to the busiest person, a tall Chinese-American guy with Frodo hair, and asked to talk to him.

His name was Luke, and it turned out he wasn't in charge, he was just a project manager. The real boss was a woman named Wendy, the one who'd called Gus in the first place. She was a major head trip . . . the whole thing had completely spun her out, and Luke was having to spend most of his energy calming her down, rubbing her shoulders and telling her it was okay. Hey, if I were his boss, I'd make him do that all day. . . . He's not pretty like the boy, though he's got all the right bumps in all the right places—but he was handsome, like drown-you-in-testosterone handsome. Think *ER*-era Clooney, only Chinese. He reminded me of the men who used to hang around Father's businesses: children of immigrants with hungry eyes, looking for a way into a world of glass. He had a smile that said: "You won't believe the day I've had."

I took my time interviewing them. Their story didn't make any kind of sense.

Wendy thinks the break-in was an attempt at intimidation, connected with the NGO's work out west. The local governors there are all into illegal logging and fishing: it's incredibly destructive, but it's the only game in town that pays. The NGO is promoting eco-tourism, but that's seen as competition: the governors don't want legitimate industries coming in and giving people alternatives.

Luke doesn't hold with conspiracy theories: he says it's either a robbery gone wrong or a vendetta by a disgruntled staff member.

The intimidation theory does seem far-fetched—are we really supposed to believe Luke and Wendy and their little project are enough of a problem for some corrupt governor to take an interest? But who tries to rob the office of an aid organization doing eco-tourism development? Stupid criminals, that's who. Still, when you break into a building, even if it's not the score you hoped for, you take what you can get. Right? There were laptops, hard drives, cell phones—stuff you could get cash for if you needed it—so why was nothing missing except $100 from the petty cash kitty? Option two is, you trash the place. But nothing was smashed aside from the window, one PC monitor, and the cabinet drawers, which were all jimmied open.

So I see two possibilities. A) The break-in wasn't about robbery or vengeance, it was about reconnaissance. Someone wanted a look at something in that office—the files, the employee lists, the access to another building—and they wanted it bad enough not to care if they made a mess getting their look. B) Perhaps more interesting—Luke and Wendy aren't telling everything, and something was taken: something the police wouldn't notice, and that the NGO wouldn't want to admit was missing.

I ran all this by Gus, of course—he laughed and said I was thinking too much. This kind of stuff happens every day. But even if he didn't see a story in it, I didn't care. . . .

I think I'm starting to enjoy this gig.

In the office, I grinned and flicked lit matches at the boys, who yelped and fought and gave me Indian rubs. Today was nothing—just a little touch of Cambo in the night—but I felt like I'd made the club. I had scars.

WILL

Gus gapes at me as I stagger through the door. He's on the couch in his apartment, laying up for a siege. Bottle of Kentucky rye on the coffee table—his good stuff, about two inches left in the bottom. Next to it: the battered old 9 mm the *NYT* correspondent left after his last trip. Ignore the gun; pick up the whiskey and take a long swallow. My cut mouth burns. I take another.

"Jesus, Keller. The fuck happened to you?"

"Ran into my ex."

"Vy wouldn't hit you, *hijo*. She'd have you shot." His face gets redder as he realizes what he's just said, and he stands and grabs the whiskey back from me. "Jesus Christ."

The day's injury list so far: one black eye, one swollen jaw, one very bloody nose. Possibly a couple cracked ribs, but hopefully no internal bleeding. Likely concussion. Can't move my right hand very well, not sure what that is. A bad sunburn on the side that was up when I passed out. One plastic sack, donated by a shopkeeper, filled with broken camera parts, and one roll of partially exposed film. The goon didn't bother with my bag, so the digital is okay.

Apparently my state is pathetic enough to warrant another drink: Gus passes me the bottle again. "Drink this, I'll drive you to the hospital."

"Later." I lower myself onto the couch.

Gus's look is pity and worry and unacknowledged contempt. "You should see a doctor."

Ignore him. Feel my eyes start to close again. That's no good.

"Stimulants," I say. "Then you're gonna tell me what I've got myself into."

Gus.

No one knows why he's still in Cambo. It's not the sort of question you ask. I know that sometime during the Dirty War his family decided Argentina was too dangerous and sent him to school in the States. I don't know who they thought was after him. Argentina got better, but Gus never went back.

When he came out here he was working for the wires, but he got fed up and started his own paper—the *Post* and the *Daily* had just got going, and he hated them both. He's kept the thing running for years on guts, coke, and an endless string of free interns.

When I landed, we hit it right off. Same interests: drugs and kickboxing and military coups. He got me work, and the upstairs room in Mun's house. We spent our mornings fighting, our nights chasing the dragon—but Gus always held back. He's a different kind of addict: his fix is answers. He doesn't want the headline, he wants the solution. That kind of desire takes you strange places. I think he stayed in Cambo because he couldn't figure it out.

It means he's going to die here.

I wonder if he's figured that out yet.

Two cups of coffee, half a pack of cigarettes, and a candy bowl full of Sudafed and 800 mg Advil, and I'm ready. Gus's girl is long gone, but we're still talking in whispers. It's hot, and even with the balcony doors open the room is an oven. Jammed with plants and stacks of books and boxing gear and caged lovebirds, it feels like the jungle. Pain creases my face when I wipe away the sweat.

"There are wheels within wheels here," Gus says. "The obvious thing would be that Bunny, *que en paz descanse,* just pissed off the wrong guy. You heard what he'd been saying about Hun Sen's so-called reconciliation plan."

"Only heard."

"Well, it was bold. Not just the usual insults, y'know, calling him a one-eyed dog. Bunny used logic—took apart the speeches to show how Hun Sen was promising everything to everyone and could never live up to it all. It was dangerous stuff. Before you got back, Hun Sen warned Radio Ranariddh they should shut up. Bunny toned it down, but maybe it was too late." He's watching me like a kid who's thrown a bag of M-80s into the campfire and is waiting to see if they'll explode.

"But you don't buy it." I suck on another Advil. My teeth feel like glass.

"Well, there are other angles, eh? Hun Sen hasn't got the seats to form a government, right—not without either FUNCINPEC or Rainsy throwing in with him. Rainsy says fuck you, obviously, he lives off being opposition. But FUNCINPEC? They're nothing without favors to trade. So they're dropping hints like mad, saying they'll give him his coalition, but they want stuff in exchange: dissidents let out of jail, better posts in the cabinet, assurances it won't be '98 all over again . . . The list just gets longer. What if Hun Sen got tired of it? He wants his job back, and he wants it now, so he starts sending a few royalists on Khmer Rouge holidays—just a little reminder where this thing could go if they keep pushing him."

"Royalists, plural?"

"A minor FUNCINPEC figure was shot and killed in Kampong Cham a couple days back. Someone took his head as a souvenir. Everyone thought this was a local grievance . . . but maybe not. Then, a week ago, in Siem Reap, an organizer was stabbed—"

"I get the idea. All a bit public to just be bargaining with Rana-riddh, though." My head aches. "Is it just coincidence this happens today? With the army and the police about to kill each other?"

He has to stop and chew on that one awhile. It's not so far-fetched: bad stuff happens every day in Cambodia, so the odds go all to hell. When he looks up, I see the idea glowing in his eyes. He's chasing his fix now, and even Bunny doesn't faze him.

"How about this, then: darker powers at work, right? Hun Sen is letting some big army guys hang out to dry in this heroin-bust thing. Embarrassing, that, eh? A four-star general trafficking junk? Makes them all look like pushers and thieves. So how hard would it be for General Peng, or someone even higher, to say, 'Fine: embarrass us, we'll embarrass you.'"

"And because he'd threatened the radio station last week, everyone knew Bunny was in Hun Sen's crosshairs. Anything happens to him, that's where we all look."

"Exactly." Gus is so jazzed, he's actually grinning. "The prime minister looks like a murderer in front of all the nice people who think he's reformed. Aid money could start pulling out, investors—could hurt his position a lot."

"And it could explain why the scene was being watched." I touch my face to see how much it hurts. "Find out who took the bait."

Gus nods. Reaches for the whiskey—as he does, I see it all come back to him. The excitement dies. He pours until it's done. "How shit would that be? If it was all just a distraction? I suppose it's no difference to Bunny, but I'd rather Hun Sen killed him. At least it would mean he shook things up." He downs his glass, winces.

I say nothing.

Finally: "There's another option. What about the girl?"

Gus looks blank: *What girl?*

"The one who's missing: June Saito."

He didn't see that coming: you'd think I'd hit him in the teeth. Then he laughs. It's a raw, hurt laugh, but he's got nowhere else to go. "*Hija de puta.* The girl." He starts to say more, but he's laughing again. I breathe a bit easier: with everything else going on, Gus forgot all about June. He still thinks whatever happened to her is a mistake or a misunderstanding; that soon enough she'll come wandering back with a sheepish grin on her face: *So sorry for the trouble.*

It means he had nothing to do with it.

"So she found you," he says, when he's calmed down. "The sister." He's looking at my cigarettes: bad sign. "I meant to warn you, but the day was so . . ."

"You needed a drink first." He nods. "Tell me everything she said."

He stands up, then sits down, not sure what to do with himself. "It was about five thirty, in the middle of deadline. You had just left. And this woman walks into my office, asking if I know where June is. I said, sure: she's taking a few days to go to Siem Reap, see Angkor, maybe go up to Laos. I haven't heard from her. Why would I? She'll be back to get her stuff when she's done. Except then I realized, she's been gone for two whole weeks. And the woman—the sister—says yes, June didn't make her plane home, they're all concerned."

"So, any reason someone would target her and Bunny?"

"You have Cambo on the brain. Am I worried about June? Of course, but not like that."

"Why not?"

"The girl was bright, okay? Focused. But not so great when it came to taking care of herself. She got in a moto accident, some little scrape, and she got a tiny bit of a cut on her leg. She just wraps it up, doesn't mention it to anyone—a couple weeks later she winds up in hospital in Sihanoukville. She'd been wandering around in the swamps and thing's got infected. This'll be the same, or something like it."

"Humor me." For some reason, I don't want to tell him about the suitcases yet. "We have a dead journo and a missing one, and you're saying no connection?"

He thinks a long time before he answers. "You put it that way, it looks odd, but they're too different. Bunny . . ." He pauses, giving me that firecracker look again. I wait. He breathes deep. "You said it yourself: Bunny was public relations. Whoever killed him wanted everyone to know. June just never came back. Now if—*if* something happened to her that wasn't an accident, then it was timed just right, eh? So no one would notice for days, weeks even. I can think of lots of people who might go after journos, and lots of reasons why, but I can't make those two things sit right."

"And they didn't know each other? We've got nothing that puts them together?"

He shakes his head. "I can look, but it'll be hard without telling everyone she's gone."

Kara whispering in my head: *"I want it done quietly."* "It bug you the sister didn't want police?"

He nods. "She'd heard the cops could be into trafficking, she was worried about a blond half-Japanese girl."

"You saw June. Think that was likely?"

"Who the fuck knows, man? She was no beauty queen, but with the sick bastards out there, who can tell?"

"I'm guessing you called the hospitals in Siem Reap already?"

He nods. "And the ones along the way—as many as I could without getting noticed. Nothing yet."

"When did you see her last?"

"Night before she left. Right here. She was packing, came down to bring me some kitchen stuff she wasn't going to need anymore. Said she would sleep in before getting the boat, so I wouldn't see her in the morning."

"And you didn't?"

"Went to the club at six, then the office."

"So we don't even know for sure she went upriver. She could have hit the airport, be in Djibouti by now. Any reason she might take off? Family troubles, love, money?"

He shakes his head.

"Drugs?"

"Never that I saw."

"Boyfriends, any reason to skip out?"

"Don't think so."

"What *was* she into?"

"Just—quiet? I didn't see her out much—kept to herself, except for work. She was a good writer: clever as hell, kept at a story until she got it. Not much else."

"You're a real lifesaver here, Gus. You call yourself a journalist, you might try asking a question or two of your staff sometime."

"Well, I didn't know she was going to fucking vanish!"

From nowhere, I'm furious. Feel the ache in my bones, blood in my eyes—I think I'm shouting. "The fuck country do you think this is? You think we're in Switzerland? We're where every backpacker and junkie and psycho on the planet comes to die—"

"And you're the fucking expert on that, aren't you?"

—and then it's gone. My head hurts. I suck on another Advil and watch the lovebirds, who appear to be screwing. "Paying a little attention wouldn't have killed you."

"Well, too goddamn late now."

We stay like that a minute or two, staring at the walls. Gus pulls a cigarette from my pack. Lights it, inhales—the deep drag of a long-time quitter who's come back to the fold. Lets the smoke out slow.

Once he's got his nicotine, he turns back to me. "I shouldn't have got you into this." He's got that pitying look on his face again. "Try not to let it get to you."

Try to stay calm: "Why the fuck would it get to me?"

He's about to answer, then changes his mind. I almost ask him—
You don't want to know.

"Widen the net with the hospitals. Call 'em all. I'll cut you in for your time." He waves the offer off, takes another cigarette. "While you're at it, ring that friend of Klein's in Bangkok. Let's hack her e-mail, see if there's anything useful there." He nods, and I have a moment of not hating his guts. "Why *did* you get me into this?"

He turns, stares, says nothing: waiting for me to have whatever realization he thinks I should be having. I stub out my cigarette on his coffee table. One more scar.

He sighs. "Anything bad happens, you're the first one there."

After that, I let him drive me to the hospital. I need drugs, in quantity, and given my state, scoring them isn't hard. Two ribs turn out to be cracked, but not bad. On the plus side, the fingers aren't broken. I'll heal—if I can avoid getting the shit kicked out of me again.

I know what I should be doing now: I should be buttonholing June's friends, asking what they know about her. Most of the time, when family report someone missing, there's a love interest they don't know about, or an addiction. Someone knows, though—a friend, a work buddy. Poke around a bit, the answer pops up. But June's mates are journos: I start asking questions, ten minutes later the whole thing's on CNN. Kara wanted this quiet. She has a reason—and I'd like to know what it is. For now, at least, I play along. Two weeks out, it doesn't matter if I keep things close for a few days.

Also: I'd like to get paid.

I can't ask around, but maybe I've got something better: I've got a diary. A part of me is aching to go back and take a look, but there are things I need first. Cash. Possibly divine intervention. Time to call on the Angel Gabriel.

———————

Heaven is poorly lit and smells of vomit. It's about 3 million degrees inside, tinfoil and duct tape over the windows. There is no vileness like a real junkie's lair, but the man has what I need.

Before he was a junkie, he was a journo, I know this for a fact. Before that, they say he was a priest. At the moment he's a sweaty, scratching mess, trying to control the effects of the recent drought with various painkillers: a man on the edge of a fix but not quite able to fall in.

"Brought you some Percocet."

He bolts the door behind me and collapses against it, snatching at the remains of his beard with stained fingers as he inspects the packet. "Waddaya want for 'em?"

"Work. I need cash, and fast. What you got? Anything moving in the city?"

He looks me up and down like he's trying to remember who I am. "You're presentable these days," he mutters. "Except for the face, that's a bit of a problem, huh? Oh, and the arm . . . Actually, you look like shit, it's this town, huh, does that to you. . . . But you know your way around, I guess—got a joint?"

I look for a place to sit. Dirty mattresses, spotted with mildew. Pizza boxes and beer cans. Six broken televisions. Piles of books everywhere, on the floor and against the walls, bristling with black-and-green fungus. Gabriel paces, never stopping his low, murmured monologue: hard to tell if he's talking to you or himself.

"—little fuckers are supposed to clean, but half the time they just take their pills and run, I'm afraid of moving half this stuff, I don't know what's underneath, but I figure it's all a metaphor—hey, welcome to Cambodia post-government—like that's new—are we having fun yet?" I sweep the spoons and candle ends off a cracked end table and start rolling. "This whole situation is fucked, fucked, fucked, like rusty chainsaw—" He stops to breathe and grins, a jungle ruin of gray-and-yellow teeth. "I got something you could do, but you won't like it."

"No kids." It's starting to hurt to talk.

"Relax. I just want to utilize your photographic skills—"

"No kids."

"Heh, hoo, oh, this is worse, worse, but I think you go for this kind of bad. Ever hear of a guy named Van Chennarith?"

"Nah."

"One of those little fuckers, boy-band gangster, dresses like NSYNC and acts like Pol Pot, but—but his father is who you worry about, he's po-lice, and high up, sure, I mean this guy—I've heard shit, okay? Serious shit—but politically not really a power on his own. He's a gofer for bigger players, gets to stick his fat thumb in every dirty cunt in the city"—Gabriel matches the gesture to the obscenity, hand twitching like a palsy victim's—"guns, drugs, you name it. Unfortunately for him, his son is a genuine back-door boy, takes it in the ass on a regular basis, mostly from foreigners—and for pleasure, apparently, not cash—yeah, that one always bewilders me, too, so"—he catches his breath—"I want pictures."

I whistle. "On second thought, I'll take the kiddie porn. That'll just get you prison. This'll get you dead."

"It's the job I have."

"What's it worth to you?"

He names a figure—it's satisfactory.

"How long I got?"

"Five days."

I nod and light the joint.

"There a lot of stuff moving through the city now?" I ask again, trying to be casual. I'm sure he sees right through me.

His smile comes back as he leans forward. "Shitloads. More than anyone's ever seen before, or anyhow that's the rumor, because no one's actually *seen* it: no one's selling. All for export."

"This the stuff they bagged on Friday?"

"Maybe." He fumbles for a lighter. He doesn't know.

That's why he needs me. "I need an advance." Pass him the pot.

"Pick me up more Percocet, and I'll give ya two thousand up front." Gabriel never leaves his apartment, has to have all his drugs couriered in.

"Four. You don't want this traced. I'll have to buy a plane ticket."

He rises, suddenly tired looking, and stalks off into some indescribable kitchen in search of cash.

Doing a job for him is a bad idea. Doing *this* job is a really bad idea—but I haven't had many good ones lately. It works out all right: Either my luck comes back or I'm dead in a week.

"One more thing," I say, as the junkie trots back with my money. "Got any roofies?"

———————

By the time I get free, the world is fraying at the edges. Gabriel wanted to rant, and I was in that vile hole for hours as he smoked joint after joint of my stuff and shouted about useless American politicians and the war in Iraq and the war on drugs. The swan song of the world's last great junkie philosopher.

The street outside is pitch-black, and I cling to the wall, trying to get my bearings. Head for the river. Even with the drugs, the pain has grown into a living thing, spreading out from my ribs until all I can think about is how much I hurt. I can hardly stand up straight. I need rest, and food—can't remember when I last ate.

In the corner of my eye, a shadow moves. I try to walk faster, stumble, slide nearly to the ground before I catch myself on the wall again. The motodops across the street rev their engines and mutter—who knows who they're working for?

Christ: getting paranoid. Too long in the dark. Got to get to the river—

Two blocks feels like two years.

The Edge is a mirage, glowing. Channi's eyes go big when she spots me, and she runs out from behind the bar to take my ruined face in her hands.

"What happen?" Her voice is husky with concern.

"I thought I'd try kickboxing," I say, in Khmer.

"You're even dumber than most foreigners," she snaps. She's older when she speaks her own language. Tougher. I try to laugh, and my face twists in pain. She puts her hand on my shoulder, smiles like she knows the feeling. For a second, she's another person. Then she switches to English, and the pixie girl is back: "I get you beer."

"Food," I mutter, and collapse in a chair. It's getting cooler. The rain must have come while I was inside, and a breeze sweeps away the day's stale heat. Beer helps. I want a burger, but my face won't move much, so I settle for rice and fish soup. Pop the last of my Advil. The place is empty, and Channi sits with me while I eat. She doesn't ask any questions, just watches as I ladle the broth onto the rice and chew, painfully.

I take a good look at her. She's as dark as the polished wood of the bar, and her profile has the placid curves of a stone Apsara. She dresses to keep the wolves off—no halter tops and cutoffs for her. Tonight it's a loose white blouse with a plunging neck, over skinny jeans and simple black flats. It says, *No, really, I'm a waitress*. Lacquered bracelets clatter at her wrists. Her eyes are huge and bright, and when she turns them on me I forget who I am for a minute.

She's got Tom Waits on the stereo. The drums dance with the twinkling lights of the bar, and some of the knots in my head come undone. I could sit here forever, just watching—but I'm going to crash soon. I need to get back to the house.

Order another beer.

Channi gets it and goes back to cleaning glasses.

For as long as I can, I just sit, aching fingers tracing the wicker strands in the arm of my chair. I'm realizing I don't want to go back. I might even be avoiding it—avoiding *her*. June and her journal. For some reason I can't put my finger on, they frighten me.

But it's too late: nothing else left.

I give Channi a tip as I leave, and she reaches out and presses my good hand: gentle, unsmiling.

"Be careful," she says in Khmer.

———————

My bedroom. Bats screaming outside the window; June's notebooks on my desk. I take the one on top of the pile. On the cover, a Rapha-elite sort of angel, drawn in ink: pendulously male, limp wrist and bloody sword. Radiating out from him, a starburst of color, razored from magazines in tiny strips, so only hints remain of the original image—glimpses of desert, sea, of strange machinery.

Now, with June's history in my hand, the feeling is stronger than ever: I don't want to read it. Whatever happened, I don't want to know.

I could walk away. Turn around and dump this all on Gus's doorstep, find some way to pay back Kara; I could come up with a reason—

The reasons make no sense. The only way out is to go on.

I open the book.

It's worse than I thought.

The pages are thick with pasted-in pictures, tickets, notes—little tokens, fetishes. Words go up, down, any way that fits: written between lines and in margins and over other entries in different colors, even different languages. I see English, French, Italian . . . characters that must be Japanese. In places, great chunks of text are blacked out with marker. She doesn't say where she is, or when: time and place come as Paris metro fares and Brazilian train tickets. I find Cambodia by the newspaper clippings; it takes up most of two volumes. Her boarding passes are right there, the stubs glued to the page.

"A tiny plane, smelling of cigarettes . . ."

She arrives late, on the last Saturday of June. In thirteen weeks, she will be gone.

Except for this.

DIARY

July 5

God, *God*, why do I do this to myself? I knew, I must have known, what waited here—did I really think I could steer my way past all the bitter, sharp, and poisonous things that give this place its reputation? And yet I let myself be drawn, again and again, to these . . . these excrescences of death.

It only took a week for them to get me to the torture chamber.

On Saturday afternoon, I hired a moto driver to take me around the city. It was only supposed to be a tour. I remember the rest of it like some distant dream: cruising through the beautiful old parts of Phnom Penh under a blue sky, around buildings in a hundred states of gorgeous decrepitude, pagodas and temples with roofs guarded by naga, the nine-headed snake-angels that are supposed to protect against evil spirits. I visited the wat in the center of the city, and it was like a tiny slice of forest, quiet and serene, while in the nearby streets angelic monks wandered through traffic unscathed with their tame elephant. When the driver told me the name of the last stop, I didn't understand it, I just nodded and let myself be taken to Tuol Sleng.

The name means "poisoned hill," and when properly pronounced it sounds like a curse. At first it was a school, now it's a monument . . . but for a time in between, it was Hell.

In 1975, the Khmer Rouge took over this country, instituting radical agrarian communism. They called it Year Zero: history ended and began anew. Overnight they emptied the cities, sending whole populations on a forced march back to their home villages—villages they might not have lived in for generations. How many died on that march? Thousands? Tens of thousands? They slaughtered anyone with any kind of education, and when it came time to build their agrarian paradise there was no one left who knew how to build, or dig a sewer, or run a functioning farm. Over the next three years, millions succumbed to famine and disease. Leaders grew desperate for someone to blame, and supposed spies and enemies of the state were taken to Tuol Sleng, and places like it, where they were interrogated about imaginary conspiracies, tortured and executed. Their piled skulls reach the ceilings.

By the time the Vietnamese invaded and drove the Khmer Rouge back to the hills, a third of Cambodia's population had been killed. Those who survived were changed: their identity was bound up in death. They had nothing left, save the knowledge that something terrible happened to them. You cannot understand us, they say, unless you have been to Tuol Sleng. Unless you have seen our skulls in grinning piles; seen the iron bed-frames to which our uncles chained our parents for torture; seen the flesh still hanging from the hooks like leather, the blood still on the floors . . .

It's not even death, death was something that happened long ago. Cambodia is what remains: the place of the skull . . .

> . . . Dried bones in salt earth . . .

> > . . . Sun on black water . . .

> . . . Rivers of mud . . .

> No shelter.

How could I expect the journey to end anywhere but here?

WILL

Everything hurts. I drift for hours through dreams of being kicked by hobnail boots. Eventually I wake up enough to crawl out of bed. It's 7:00 a.m.

Make a packet coffee. It doesn't help, so I pour some whiskey in it, chase it with a handful of 800-proof Advil, and curse myself for giving Gabriel all my Percocet.

June's diary: face down on the floor. How long was I reading? I can't remember. I stayed as long as I could, trying to follow her story through those tangled lines. Read the end first, hoping for an easy clue: nothing that made sense. The last legible entry was an essay about visiting the Killing Fields. So I started at the beginning. It was hard going, easy to get lost among the overwritings and interruptions—and when I did, sleep took me.

I pick the book up and set it back on the desk, smoothing out the creased pages.

My apartment feels strange. I keep looking at the door, like I'm expecting her to walk through it. The way she talks about this place—

My life, with someone else living it.

It makes me edgy—but what have I really learned from her monologues about airports and descriptions of the city? June is like all the new scum: she thinks she's got a place in the world, and she's dead set on finding it. She's full of clever ideas, so she thinks she's a writer. She's got a morbid streak. But she's not telling me what happened to her. Most likely she doesn't know herself—even if she is still alive.

I finish my coffee in a long gulp. No more losing sleep trying to suss this girl out. I'll find June the same way I find anything else: by looking. And the first place to look is the river.

────────────

After the first hour of showing June's picture around the boat companies, I've stopped wincing at every step—I think maybe my body is warming up. After the second hour, I feel like there's a drill bit stuck in my ribs on low speed; I'm out of Advil and out of leads.

June told Gus she was going to Angkor. The drive is hours of slow-motion misery on dirt roads with potholes like swimming pools. Flying is expensive. For most folks, that leaves the boats. The companies that do the run up to Siem Reap, they copy your passport when you buy a ticket. A few bucks in the right hands will get you a look at the manifests. If June really went north like she said, I could find the boat, the arrival time—I'd have a trail to follow.

But there are no hits on her passport, no one believable remembers her, and as the pain in my side gets worse, and one company after another comes up empty, I try to ignore the obvious: I knew this was a dead end. Air travel is harder to check if you're not the law, but Gus has a friend who can do it. I'll call in that favor, but it'll be a bust, too. June didn't pack for a tourist jaunt. She was planning to go *somewhere*, though—somewhere the river doesn't know.

At least by now the office will be open.

The moto ride isn't long, but it nearly breaks me in half. I'm gasping as I stagger up the stairs—reception area still jammed with boxes of last week's issues, so I sit on one to catch my breath. Listen to the chatter from around the corner.

Bland sixties rock on the radio. Phones ringing, overtired scum answering and trying to sound cheery. Number Two and Barry debating whether Cambodia's leaders really want to trade in organized crime for garment factories and call centers.

Could be any morning, ever.

I stay in the hall. The archive is here, slotted into three-ring binders on floor-to-ceiling shelves. Ten years of paper, but I only need the last twelve weeks. I carry the binders back to the photo office; start flipping through, looking for June's byline.

Her first week, there was another big drug story. On July 8, a Jakarta-registered cargo ship docked in Sydney harbor with a load from the Cambodian port of Sihanoukville. Aussie police were waiting. They jumped in and found twenty-two kilos of Burmese heroin, and a bunch of guys from a local syndicate busy unloading it. Bit of a black eye for Cambo, but everyone played it cool: law enforcement agencies will cooperate, all that. Then, out of nowhere, a court in Sihanoukville arrested three customs officials, saying they were responsible for the smuggling. Three days later the prime minister let them out of prison with official pardons. All the opposition groups went nuts, screaming that Hun Sen was protecting the drug trade. The police stayed quiet.

June isn't the only byline, but she gets some play. The timing interests me, too: it couldn't have been long after this that the local drug market started drying up. Was the Sydney operation the start of something? But June never gets to it: she does three or four pieces as the whole mess is developing, then the story dies. With no one talking, the paper just runs out of stuff to print. June moves on to other things.

She's ambitious, I can see that. Lots of enterprise, lots of features: she's going out and finding stories, making them hers. They can be about anything: business, the environment, sports, archaeology. She's got a gift for it. Young yet; her style is still rough around the edges. She indulges in purple prose, and Gus, for some reason, lets her. I guess he saw what I'm seeing: June knows what questions to ask. She'll start with something simple—say, an environmental assessment in a coastal town—and over twelve column inches she'll tie it into everything: the collapsing economy in the provinces, political corruption, urbanization, globalization. She does her legwork. The stories aren't brilliant, just promising. But give her a few more years—

Hell.

What I don't see here is a red flag: a conflict with some local figure, a sensitive political story she's sniffing around—the standard stuff that gets reporters in deep water. After three hours flipping through back issues, I'm not sure I'm any further than when I started. Her last byline is a goddamn press release, about the graduation ceremony at a school for kids injured by land mines.

Shove the binders away, light a cigarette. Desk covered with ash. I stare at it for a while, but nothing's happening in my head. Finally I head back to the newsroom. It's mostly empty—everyone's out interviewing. I don't see Gus.

The Khmer reporters have their own room, side by side with the main one. No desks in there, just old couches melting into the floor. TV in the corner, for the fights. When I come in, a couple of the young guys are sipping Cokes and watching MMA—Australian, looks like. I throw myself on the floor next to them and start rolling a joint.

One glares at me; think his name is Yun. "Come on, man. We get trouble for your shit."

"Sorry." I stuff the result in my pocket. The Khmers don't like trouble—they're the opposite of the foreigners. No one this side of the wall is on a mission from God. I light a cigarette instead, letting it burn away the sour, sticky taste in my mouth. The fat fighter gets the other one in an armlock, and the guys next to me start shouting in the tones of men with money at stake.

The new scum hate this room. They stick their faces around the door, all they see is lazy natives lounging in the shade. Half the time they get racist; the other half, they lecture Gus about it: How are the Khmer reporters supposed to *build capacity* if they spend all their time sitting around, and then *colonialism, imperialism,* some more -isms.

I got most of my Khmer in here: endless hours listening to them shout back at the television, trade sources, argue over politics. These guys are old pros. They see the foreigners come and go, but they stay. They know what lines they can't cross, and don't ask questions that won't get answers. Why should they? Even a guy like Khieu, who speaks mostly fine English and can tell you what the cops are doing an hour before they know themselves—he's still going nowhere. He might string for AP or Reuters, but he'll never get hired. He'll never make it to the foreign desk at the *Times*. He thinks his job's important, but he plays it safe.

The highest honor Cambodian journalism offers is a bullet in the head.

Light another cigarette, ask Yun if he knew June.

He shrugs.

Did he ever work with her?

Shrug.

He'll never ask why I wanted to know.

The wrestlers get timed out, and the announcer lines up a new match: some skinny Canadian kickboxer is taking on one of those big Brazilian grapplers. This should be good.

Half an hour later, Khieu rolls in. He's been at the Interior Ministry, getting jerked around, and doesn't want to go over two months ago's news.

"Heroin," he says, like he's talking about what he had for breakfast.

"A lot, twenty kilo. Australians find it on a ship from Sihanoukville. They make investigation. The judge find evidence, he find papers, for shipping, sign by customs men in Sihanoukville, so he arrest. Three days, they in jail. Then Hun Sen let them go. Everyone very upset, the human rights very upset—they say this show our judges not independent." Khieu gives a little snort: *Like that's news.* "Nothing else. I think they still looking."

"Did the thing in Sydney lead to the raid on Friday?"

"Police not say. All we know is they still question the people they took at that house, the army people. Say more arrests soon."

"What about June Saito?"

"What about?"

"She worked on the Sydney story with you. Know who she talked to?"

"United Nations, mostly, I think."

"Anything strange happen?"

"What strange?"

I switch to Khmer. "Did June talk to anyone who could be dangerous?"

"The United Nations is very dangerous for my country." He smirks. It's the "crazy *barang*" look, the one they save for wacky newcomers with no idea where they are.

I'm getting desperate. "When she was working with you, maybe she found something out? Something someone didn't want her to talk about?" It sounds just as silly in Khmer.

Khieu's face has gone dark: anger brewing in him now, anger and something else— "Come on," he says, in English, then switches back. "You know how things are. There are no secrets. Suppose you found out Hun Sen was dealing drugs, and stealing money from the country? So what? Everyone knows that already. The people with real power, you don't touch them. They don't care what you say. If you become political and oppose them, then they shoot you." His voice is bitter. We're not talking about June anymore. "If you're a real journalist, they're only dangerous if you get in their way in the street." He turns to go.

"Bunny, which was he? Did he die because he was political? Or did he just get in someone's way?"

Khieu stops walking for a second; doesn't look back. "Does it make a difference?"

Ray is at his desk, starting layout. I stay in the doorway a second, watching him as I light my cigarette: nearly seven feet tall, skinny going on dead—sitting folded up in front of the computer, he looks like some giant, easygoing stick insect.

He hears my lighter and turns, gives me a faceful of giant white teeth. "Hey, man. How are ya?"

I have to be careful with this crew—not just because I don't want to give too much away about June's disappearance. I can't discard the possibility that one of them had something to do with it. I'm starting with Ray because he's the safest: been out here for ages, likes his dope and his backpacking, and no funny stuff. He never hurt anyone except by accident.

He has a lot of accidents.

"Talk to me about interns. I need more shooters if we're gonna have a war on."

He furrows his brow. "This bunch is weird. They're all out of Syracuse, don't ask me why Gus took a whole class, but they all want to do, like, new media, Web video projects and stuff, uh . . ."

"Christ. Can any of them work a real camera?"

"Beats me, man. You see the girl with the eyebrow ring? You should talk to her, she's pretty gung ho. She's got a little point-and-click thing, at least. Her name is—"

"Eyebrow ring. Got it. She any good with a story?"

"Dunno yet, man, they've only been around for, like, two days."

"Sure. What about the last bunch? Wasn't there a girl shot film?"

"Last bunch? The only girl was June, and I don't remember her having a camera, man."

Interesting. "Yeah, she's the one. What's she like?"

"She was a sweet kid, totally. She'd come out with everyone, have a laugh. Real smart, man, like, impressive. I don't know if she could shoot, but I bet she'd be good at it. But she's gone, anyway, man." There's no nervousness about him, his face is as blank and guileless as ever.

"Isn't she coming back?" I ask. "Gus said she was coming back, she left some stuff behind and everything."

"I dunno. Maybe she just abandoned it, man?"

"Well, shit, you're the one who knew her—she say anything about her trip?"

He looks blank.

"What *did* you guys talk about?"

"I . . . I dunno. Just, y'know, what was the what with Cambo. She wanted to hear about everything, man." He shakes his head, as if trying to clear it. "I thought she was out, but you should ask Number Two and Barry, she hung out a bunch with those guys." More interesting. "They should be back in a minute."

"Right. I'll figure it out. Anyway: eyebrow ring?"

"Dude," Ray says, suddenly puzzled, "what's with your face?"

"June?" Barry says, barely glancing up from his spreadsheet. "I'd have done 'er. Those skinny girls can rock it in the sack. But it might not be worth the effort . . . she was a bit of a freak show, know what I mean?"

I don't. Raise an eyebrow.

"That chick had fucked-up shit in her head, and, man, she liked to show it off. Not too bright, either. Get this: We're out drinking, right, her and Two and me and Ray, and she's going on and on about this drug story, like no one in this town ever heard of heroin before, right? I don't even remember what she was talking about, but Two starts shutting her down because she doesn't know shit. And then *she's* trying to correct *him,* like, "No, a courier would do this" and "The organization will be structured like that," and all. I mean, I guess she had some balls on her, but, man, the ego. She was a pain in the ass. Still . . ." His eyes meet mine, and he mimes someone giving a blowjob.

Barry.

He looks like something Frank Bacon dreamed up after a night of bad acid and sodomy, and he acts like a seventeenth-century planta-tion owner—but he's got a sweet, shit-eating grin, and somehow he suckers folks into believing there's a heart of gold in there. Cambo's a playground for guys like him. I had him pegged for a garden-variety predator, out here to smack whores around and score cheap coke, but watching him leer about June, I'm starting to wonder. Has Barry moved on to rougher games?

I light a smoke; give myself time to think.

"Whatever," I say, "I don't need a charming personality, I need someone can use a fuckin' camera."

"Beats me." He shifts his bulk in the chair and shouts down the hall. "Hey, Two!"

Number Two has been in the kitchen, getting coffee. I wanted to talk to them separately, but before I can think how to stop it, Barry's got him back. When Two sees my face, he starts jumping up and down and shouting, "Holy fuck, man, what happened to you?" I shrug. He keeps going: "For God's sake, man, what did you—" He sounds like he's doing the *Hindenburg* disaster for Radio 4. Barry's grinning.

"I was shooting at Radio Ranariddh. Someone didn't like it."

"For God's sake," Two says again. "Trouble does find you, doesn't it?"

"Never even buys me a drink."

"Keller was asking about your girlfriend, Twoey," Barry says, bored already. "Or maybe she was your boyfriend, you know, it's hard to tell."

"Ask your mother," Two says, not even blinking. "She knows." He thinks Barry is joking. He thinks this is banter. "Which one is my girlfriend now?" he asks me.

"Little, yellow, different?" says Barry.

"June Saito," I say. "When's she back?"

Two looks puzzled. "She isn't coming back." Is there something else in his eyes, some nervous edge? "She went home." He starts to turn away, as if that was that.

"Weird," I say, to stop him. Trying to be normal—what now? An impulse: "She left all her stuff behind. Her suitcases are still sitting on my landing. Tripped over them this morning, nearly died."

I don't even get to the diaries: Two's gone corpse colored. I can smell the fear coming off him, and my fingers start tingling. Barry's looked up from his screen and is watching us with quiet amusement. Has he guessed my real interest? No choice now. I keep going: "Who told you she left?"

"Sh—uh . . . she did," Two says weakly. "Said it was a family emergency, so she wouldn't make it to Siem Reap after all."

"Awww, looks like someone got dumped," Barry says, rubbing at his eyes.

"Would you please get a bloody sex life so you can quit imagining mine?" says Two, recovering himself.

"Touchy," Barry says, with little mince. Then, turning back to me: "See, told ya that girl was full of shit." His eyes narrow. "If you're really interested, there was some Khmer guy she hung around with."

"Who?" Try to act like I just think that's weird.

"I dunno, some older guy. I saw them arguing once, in the Heart, they thought nobody was around. They seemed close." Is he lying? I can't tell, he does it so easily.

Hell. I have a million questions—Two is hiding something, and I want to know what. But Barry has derailed the conversation, maybe on purpose. And if I keep pushing, it's not just curiosity anymore. Barry may already suspect something: he's as good at spotting liars as he is at lying.

I have to wait—until I can make myself another chance. "Screw it," I say. "Girl was into some shit with the Khmers, I'm not getting involved. Now, you assholes got any bright ideas about which of these new kids can use a camera?"

I'm hiding out in the paper's kitchen, wringing dregs of coffee from the filter with chopsticks. The whole day has got strange and off-key.

I wish I knew what I just saw. June's name made Two nervous, that was clear. But it doesn't mean much—if they were screwing around, that could be enough to explain the jitters: boss wouldn't like it. But then there was his reaction when I mentioned the suitcases. Maybe he was panicking about what she might have left—the journals, for example. But if he'd had something to do with her disappearance, he'd have had plenty of time to realize the journals might incriminate him and take care of them. No: he thought June was safe home. It was only when I said she wasn't that he got scared.

He doesn't know what happened to her, but he knows something could have.

Which leads me right back to Barry. Is he what Number Two was afraid of? Was he trying to shut Two up, keep him from spilling something? And what about his nameless Khmer? Is that a lead, or was Barry just muddying the waters?

Then there's June—why would she tell Gus she was going backpacking, and at the same time tell Two she was headed home for a family emergency?

So far, talking to her friends has got me nothing but paranoia and a headache. June was smart, or she wasn't. A promising journo, or a poser. I'm wishing I could remember her. Even her face, once so clear, is getting fuzzy in my mind: a picture thumbed too many times.

I need to do something solid, so I ring Clean Steve at the Australian embassy. If June was working on this Sydney heroin story, she must have talked to him. It takes some persuading, but he agrees to meet me at the Russian Tea Room after work.

I'm still sitting in the kitchen when Gus finally shows up. He's munching pad thai from a take-out box with chopsticks, but his face has bad news all over it.

"Hospitals a bust, then?" I ask.

He nods, thoughtful. I wait.

"We need to get the cops," he says, at last.

I don't argue—not the way he's looking. "I'm going to see Steve in an hour."

He nods again: good enough for the moment.

"What did you find?"

Silence: I realize he's embarrassed.

"Our man in Bangkok got into her e-mail last night, easy. But here's the thing: that account's been active less than six months. All that's in there is job applications. That's a bit funny, right? So I ring Paris, recheck her references. The study-abroad-program supervisor remembered her, he was the one who recommended her before. So I started to ask about the personal stuff—love life, drug problems, anything that might have set her running. That's when it started to fall apart."

He pulls a folded sheet of paper from his pocket, lays it flat on the table. It's a photocopy of a US passport, printed from a fax machine. The photograph is of a stunning Japanese girl: straight black hair, apple cheeks, dimples. No glasses.

The name on the paper is Jun Saito.

"That's the real one. I people-searched her, her details check out. Our June said she was from LA, this girl is from Burlington, Vermont. I had to wait for the States to wake up so I could call. The real June is happily back at school at Northwestern. She had a lovely time at the workshop in Paris, then did her internship in Germany." He stops, letting this all sink in. "We're not ready for this. We check references to make sure the kids have a work ethic, not to screen out identity thieves. Now we've got a girl missing, and we don't even know her real name. We need to kick this one along."

"We can't," I say, voice too sharp. "Not yet." I'm still staring at the passport, like it's put a spell on me. June isn't really June—

So who the hell hired me to look for her?

DIARY

July 5

Have I told you about the Heart of Darkness? A nightclub named after a novel about the corruption of the human soul, and without a stitch of irony anywhere. I know, I know: no surer sign of genetic un-fitness than writing in one's journal in a bar! Well, I'm glad I'm a beta. . . . And I needed a drink, didn't I, after that disaster? I'm embarrassed even thinking about it: sitting in my apartment, listening to the rain pound the roof and brooding over all that old childhood stuff. . . . I don't know what it is about this place that makes me think about those times.

As soon as the weather let up, I had to go out. Fortunately the drivers on my street all know where the Heart is. It's still Saturday, and I thought the guys would be here—but so far, I'm alone. Perhaps it's too early for them. They'll still be at the river or the Bar with No Name. I could look . . . but somehow I can never get over this place.

Tiny, no lights except for these red spots picking out faux-Angkorian carvings on the walls, a graffiti-covered back room with a pool table. It was throbbing when I got in—the whole place pulsing like a living creature, a real heart beating in the dark back streets of the city. Inside, it's girls, girls everywhere . . . little Cambodian girls smiling up at their men, hanging on their arms and hips and chests, laughing at jokes no one made.

If you weren't careful, you could think they were out having fun, like the girls on the Strip on a Saturday. On some level maybe they are . . . but I remember Ray's rule:

"If a Khmer girl is out after dark, she's a prostitute . . . one way or another." The boy, who gets a list of arrests read to him every day, can reel off the ways like some exotic taxonomy: The bar girls and the taxi girls and the hostesses, the hookers in the midtown brothels and the Vietnamese whores trafficked into $5 sex shops on the edge of town, the sold children and the professional girlfriends . . . Who knew such a simple transaction could spawn such variety?

Those that inhabit the Heart are the elite. They smother their ocher skin with iridescent powders, until they assume the appearance of some species of giant butterfly larvae. Packed inside their vinyl dresses like department-store chrysalids, they await the moment of metamorphosis when the turgid form bursts wet and writhing into the world. Beautiful monsters, no rules but hunt, mate, feed—

I like to watch them.

They're different from prostitutes back home. These girls are mirrors and plastic, slick and pink and reflective. There is no bottom to them: ask a million questions, you will never find the real girl, just one Barbie doll nested inside another. They are dependent upon the role they play in a way few of us can comprehend: their inner life has been completely erased.

Can it be I feel jealous of them? I scratch absent-mindedly at my arm, hoping to see the skin part and shining chrome beneath. . . .

Thank GOD . . . the guys just came in.

No, funny . . . just him. And he doesn't seem altogether pleased to see me—

WILL

The Russian Tea Room isn't Russian and doesn't have tea. It's the nickname of a grisly tiki bar off Monivong owned by a four-hundred-pound Kazakh named Sergei. It's also a hangout for the pedos, which means Sergei never says anything to anybody about who was there. This can be useful to all sorts of people. Clean Steve is leaning against the doorjamb when I arrive, looking about as hangdog as a six-foot-seven ex–Special Forces guy can look.

"It's not empty," he mutters.

"Flip you for them."

Steve just shakes his head. He used to be more fun.

"Suit yourself." I push past him into the gloom of the bar. It's lit only by Christmas lights and tiki torches, and the gleaming pig eyes of a couple of fat, sixtyish Europeans in sandals and shorts, huddled in a booth in the corner.

"They hit me, Sergei, they hit me," I scream in sudden, forced hysteria. My face makes this pretty believable, if you don't know much about tissue damage. I knock over a stool as I stagger to the bar. "They looked like cops, but I don't think they were cops. They said I fucked an eight-year-old boy and they weren't going to let me get away with it. You've got to help me." I lean across the bar until I'm right next to the fat Cossack's unshaven mug and stage-whisper, "They say they're going to attach wires to my penis. You can't let them, Sergei! Tell them I'm innocent—"

The other guests quietly exit through the kitchen.

"You are fucking asshole, Keller," Sergei says. "With infection."

"I need the room."

Clean Steve.

He earned his nickname in Lebanon in the early nineties. Back then it was ironic: he was Australian military, part of the UN peace-keeping force, working every angle there was and a few they didn't have names for yet. I was a kid, jaunting through the Bekaa to hang out with Hizbullah, waiting for things to explode. God knows how we got to be friends—I think drinking was involved.

Eventually I moved on to places where the wars were hotter. Steve quit the army before his sidelines caught up with him—got a job with the Australian Federal Police, part of one of those international drug-enforcement "assistance" programs. A couple years back, they posted him here.

He's trying to live up to his name these days—even on a barstool he sits arrow straight. He's got two daughters who don't talk to him, and child-support payments his ex-wife won't let him forget, but he's not a corrupt junkie bastard like all the other narcs in this town. You could say we're friends—but if there's one thing he hates about Cambo, it's me.

I'm from the old days.

Right now, though, Steve is my best play. I need to know who

June was, and why someone would be hunting for her. Whoever "Kara Saito" is, she's got my home address. Steve can get me information and will hopefully agree to do it on the DL. I order us Zombies: you can't sit in the Russian Tea Room without a shitty fruit drink. We finish them in silence; order two more.

Finally he speaks: "We off the record?"

I nod.

"Say it out loud."

"Off the record."

He gives me a sour smile. "You said this was important?"

"One of our interns, June Saito, wrote a story about that heroin bust in Sydney a few months back. Did she talk to you?"

His face gives me the answer, even as he puzzles out the question. "I don't usually talk to journalists about which other journalists I've talked to, even if they do work at the same paper. Why do you wanna know? She get something wrong?"

"Her name, among other things."

Steve's eyes go black, under knitted brows. "What do you mean?"

"I mean we don't know who she is. She was using a fake passport, with a stolen identity. She's up in Angkor now, and we'd like some answers before she gets back."

I can see him struggle. His cop instincts are screaming call the police, the embassy: make it official—and someone else's problem. But his brain is churning through what June might have been doing here, and why she was asking him questions. What he might have let slip; how much trouble he could be in.

I help him along: "What did you tell her?"

"Christ," he mutters. "Nothing sensitive—who am I going to be more careful around than a kid reporter?" He pauses. I wait. "You're right, she was asking about heroin. But she had most of the story already. She thought those customs guys had nothing to do with anything, wanted me to confirm it, off the record, so she could kill a piece that was barking up the wrong tree. She seemed like a conscientious type, so I did." He gives a little snort.

"How did you know the customs guys were innocent?"

"Because that was our op. We've been telling the Cambodian police to get smart about this stuff for years, do some controlled ops, maybe get something bigger than just street punks. Well, now they got a special unit, anti-corruption, hand-picked by Hok Lundy. In July they caught wind of a big shipment going out, so they flagged it for us. We checked it out, got an eye on everyone, and then let it go ahead to Sydney, where they grabbed it. I understand it was quite successful."

"So did that lead to the big bust last Friday?"

"That's the Cambodians' bag, mate. We shared what we learned, that's all. But it seems pretty likely, doesn't it?"

"Right. So how do the customs guys get into it?"

"They don't. It's this bloody legal system. They got this 'investigating judge' business here, you know. From the French. These guys are cop, judge, and jury—but most of 'em can't find their bums with both hands and a flashlight. Totally useless. So while Sydney was working on getting information from the people they'd pulled in over there, one of these judges sees the signatures of some customs officials on the shipping manifest and thinks, 'Hey, we've caught the smugglers!' Fuckwit. Never mind those guys sign off on hundreds of containers a day and probably look at less than one percent of the cargo—they just arrest them."

I'm getting the drift now: "So you have a few words with the interior minister, and they cut the guys loose. Causing a ruckus."

"They could have been a bit softly-softly about it, eh? Anyway, that makes it sensitive—no one wants to give the impression foreign powers are pulling the strings here."

"That would be terrible."

He glares. "It's not really very hot stuff. I don't see where your girl could go with it, even if she was . . ." He trails off. Who knows what June was?

Now Steve's spilled, it's time for softball—before he comes back to calling in the authorities. "I don't think she was up to anything. I've looked through her stuff, talked to folks at the paper. Sounds like she was just trying to do her job. It was an accident we even found out about the fake ID." I can see him softening. "She's a kid, Steve. Says she's twenty-one, we're not sure—we're only assuming she's not still a minor. Maybe she's scared, on the run from something. We want to know, before we throw her to the dogs."

Steve can see where this story goes: a stolen identity means no idea which embassy should be involved. They'll all stand back with their hands up. She'll be called stateless and tossed to the Cambodian police. Steve doesn't like the picture—he has daughters.

After a minute he waves Sergei over. Starts to order another Zombie, then changes his mind. "Fuck this. Gimme any Irish whiskey. No ice." He looks at me. "Make it two."

After the drinks come, and he's had a long pull, he speaks. "It's hard without a name. You can't just get a mate to do a lookup, those kind of searches take effort. Bright side is, your girl stands out. What's she, just over five feet?"

"About that, yeah. Can't be more than eighty-five pounds."

"And a natural blonde, but East Asian descent?"

"Yes. Said she was from LA, I'd bet she at least lived there. She knows the city."

"Well, should be easy to ID. If she's got a record, I'll see if I can find it without getting official. Anything pops up, you'll hear me shouting."

"Thanks." I watch him sideways as I down my drink. He's playing it cool, but his face is full of trouble.

———————

The InterContinental Hotel is in a neighborhood that's trying to be fancy, but settles for deserted. The sun is down, and steel grates already cover the glass windows of the Euro boutiques. The hotel is owned by a big Chinese-Cambodian businessman—one with more than a finger in the local heroin trade, and a habit of shooting up buildings when he gets mad. Rumor is, when the place opened, the guys from the parent company came for a visit and found him putting up a stage in the lobby, with dancing girls wearing number cards like marathon runners. Guests could order them up with room service. I can only pity the brand manager who had to come out from Oxbridge to tell his Uzi-toting franchise holder this wasn't the InterCon way.

It's quiet when I come in: all soap-slick marble and silk, off-white, and bland. Some dancing girls might improve it. The downstairs bar is like an out-sized conference room, huge and empty. Off in the corner, a group of singers in neon latex dresses are belting out the top hits of the eighties in Thai, accompanied by a Filipino with Metallica hair on a vintage Casio. They're on "Uptown Girl." If Billy Joel doesn't already have a smack habit, this would give him one.

Double whiskey: I'll need it.

Senn wafts in like a cartoon character on a floating cloud: white pants, white jacket, radioactive-green silk shirt that he looks to have coordinated with his shoes.

"*Cool,* I *love* this band," he gushes, draping himself on the stool next to mine. I've already got him a grasshopper; it matches the outfit. Got to make this quick, they're starting on "November Rain."

"Know a kid named Van Chennarith?" I ask. "He might not use his real name. He's tallish for Khmer, maybe five-eight. About twenty-three. Has a diagonal scar on the corner of his mouth and an old bullet wound in his thigh. You definitely hate him."

"*Hello,* how *are* you, so *nice* to see you." Senn purses his lips around his cocktail straw. "You don't call for months, and now it's all business."

I shrug. "Out of town."

"That's what they *all* say when they mean shacked up," he coos. "You look like shit, by the way."

I don't respond, just tug at my whiskey.

Senn throws his hands in the air with an exaggerated sigh. "Yes, *yes,* I know him. He calls himself Charlie, I call him something else. So go on"—he rests one manicured nail on the back of my bruise-yellow hand—"you know I love it when you talk dirty to me."

Senn is my connection to Phnom Penh's gay mafia. It's a strange little world: open enough to those in the know, invisible to everyone else. Cambo isn't known for tolerance—but most Khmers wouldn't recognize a screaming queen if one tried to pick their pocket, so Senn and his friends can vogue all they want, as long as the sex stays behind closed doors. In their back-stair bars and secret house parties, princes and sons of high officials rub shoulders (and other things) with boys right out of the provinces. Senn himself is the offspring of some big hoo-ha in the customs department. He has a degree in eighteenth-century French literature from the Sorbonne and no brothers, which means he's stuck here—useless at any local job, and forever complaining about the new anticorruption laws eating away at his family's income.

"Honey trap," I say. "I gotta get him somewhere we can do a little photo shoot. Got any ideas?"

Senn feigns shock. "You want me to out a brother? *Tu me prends pour une racaille, ou*—"

"It's not for the papers. Someone wants info from Daddy and is willing to pay well for compromising pictures of the kid."

"*C'est ça—pour finir en petits morceaux dans un sac plastique au fond de la Tonlé Sap.*"

I get the gist—something about dismemberment. "That's the client's problem."

He sips his drink again, lost in thought. "With Charlie's taste in boys, I'd say we'd have to use you as the bait. But that's no good, with your face looking like something from Sophocles." He pauses, lips pursed. "I know a guy, if you've got the place. But we have to do it *very soon. Garçon—*"

He screams for more drinks. The band strikes up "Eternal Flame." This can't possibly end well.

The river's bank is quiet. Saturday is somewhere else tonight. A few lifers droop outside the pizza joints. In the murky water, a splash and a shout, and the smell of it wafts over: urine, garbage that's been in the sun too long. The lights in the Edge are bright and yellow. I can see Channi smiling at me from behind the bar. Go in.

"Your face better."

"Give it time. It'll get worse."

The corners of her mouth turn down a bit as she slides me the peanuts. Laughing? Tom Waits on the stereo again.

I watch as she hands out beers and talks up the one other lonely punter in her broken English, Tom growling away behind her. She says she's nineteen, but the girls all know that's the magic number. From her face I might almost believe it, but her eyes say different. She could have five years on that, or fifteen—but they weren't all easy.

She watches me watching as she brings my drink.

"What you work?" she asks. Serious.

"I take pictures."

"Where you camera?"

"Someone threw it off a roof."

"They no like pictures?"

I laugh. "Guess not."

She's silent a minute. "You no like take pictures."

"I used to," I say, surprising myself. "Guess I don't anymore."

"What you do now?"

"I'm looking for a girl."

I realize this sounds like a come-on, but she takes it as meant, her brow lining with concern. "What happen her?"

I shake my head. "She's lost."

Channi's huge eyes are locked on me, expectant. I didn't want to think about this. Don't want to talk about it, so I reach for something else. "Do you like Tom Waits?" I ask, switching to Khmer.

"I'm in love with him," she says, changing languages with me. She smiles, but her eyes are still worried.

"How do you know about him?"

"My friend Ruth played him for me. A long time ago. His voice was so sad. . . . He could have been Cambodian."

I got nothing to say to that. Tom's singing about girls who look like Cadillacs, and Channi's fingers are lingering next to mine on the counter, like she's waiting for me to take her hand. It's a bar-girl move—I didn't think she'd be the type.

I'm paying way too much attention.

The other customer has vanished, and Channi unfolds her story: the neighborhood she grew up in, out on the edge of Phnom Penh where it's not really city, just what happens to farmland when it dies. Ruth and her folks fixed up a little school in one of the old houses— they used song lyrics to teach the girls English. Religious stuff, or pop hits if they were lucky, Celine Dion and Faith Hill. The girls loved that. But Ruth had a bit of rebel in her, and when her parents weren't there, she'd play Tom Waits and Bob Dylan and the Eagles, and Channi fell for them because the songs were hurt and lonely and strange, and here in Cambodia we understand those things.

She was sixteen when she became a Mormon. Ruth's parents told the girls that when they were twenty-one, they could go to the States as missionaries, and it was an easy sell.

"I wanted to see the moon in America," Channi says. "I was sure it must be a different one to the one we have here. A whole different sky. Better, maybe."

But she's still here. Wonder why? Things changed after 9/11, maybe the missionaries just couldn't deliver. Or it was the usual: a sick relative, a sister needing school fees—something she had to work for, something she couldn't leave behind. What a number they've done on this girl's head. Cambodia, the Mormons, the tourists in this damn bar—

I realize she's taken my hand as she talks. Tom says he's irresponsible, and he's ruined everything he does.

"In America you never see the sky." I drink deep. "They light up everything like it's Water Festival all year round, and there's nothing up top but black."

She smiles, some sadness in her eyes I can't understand. "Let me read your palm." She pulls my hand across the backs of the carved snakes and studies it like an archaeologist. I take it back.

"I don't wanna know my future." But there's a strange expression on her face, and I wonder what she saw. The intro to "Jersey Girl" comes on. Outside, the rain starts again.

"You want beer," she says, in English, and slips away to get it. I feel something big and dangerous happening, just past the corners of my vision.

I don't move. Sit hunched at the carved bar, waiting for something I can't explain. Sip my beer.

Just until the rain stops.

———————

Another late night.

The uneasy feeling that came over me in the Edge has followed me up the stairs to my room. I open the cage door and stand a minute, looking at the unmade bed, the white walls, the bare bookshelf. Nothing there—nothing but the journals on the desk.

My room is full of *her*. I'm barely here at all.

D I A R Y

Damn Gus, and his damned judgments and instincts. It's one thing if he doesn't want to listen to me, but to *punish* me with this picayune nonsense? I had been doing exciting stuff, with the break-in at that NGO, and then the heroin in Australia, and those customs officials getting arrested . . . I was sure I was onto something good.

But for the past week, he's been sending me to every pointless press conference and NGO ceremony celebrating another year of achieving nothing. Now I'm spending the entire day on this press bus with a dozen Cambodian reporters, headed down to a village on the Mekong to check out some Red Cross project. . . .

The road to the southeast is pretty much a dirt track, and we had to crawl along at 15 miles per hour, rocking back and forth like a carnival ride. All around us, water country: stippled with ribbons of reeds and cattails, houses rising on stilts and tiny islands of hills. Even the poorest villages had temples: wats hundreds of years old whose roofs glistened with new yellow paint, the eyes of their giant bodhisattva faces brilliant lime-white. Religion is life, and spirits and devils are to be feared. How could it not be so?

––––––––––

The town, when we finally got to it, seemed to have been sucked down into the thick brown mud of the riverland. Just a few reed houses, poking their way through silty earth on either side of the road. We got off the bus, all the reporters' shiny shoes squelching in the mud, and the Red Cross woman started talking in Khmer about the project, whatever it was—Samean was supposed to be translating for me, but he just stood there, smoking and occasionally chatting with a photographer from one of the Cambodian dailies. No one was listening. Perhaps there was no project. The Red Cross here is run by the prime minister's wife, and the boy says it's pretty much a front organization for political propaganda.

A little way up the road, a couple villagers, naked except for their *kromah*-sarongs, were struggling to get a donkey to pull a two-wheeled cart out of the mud. The animal struggled, the men sweated; the cart moved half an inch. It was piled high with what appeared to be the exact same brown dirt it was stuck in. There's an economics lesson in there somewhere. That, I felt sure, was the story I ought to have been writing. . . .

The Red Cross woman kept talking. I pushed up to Samean and asked him what was happening.

"She saying . . . the project," he said, with a shrug, and offered me a cigarette. I found myself wishing I smoked. It seemed to pass the time, so I took one and lit it, then coughed and dropped it in the mud in a wave of nausea. No one even looked at me.

The woman started walking, and we followed her to the edge of the river, where her excited chatter ramped up a notch. She was gyrating like a cheerleader now: either her Ritalin just kicked in or we were about to see something very important.

"What's that about?" I whispered to Samean.

"Big water," he said, and walked away.

The river was narrow enough to throw a stone across, but deep and fast. A farmer in Nike shorts was trying to coax a half-submerged donkey onto the bank. Skinny men pushed skinny boats into the frantic current. Their tiny outboard motors looked like the things you use to trim weeds in your driveway back home.

The Red Cross woman gestured proudly to a tall concrete cylinder on the river bank, and we all lined up to look inside—apparently whatever they'd made or built was in there. Even the Cambodians had to stoop to peer in, then nodded sagely to the woman and moved along. A few made comments with the tone of congratulation. I was last, and when my turn came I bent down and squinted into the darkness like all the rest. There was nothing there.

The woman smiled at me and said something in Khmer. I smiled back. Then she led us back to the bus.

I thought that was the end, but five minutes away from that doomed town we stopped again, this time pulling off the road to a clearing in the woods with a concrete pavilion. The other journos seemed excited, but I was groaning inwardly: another slog through the mud to see nothing. Then I realized the pavilion was filled with tables, all set with bright silver and red satin napkins. This was lunch.

It must have taken three hours, course after course after course: spicy Tom Yam soup floating with fat prawns, chilled seaweed salad, crisp and salty. Fried noodles sweet with sesame oil, plates of brazed bok choi, chicken salad with mint and peanuts, pork spareribs Cantonese-style, hot-pots stuffed with steamed crayfish the size of small cats (the local delicacy), sweet pastries and mango sorbet and plates of chilled fruit . . . a couple of the Cambodians had brought their own beer and were getting sozzled down at the end of the table. Everyone, I suddenly understood, was going to go back and write about what a great project this was, and how much good it was doing for Cambodia.

Perhaps Gus was trying to show me something important, after all?

I have to figure out how to convince him. I feel so sure I could do something great . . . something *real* . . . if I could just get the space. But lunch has weighed me down, and I'm having trouble thinking. The only thing keeping me awake is that cut I got on my leg—it's throbbing and itching like crazy.

It's nearly dark out now. Everyone else on the bus has drifted off—either sleeping, or smoking, or both. The only other person not in a coma is the guy in the seat behind me, a tallish Cambodian with a Ritchie Valens 'do and terrible skin—worse than mine. He's in the uniform: a short-sleeved shirt with an ugly pattern, no tie, shiny shoes. His camera and cigarettes stick out from a faux-leather fanny pack, and he's eagerly paging through a Khmer-English dictionary.

And as it did after Tuol Sleng, my mind keeps swinging back to the night my mother left. I don't understand—I seldom think about that time anymore, and I don't know why it keeps coming to me now. Was it something she told me? I was only six, but I can see her, face still tracked with tears, sitting beside my bed. I can see her lips move, but I don't know what she's saying.

I like to think she said she would take me with her (though Father would never have let that happen). Sometimes I imagine there was a clue she left, if only I could remember: *Here is the lock, break it. This is how you get out.*

I don't remember her leaving. One moment she's there—the next she's gone.

Out the window to my right, the reeds part to reveal another great, shining stretch of water. Across it, on a tiny island or spit of land, I can see the first old thing that looks properly ancient and neglected. A temple of some kind—just a glimpse of crumbling gray stone wrapped with vines, like the head of some slumbering, cyclopean creature. On the pagoda top, instead of bodhisattvas, the faces are bug-eyed, tiger-mouthed. I can't turn away.

"Not look," says a voice. I turn and there's Ritchie Valens, a cigarette caught between two long, yellowed fingernails. He's looking intently at me, dictionary open in his hand. I can't say anything. "Not good look," he continues, then looks down at the page for the word he wants. "Demon," he says. "Demon. Not look."

WILL

In dreams, I'm following a blond shadow down dark alleys. She doesn't run, but she's always ahead. Can't tell if she knows I'm here. If I could just catch her eye, I'd know what she's running from, but she never looks back.

I drag myself out of bed and pour a whiskey, still chasing June in my head. Can't remember where I stopped reading: where real June ended and shadow June began. I remember nighttime walks, tropical fevers—

Drugs.

Malarone: it protects against malaria, but the price is dreams that are vivid, violent—dreams that hold so hard you can't wake up. If you're careless, or unlucky, they can follow you right into the waking world. June had bottles of the stuff in her bag, mostly empty. And she said she was unlucky with drugs—

"I could wake and discover I was someone else altogether."

June was a fake—but her diary feels real. She cared about her work at the paper. I'd been focusing on what she wrote about Cambodia, but after what I learned yesterday, I went back to see what came before. In Paris, she describes going to a university—or at least hanging around one, it's not clear she was studying anything. That must have been how she came across Jun Saito. Something happened while she was there. I don't think she says what, but I get the impression it gave her a fright.

Before that, it was Italy, where she was helping out on some archaeological dig. In Greece, she was feeding the homeless. She traveled around South America for a while, as some kind of assistant to a documentary filmmaker named Rafe. It doesn't make any damned sense.

But it will. I'm learning her like a foreign language. I see how her stories dance around the edges of the real story—like in her photographs: the real subject is always just out of frame.

You're looking in the wrong place.

Hell. For all I know, I'm reading scenes from her great American novel. Maybe her ma's really a schoolteacher in Pasadena. What I need is facts. And I know where I could get them—

No.

I'll find another way. Anyway, it's seven in the morning—not much I can do now but think, and I'd rather not.

Head downstairs to see if Gus has anything to eat. Find him perched in the kitchen; he's picked up fried fish and noodles on his way back from the club, and he's eating them out of a paper bag. I start going through his fridge, find the remains of a stir-fry and a Black Panther.

"You could at least shower," he says.

"Buy me dinner first."

"I'll make you a coffee if you change your shirt. I think you've been in that one since Thursday. It's still got blood on it." He's fucking chipper. Beating the hell out of somebody usually puts him in a good mood. "Then maybe you can shoot the opposition protest out by the monument." Say nothing. He pauses, looks over at me as he puts the coffee on. "You recall having a job, right?"

"A job."

"Yes. You take pictures, and I pay you."

"And the girl?"

The look he gives me is dangerous. "I thought you'd got Steve on that."

"All Steve can do is try to ID her. Could take days."

"Then we go to the Americans—"

"How do you know she's an American?"

"This much trouble, of course she's a fucking American."

"And you think more of 'em are gonna make it better?" He glares at me. "Until Steve comes up with something, we're on our own."

"Then leave it."

"Whoever this Kara woman is, I don't think she's gonna let it lie." There, I said it. Hell.

Gus is still frowning, but he knows I'm right. We don't know what June was mixed up in. I can't sit around here reading her diary, hoping she'll hand me the answer.

Like it or not, I've got to talk to Kara Saito.

I stall until ten, pacing Gus's room and hoping the harsh light of day will banish whatever irrational paranoia has got into me since that morning on the quay.

Really, I'm looking for a better option.

Kara wanted this whole thing hush-hush. That might have nothing to do with June: maybe Kara was afraid of being recognized herself. I've toyed with asking around, but that seems even riskier: word could get back to her. Whoever she is, she's dangerous. I've got to figure out my approach. I'll only get one shot.

She's staying at Le Royal, the most expensive hotel in town—the gangsters like it because it's got good security and private entrances. A couple guys there owe me favors from the Vy days, and I've thought up a dozen ways to catch Kara off guard, get myself some advantage from the location—

The memory of the quay stops me. Kara's running this show: the most dangerous thing I can do is try to take away her control. Tricks and pretenses won't help.

The only way to come at her is straight on.

———————

The bar in Le Royal is a sun-lit alcove filled with tasteful rattan furniture, high colonial ceilings, and wide, arched windows that open onto a garden patio. The waiter gives a deep bow when I arrive and silently sweeps me into a chair. If my appearance troubles him, he doesn't let it show. Nhem, the bartender, hovers in the background. When I come in, he busies himself chopping limes, careful not to look my way. Kara's not here yet, so I order a bourbon—then change my mind and go for some expensive Scotch with a lot of syllables in the name.

Who knows, could be my last drink.

I finish it in three long swallows; order another.

Fine: my second-to-last drink.

Not a huge crowd at half past eleven. A pair of fiftyish white guys are chatting over peanuts. They're dressed in the same ready-for-the-jungle casual: rumpled safari shirts, blue jeans, tastefully chosen indigenous jewelry handmade by the tribes of wherever. They look like UN, or government—the kind who used to be aid workers and never quite got over it. In the far corner, a heavyset, nervous-looking businessman eats a late breakfast, making increasingly urgent-sounding calls on his cell phone in Chinese. By the door, a slender, gray-haired woman in a pristine white walking outfit and expensive sandals has stationed herself with her cappuccino and *Lonely Planet,* a huge white sun hat tossed across the table.

No reason to think Kara is here alone: any of these people could be working with her. I watch them sideways, keeping my eyes on the brochure I've picked up about Angkor tourism.

She's ten minutes late coming down. Here in the hotel, she's ditched her street clothes for a thigh-length yellow sundress and fashion-forward flats. I'm struck by how young she looks: with her legs bare and hair scattered, she could pass for a schoolgirl on holiday, except for the exhaustion hanging around her eyes.

"I'm sorry," she says, out of breath. "I've been on the ph— my God, your face! Are you okay?"

Feel myself flush as I fumble for an answer. "Art critic. I'll be all right."

She sits, and her brow furrows as a thought hits her. "Was that from . . . ?" *Was that from looking for June?*

"No." I try to be reassuring. "Nothing to do with your sister. Just a rough day at the office."

"Oh." She lets out a sigh of relief—then stares at her fingers. "I've been so worried." How did I think this girl was a threat?

From across the room: a sudden, sharp bang.

That's what saves me.

Everyone jumps—Kara practically falls out of her chair. We all turn to look for the source of the noise. All but one: for a tiny moment, the woman in white is looking the wrong way. She's watching Kara. Her hand has slipped underneath her sun hat.

Behind the bar, an embarrassed Nhem is saying sorry, holding up the wooden cutting board he just carelessly dropped into a steel sink. Not a gunshot, but it was loud. The aid cowboys actually clap.

But I'm awake again.

Kara's face had gone pale; now her cheeks are starting to flush with embarrassment. "Wow. High-strung, I suppose!" Self-deprecating laugh, then her eyes grow tired again. "You can imagine what this has been like."

Fucking hell, she's good. That breathless entrance, the schoolgirl look: making herself vulnerable. Without a word, she's been begging me to protect her, cutting off my questions before I even ask them—and I've been falling for it. Three sentences in, I'd already half convinced myself the quay was just the speed talking. Another five minutes, I'd have told her anything she wanted.

I'd even forgotten about asking Nhem to make something go bang. At least my surprise was genuine. He played it well—make a mental note to get something nice for his wife.

"So," Kara says, "what did you want to talk to me about?"

"I'm sorry." I shake my head as if I've lost my train of thought. Tack left: try to recapture the breathless idiocy of my first reaction to her. "Sorry, it's been a long week. You said you were on the phone?"

"God, all morning. Our parents are going completely *insane*. They keep threatening to come out here, and I'm trying to tell them to wait. Our dad has been sick, and I don't want to put him through the stress—"

Most liars are lousy at it, cruising by on bluster and people's desire to believe. The woman across from me is something else: an artist, spinning fantasies so real they show in her hair and her complexion and the curl of her toes. Even now, when I know she's toying with me—because she wasn't fooled for a second by my trick with the cutting board—there is nothing in her face or voice or posture except Kara Saito, worried big sister. Every second, I have to fight the part of my mind that says I've somehow made a mistake.

"I can't imagine what you must be going through," I say.

The waiter slides over to our table, hovering. Kara orders her tea without looking at him, her eyes still fixed on me.

"Beam, no ice," I say.

I am miles from good enough to play with her. I'm pretty sure I can't even stall her, she'll smell me lying a mile off. That leaves one option.

"What was June to you, really?"

"What do you mean?" No bogus shock, just confusion. "Okay, fifteen years, we're pretty far apart, I don't know. . . . Are you asking if we were best friends and whispered secrets to each other in our beds after dark? No, of course not. But she's still my sister."

"You know that's not what I mean. She's not who she says she is."

"I . . . I don't understand. Is this some kind of 'Does anybody really know anyone' thing?" She gets suddenly worried. "Was June in some kind of trouble? Did she do something wrong?"

Still not a crack: she's going to play her bluff to the end, make me show my whole hand before she gives it up. So I do. Lay it all out: the dummy e-mail, the fake passport, the phone calls back to Northwestern to make sure it wasn't a crazy coincidence. "The girl you say is your sister is not Jun Saito. So you can't be Kara Saito. So, again: who are you, really?"

She looks down, deflated. Then up, hopeful:

"Do you need more money?" She's reaching for her handbag. No sudden moves—but if I let her pay me off, I'm pretty sure I won't leave this hotel alive.

"No," I snap. "I know you think I'm dumb, but I'm not dumb enough to shake you down." Take a breath, sell this hard. It's the truth, and I need her to believe it. "Whoever you two are, whatever you're involved in, I don't care. I guess you can tell that just by looking at me. You offered me a lot of money if I found June alive, I'm trying to earn it. But whatever she was really up to, that's the thing most likely to get her missing. You want her found? There's stuff I gotta know. Maybe you don't: maybe you just want it to look like you're looking. If that's the play, I'll go along: poke around, be just discreet enough to be noticed, and never bother you again. I just don't wanna be looking over my shoulder."

She lowers her head into her hands, sighing deeply—like listening to me has exhausted her all over again. Then her fingers start to run through her hair: they move fast, expertly smoothing and straightening and twisting the unruly strands into a tight, shining knot behind her head. She stretches, and I can hear the joints in her neck pop; claws flex and retract. When she looks back at me, she's a different person, with a face carved from bone and eyes that slice like scalpels.

"It was a cheap pretense," she says, in a voice that's brand-new. "June was always careless about details." Her eyes flash. "We really did call her June, she got lucky with that girl in Paris. She is my sister; I do want her found. And you are definitely better off not knowing our real names. But I understand you might want more information. Who knows, you might even be able to use it. So, fine"—she leans in and smiles, wide and white and sharp: a tiger smile, her tongue playing gently across the back of her teeth—"let's play twenty questions."

I give up on the idea of getting a grip on myself. Drain my glass, gesture for another.

"You shouldn't drink so much." She's still smiling.

"You shouldn't lie so much." Lean in, before I lose what's left of my nerve: "Was June involved in something criminal?"

"I don't know."

"Does she have a record?"

"Not under her real name. I couldn't say about the aliases."

"Was she into drugs?"

"I assume you mean 'consumption of.' I never saw it, and I'd say it was unlikely."

"What about 'trafficking of'?"

"I don't know. I would be very surprised."

Something's coming clear; I change tack. "Did June really miss her flight home?"

"No."

"I'd say she wasn't coming home at all. And hadn't in a long time."

"You might be right."

"How long? Months?" There's at least a year in the journals.

"Almost five years."

"How old is she?"

"She was twenty-three this summer." Kara watches me do the math. "Yes: eighteen and out. She went to college—a good one. She was young for her grade. Did most of a year, then vanished."

"Why?"

"I wish I knew."

"Why didn't you find her?"

"She's good."

"You're better." Our faces are getting closer as we bat this back and forth, and now I feel, more than see, something flicker across Kara's mind: something dark and worried.

"We weren't trying that hard. I knew she could take care of herself, and I thought it would be better if she came back on her own terms."

"She had money?"

"Plenty. She specialized in hiding it."

"You said *we* a minute ago."

"Me and Father."

"What's he do?"

"He makes sushi."

"An artist with a knife, then."

She just grins. I think again about the cutting board: Kara never even glanced at her bodyguard. She looks after herself. I wonder where she'd hide a gun in that outfit—or if she's a knife girl, too.

"Get your mind out of my skirt," she says. "That's not where I keep my weapons."

"June's mother left when she was eight?"

"Six." Dangerous eyes: the tiger knows a trap, wonders how I know. Be more careful.

"Why?"

"Her *mother* was a pill-popping refugee from the *Valley of the Dolls* who spent her life on a desperate quest to get more of things she already had too much of. Father caught on, finally, and firewalled her.

So she bailed." The bitterness is the first emotion to pierce the veil she's worn our whole game.

"Sounds like you didn't care for that branch of the family."

"I could never hurt my sister." There's something off in how she says that, but I don't have time to think.

"How much did June know about the sushi business?"

"I couldn't tell you. June was sheltered. Doted on. She was supposed to have a different life, but clearly she knew more than we thought."

"Maybe that's why she left."

A pause. Lies and truth both come easy, but now Kara is actually thinking about what to say. "June loved Father when she was young. She would follow him everywhere. After her mother ran off, they were closer than ever. But then . . . I don't know. June never found her place. In school, she excelled when she felt like it, but often enough she didn't. She'd go from one clique to another, every week she was someone new: no one got close to her. Student groups, environment groups, political groups: she joined everything, stayed with nothing. The only thing she was never willing to try was family."

I resist the urge to lean back, to cross my arms or push my chair away: anything to put some space between me and the quiet rage in Kara's voice.

"So if she didn't miss her flight home, and you hadn't seen her in years, how did you find her?"

"Carelessness. Nostalgia. I'm not sure."

Don't respond, just look. Kara continues:

"She put Kara Saito down as her emergency contact. The phone number was mine. Maybe she'd been doing it for years, but this time she ended up in the hospital, and I got a call saying June Saito had an accident in Cambodia, but she'd be fine."

I can just see it. This woman gets a call from someone she's never heard of, halfway around the world, saying that someone else she's never heard of is in the hospital. She doesn't say "Wrong number" and hang up. She plays along. Finds out who she's supposed to be and inserts herself into the story.

"Did you talk to June?"

"No."

"Then what?"

"I waited. Your boss told me when she was supposed to leave, and I came to try and convince her to come home—but she was already gone."

"You said before you weren't looking for her. Why now?"

"Father's dying. It's time. She should come home."

I play a hunch. "He doesn't know, does he? 'Father.' He thinks you're in Saint-Tropez, doing whatever a girl like you does. But you're out here."

She smirks. "Tempe, depressingly enough. I'm in Tempe, meeting vendors about quality assurance."

I don't want to know what this woman's idea of quality assurance is. "Just one more thing. Why me?"

"Why not?"

"'Cause it stinks. Whoever you are, you've got money. But you show up here without a cop or a lawyer in tow and hire a washed-up photographer to play Sherlock while your sister is missing? You should have the army out."

She laughs, and I'd swear it's real this time, because it makes the hair on my arms stand up.

"Mr. Keller, I think you underestimate yourself. You have been far more difficult to play than most people, which, I have to say, has turned out to be a relief. And I don't think you realize how limited my options are. The police don't love me—sushi is a bit rarefied for their tastes. The embassy is entirely populated by the kind of boys I went to college with. Private detectives in LA are usually scam artists, and inevitably lowlifes—I have nothing against lowlifes, but these all sideline for the tabloids. I could use my own staff, but the good ones, like Miss Eyre"—Kara makes no gesture to the woman by the door; she knows I know—"well, my sister would recognize them in a heartbeat, and she would move on. And anyway, this country is . . . different. I wanted someone who knew the territory. For better or for worse, you're my man."

I almost believe it. It's close to the truth, close enough she means it. But it's not everything. Thinking fast: I don't know what to believe out of what I've just heard, but I believe Kara really doesn't know what happened to June. And that means she doesn't know how close it gets to her, or "Father," if he exists, or whatever business they're in.

She wants the digging done by someone disposable.

And now, just watching me, she knows I know. "So, Mr. Keller," she says, still with that playful edge in her voice, but I can feel the steel underneath, "what do *you* think happened to my sister?"

DIARY

July 14

Gus said yes!!

It wasn't even all that hard, it's just not like in the movies. You have to figure out the rules: An editor is like a banker, he won't give you a story unless you already have one. (All right: I got some help from the boys at the paper! Barry was particularly good for the outlining. I didn't tell him why I wanted it, of course. . . .) In the end, all I had to do was figure out why Luke and Wendy's NGO was *already* a story.

They work in this beautiful area out west, Koh Kong. Apparently it has amazing coastline, acres of mangrove marsh, it could totally be a paradise . . . but it's just a bunch of dirt-poor villages full of people who are slowly tearing it all down just to stay alive. A couple years back, the government built a huge bridge connecting it to Thailand across the gulf. Some Thai mogul put a casino right next to it, everyone expected the money to start rolling in, and soon enough Koh Kong would be Monte Carlo. But nothing happened . . . those pesky trickle-down economics just didn't trickle.

Maybe it was poor planning: Koh Kong just didn't have the infra-structure to support big resorts or hotels: the electricity is sporadic, there's no proper port, the roads there are a shambles and there's no direct route to Phnom Penh, you have to go south almost to Siha-noukville. Gamblers would come over the bridge for the day, then go home, and no one benefited but the casino owners. Maybe there was a bit of corruption thrown in as well. And bad luck: relations with Thailand haven't exactly been swimming along. So the people stay hungry, and keep over-exploiting the environment, which only makes life harder in the long run. . . .

That's the story: the years of money and effort that have gone into trying to develop this place, and the reasons they've all failed. Paradise lost. Throw in a few paragraphs about a plucky little group of photo-genic Americans who are trying to break the cycle of poverty, and you have exactly the kind of story an editor will go for.

That's how I sold it to Gus, anyway, and after about fifteen min-utes of maybes and eye rolling, he agreed. Of course I have to wait until after the elections—that's going to take up the whole week. But he'll let me go down with the boy and help him do the election stuff in Sihanoukville, and then I can go up to Koh Kong afterward.

My conscience is clear: it will be a good story. It's just not the point. I know there's something strange going on out there in that swamp. Now I'm going to find out what it is.

WILL

OCTOBER 7–8

It takes three beers to get anything close to steady.

I flagged a moto, had it take me to the river—by the time I got off, my legs were rubber and my hands were shaking. Kara worked me hard, but I think I kept my edge. She doesn't know about the diaries. I told her the truth about June: that there were too many angles to pick one. That I was pretty sure that she hadn't gone to Siem Reap, but I didn't know where. That there were stories she was chasing that might have got her in trouble, as well as strange relationships with coworkers. I stalled on specifics, said I didn't want anyone garroted until I had a good reason.

"Garrotes are for Mexicans," she said.

I've still got a head start. A narrow one—but I'll need it. Staying alive means finding June first.

I stagger over to the nearest Internet café, open a dummy chat account, and spend a few minutes checking in with Senn: we've got to pull off the photo shoot for Gabriel tomorrow and can't afford mistakes.

Then I call Steve, tell him I have a possible KA for "June Saito" and give Kara's description. "They might be relatives."

"I still need a day or so," he says. "I'll let you know."

That done, it's time to take another look at Number Two and Barry. I spend the next few hours doing people searches on incredibly slow Internet.

Number Two is interesting. His real name is Christopher Grimsby-Roylott, sad but true, and he spent the first fifteen years of his life in a house near Hyde Park that could pass as a midsized museum. He's from an old, important family; his dad was a columnist for a big Conservative paper. Then things changed: suddenly our Chris is living in a flat in a much less savory area with his mother and younger brother, who've changed their surname back to Rigby. I can't find details about the split, but I doubt it was pretty. He still went to the top schools, presumably with his dad's connections, but there are signs of trouble. He leaves a very good university, presumably not by choice, and finishes his degree at a pretty bad one. Digging deeper, it turns out he has a record: larceny, larceny, drugs, more larceny. I'd guess it goes right back to juvie: few folk take downward mobility lying down. His last UK address was the kind of place where you get yourself home before dark, or you think twice about going home at all.

It's not pretty, but it doesn't set alarms ringing: It's about what I expected from Two. Rich kid takes a bad break, decides to reinvent himself.

Barry is a different story. He's been out here almost as long as me and Gus—I think he was teaching business in Thailand before, but there's not much to track. His last name is Strong, which I always thought smelled of bullshit. Sure enough: between '93 and '95 there's a Barry Strong who looks like our guy bouncing around a few addresses in Northern California. Before that, nothing. I have to go into some fairly esoteric resources to find the story: Sacramento, legal name change. And in a bit of luck, a city paper that's put its archives online. Not whole stories, but I can search headlines and abstracts, which is enough to find Barry Krieger, local business reporter, arrested and tried for burning down his girlfriend's house with her inside it. There was a history of violence—the neighbors all had the local cops on speed dial. The state said Barry beat the woman near to death, then set the place on fire to cover it up. Barry said it was an accident, and the prosecution could never quite prove otherwise.

Light a cigarette, realize my hands are shaking again. For some reason I think of Gus, talking about Bunny:

"I'd rather Hun Sen killed him. At least it would mean he shook things up."

The shaking is spreading through my whole body, pulse pounding in my temples, and it feels for all the world like there's someone banging on the back of my head, insistent—

Like she's trying to get back in.

I find them at the Bar with No Name, huddled around the lone plastic table: Barry, Number Two, Gus, the new scum. Guzzling Beerlao, listening hopefully for gunfire. It was the first place I looked: June again, talking in my head.

The girls from the brothel next door are out on the curb, smoking in their matching satin pajamas. They giggle and wave at me as I get off the bike.

Twilight now. The rain is done, but the road is still wet; in these back streets, it's just mud and holes. In the distance, neon signs flicker to life as the clubs start up for the evening; darkness breeds between them.

One of the new scum is the girl with the eyebrow ring Ray mentioned; she sees my face and starts the obligatory round of screaming.

"Washing-machine accident," I say. Gesture to the owner for two beers.

"We were wondering when you'd show," Barry says. "Tell me you have candy?"

Reach into my pocket, drop a baggie on the table.

"Norwegian," I say. The good stuff.

"Thank Christ," says Two.

Tuesday night. Tuesday nights are fucking boring, and this crew will do anything not to be bored.

All it takes is a little push. I don't even need to suggest moving the party to the Heart: the coke and speed I brought are enough to make them want to dance.

At eleven on a Tuesday, the nice NGO workers are already in bed, the gangsters and hookers still sleeping off Saturday. Just us and the usual crew of seven-nighters, aging filth grimly drinking their way through what's left of their second chances. Gus cozies up to the DJ and somehow gets him playing "Blue Monday." I order apple juice in a whiskey glass and settle in to watch.

By half-past one, things are winding down. Gus has been trying to corner me all night, get me to talk about my chat with Kara. I dodged the topic, but it's going to be a problem. Finally he went home, taking the New Order with him. The interns left fast once the boss was gone. I'm still at the bar; Two and Barry are trying to play pool with their eyes shut. I think Number Two has been avoiding me—but he's been drinking like he's on a clock.

Ray is alone on the dance floor, twisting as Britney begs him to hit her one more time.

Check my watch. *Soon.*

Ray's dance moves have been getting more and more extravagant over the past fifteen minutes—then suddenly he's lurching toward the bar, scrabbling at the edge to stay standing.

"Hey, Will," he gasps. "Wherza toilet at?"

"Same place as always." He just stares, openmouthed. I point.

He nods and staggers off, swaying way too hard.

"Guys," I shout, in the general direction of the pool table. Two and Barry look up—follow my eyes to Ray's spindly form as he tries to get the bathroom door open. Barry sighs. We're up and moving in perfect unison.

On any given night, there's a solid chance Ray will get fucked up enough to make trouble. Today I'm on a deadline, so I made sure. The Mickey I slipped him was tiny—just enough to be certain he'd cause a scene before everyone went to bed.

Ray and Barry live together, and night after night Barry hauls Ray's drunk ass home. Which is how I want it tonight: I need to get Number Two alone.

At the bathroom door, we share another look; Two follows me in while Barry stands watch. Inside it's worthy of any Village club, and we find Ray slouched against a graffiti-stained partition, dry-heaving at a broken urinal. One of the old filth, a thick-set former country director with hot-pink lipstick smudges on his ear, is at the next one, looking on in disgust.

"You okay?" I ask Ray.

"Zure-vine. Jus' bit dizzy." He's struggling with his zipper, and I look at Two: we're not helping. Finally Ray gets it, and I say, "Urinal's there," but too late, he's pissing right on the filth's leg. The guy recoils, but doesn't know what to do because he's pissing, too, so these guys just stand there with their dicks in their hands, peeing on each other. Number Two giggles: mistake.

"What the fuck," the filth starts shouting, backing away, repackaging himself. "The fuck is wrong with you?"

"Zorry." Ray looks around, all innocence. "Wazzamata?"

"You're fucking dead," the filth says, and grabs him. Ray's taller, but he's outweighed by a good forty pounds. Number Two starts spluttering.

"Hey," I say, loud, stepping forward, and everyone stops for a second. "You guys go at it here, you're both gonna be rolling in shit before it's done." The filth thinks about that for a sec, backs off. "Plus the bouncers may shoot us. Why don't we take this outside?"

The filth gets right in my face: "Fine, let's go." I motion to the door, and he turns. As soon as he does, I grab him from behind, arm across his neck to cut off the blood flow. He struggles for a second, so I ram his head into the door frame. He goes limp. Leave him lying in the puddle of piss and drag Ray outside.

"Fuck me," Number Two keeps saying. "Fuck me, that was fucking nuts."

"Can you get him home?" I ask Barry.

He stops grinning and looks at me, all the expression of a dead fish. For a second I think he's going to argue—but then he nods, sighs. "Sure." He pulls Ray into a half carry. "My cross to bear. See you in the morning."

Then it's just me and Number Two.

"We should get out of here," I say. Head for the bar, where my drink sits, untouched. "Here." Hand it to Two; reach behind, pull out the well whiskey and a glass, and pour myself a quick shot. We drink. "Your place?"

He nods.

Number Two's flat is only ten minutes away—newish building, half a block from the river. Up the dark stairwell. Two sways as he works his way through the locks. Cracks the door, and there's a second I worry he's not going to invite me in.

"Cup of tea?" I say.

"Yeah, sure."

Got to love the English.

His apartment is big, dark, and scattered with debris: stacks of work notes, books, fake DVDs from the Russian market. A hundred lighters, two on every available surface. Beat-up couches, beat-up coffee table, beat-up TV.

"Here." I toss the rest of the weed from last weekend on the table. "See if you can make a spliff without drooling on yourself. I'll get the drinks."

"Brilliant."

In the kitchen, I make tea and pour us whiskeys. I work on his a bit.

When I come back, he's putting the finishing touches on a joint that must be six inches long.

"Have you been in a lot of fights?" he asks.

"Too many."

"Shit. I've never been in a fight."

"I'm not going to hit you." It's automatic now with drunk twentysomethings: they always ask. There was some movie that was big a few years back.

Two giggles. Between the drugs and the booze and the low-level shock of the scuffle in the bathroom, he's pushed whatever was bothering him back into the depths of his mind. We're just mates again.

I check my watch as he takes his first sip; start counting. Light the joint, draw, pass it over.

I don't know what to talk about, so I talk about Vy. Not that there's much to say, but people are less suspicious when they think you're baring your soul. Start running through a list of stock stories, wondering which might encourage confession.

"How do you do it?" Two asks, at last.

"Do what?"

"You know."

I don't. He goes on, "You should hear the stuff they say about you. You are—fuck. You have done drugs and fucked women halfway across Asia. It just—" A gesture: something vanishing into air. "And Viola—those stories. How many bloody arrests, overdoses—I heard she shot up with the Russian ambassador in her hotel room and he died right there, and you had to come get her out before the cops came."

"Who told you that? That's bullshit."

"Most people, sane people, they want to off themselves after ten minutes with Vy. You spent three years with her. How?" I don't understand the question. He tries again: "The way it gets out here, dunnit . . . y'know? Dunnit tear you up?"

Finally, I realize: he *wants* to tell me what he knows. It's beating a hole in his brain, and he thinks I'm the guy to fix it. To save him.

I lean in, hand on his arm: *Hey, I'm your buddy.* "What's eating you?"

For a second I think he's going to tell me—but then his face closes, he shakes his head. His eyes talk for him: he's afraid.

His drink is three-quarters gone. Check my watch: twenty minutes already.

"You can tell me. Promise I've done worse." *How do you know what you've done?*

Two laughs. "Who died and made you Mr. Sensitive?" Shakes his head. "No, you got the right idea." Raises his glass: "Here's to not caring." We toast.

Our glasses slam on the table, empty.

"I'm serious. You can talk to me."

"I can't . . . talk to anybody."

"I'll understand."

"You would." His voice is getting thick, unsteady. "But it's no good, I . . . I feel funny."

"Good weed."

"Yeah." He laughs, then looks confused. Goes for his empty glass, almost knocking it off the table. Laughs as he catches it.

It has to be now.

"You're worried about June, aren't you?" He's not surprised—just shakes his head. "You were worried yesterday, when you heard she hadn't gone home."

"No way. She went home . . . she told me so."

"When?"

"After she left. She . . . she told me."

"Told you how?"

He looks at me now, finger pointing; his eyes filmed with booze and suspicion. "Why are you asking? Did *he* send you?"

"Nobody sent me, mate. I just want to know what happened." He's shaking his head now, like a two-year-old on a tantrum. "Who is *he*? You knew someone who was going to hurt June. Who was it?"

"No . . . Not . . . Not her."

"Just tell me, I can handle them—"

Interrupted by his laugh: "That's what I said. You think you can . . . but you can't."

I'm losing him now, and my temper as well. Grab his shoulders: "Goddamnit, Chris, she's gone, she's fucking gone, and you know why." My voice sounds raw in my own ears; I'm screaming or whispering, I can't tell.

He shakes his head.

"Who was it? Was it Barry? Just tell me, was it fucking Barry?"

Two stares at me, wide-eyed, and in that look is as much despair as I've seen in one place. Then he turns, vomits across the coffee table, and passes out.

Rohypnol: it can make you nauseous.

I light a cigarette and think about the tedious business of cleaning up. Two is highly unlikely to remember the last half hour—but if he wakes and things are hinky, he's going to ask questions. He's got to come to in the morning with a clear narrative: we came back, we smoked up, we drank. He was a mess, he passed out watching telly.

Two loves his TV shows—there's hundreds of DVDs here. I pick up one that looks well thumbed, put it in the player, let it run while I mop up his vomit. If he asks, I'll describe him putting it on.

This should have worked. He was on the verge of spilling—but he couldn't. Booze and drugs, they'll lower your inhibitions, make you suggestible, but no drug on earth can force the truth out of you, not if there's a stronger force keeping you quiet. Number Two is terrified of someone—someone he thinks could make June disappear. I can work against that kind of fear, but I need time or information or considerable amounts of plastic sheeting. I don't have good options.

Finish cleaning and give the place a quick search, but it's not much use: the piles of paper would take hours to go through. Story notes, newspaper clippings, UK bank statements—he's living paycheck to paycheck. Kitchen: empty chip bags on the counter, Coke and moldy pizza in the fridge. A couple pans in the cupboard. Not much of a cook. Bedroom: unmade bed, wardrobe full of clothes. No cash, no guns, no drugs except a little lump of hash under an ashtray.

It's well past three by the time I'm done. I consider swiping Two's keys: I could copy them, slip them back in the morning, before he wakes. But it's risky, and I'm exhausted. I'll find another way to take a run at him tomorrow.

Open the door, and—

"Morning, Will."

Freeze. It takes me a moment to see him: a shapeless mass in the dark of the stairwell. The gun he's got is an ugly little .38 special, but it'll put a hole in me just fine.

Barry. He must have been there an hour or more, waiting. He's thought it through: too far for me to reach, too close for him to miss. Silhouetted in Number Two's door, I'm a paper target.

"Hey," I say. "Trouble sleeping?"

He grins his best best-buddy grin. "Fucking get inside."

D I A R Y

Am I crying again? Why? Was it what he said, down by the river? I can't remember.

I thought I was strong; I thought I was different! I thought I knew myself . . . only to discover what a fragile, febrile thing I truly am: an image in a pool of water, shattered by a falling leaf.

I've made the club, but only halfway. I'm one of them, but now they think they own me—especially him. I end up back at his wretched little apartment every evening, chatting until he tires of my voice and turns on the television . . . I pretend to pass out and feel his fingers under my shirt. When he's too drunk and stoned to stand, that's when he wants me.

Tonight a friend of his came, and he literally picked me up and stuffed me in the bedroom, out of sight. He thought I was out then, too, but I watched through the keyhole. The visitor was an older man, Cambodian. Not well-dressed, but very dapper, hair and shoes highly polished. Curiously, he never seemed to blink. They talked for a while—I couldn't hear them with the TV going in the background, but it was probably about drugs—and then the man left. And I had to lie in the bed again and pretend to sleep as he came back, and his hand crept up under my skirt. Stifled my reaction as he grabbed me. Then he sat down in the corner, had his dose and fell asleep, leaving me to clean up and walk home alone.

I don't even want him. I don't know why I go. Why does Gogo come back to Didi, day after day? Better to wait together than wait alone? But even that simple act means giving away some of yourself.

You say to him: I want to go somewhere. He says go, if you're going. Turns back toward the seaside, where the children are launching fireworks, tossing sparklers into the churning water.

You say to him: I have an idea. He says better save it.

You say: I'm looking for something, he says what else do you need?

I could choose to forget tonight. I could let these sobbing hours drift into the white and vanish . . . black out these words, so that even if you did try, some day, to remember, you would be unable to. Perhaps you would recall this little room, seen as by a camera: the spinning fan, the shape that once was you, curled up on the naked bed. You would make up a story to explain what had so spun you. Of course it wouldn't be real, but you'd cling to it, so that you could see your life as singular, a true story, not a script that had been cut and changed and rewritten. . . .

I know better . . . I was you, remember?

Of course you don't. But I remain: the thing you've written out.

I was with you all those nights—all the way back to the night she left. I have kept them through the years, while you keep sunlight and warm air.

Shall I tell you what I remember?

No . . .

You don't want to read this. Black it out when you are done.

WILL

"You shoot that thing, it's gonna be loud." I'm edging backward into Two's apartment. In the hall, there's nowhere for me to get out of the line of fire. "People will hear."

"Yeah, I'm aware just how fucking loud my gun is, man." Barry's in the doorway now, keeping pace with me. "I had a quieter one, but I sold it. Anyway, shooting you is really plan B. *Stop*." I've almost reached the end of the hall, where it opens into the living room. I stand still: cornered. I am slow, tired, beat to hell. I don't like my options. But since Barry didn't gun me down in the doorway, I guess he really wants to talk—and I want to hear what he has to say.

"Can I turn that thing down?" I ask. On the TV, some blond chick is loudly kicking the crap out of Billy Idol.

"Sure. Move very slow."

I do as told. Feels like a million years before I can reach the volume.

Barry edges out of the hall, gun always trained on me. He lets his eyes flick over to Number Two, passed out on the sofa. "So he's not getting up anytime soon, huh?"

"Unlikely. Mind if I roll?"

Barry laughs. "Make two."

He's silent, watching, until I've tossed him his. Lights it one-handed, eyes and gun never leaving me. "I didn't do it."

"Didn't do what?"

He doesn't quite react, but I see his hairy paw tighten around the gun. "Don't fuck with me, man. I know you're looking for the girl. I'm telling you it wasn't me."

I take a deep drag off the joint.

"What makes you think someone did something to her? All I've seen so far is she's on a long vacation and not answering her phone."

Barry is disgustingly pleased with himself. "Well, now we're making progress, aren't we? What we have here, Will my boy, is the basis of a negotiation. I have something you want: information. And I'm smart enough not to let you drag it out of me for free."

I fucking hate business writers. "All right, shoot." *Poor choice of words, Will.* "What do you want?"

"What does anyone who comes out here want?"

"To be left alone."

"Bingo. That's it, okay? I like it here. Nobody cares that I'm a fat fuck, or that I like computers too much, or that I'm not fucking executive material."

"I definitely think you're executive material."

"You always were a dipshit, Keller. But I don't actually care what you think, anyway. It's *them.*" I must look blank, because he goes on, "The women, man. Back home, they could fucking control us. We were nothing without them."

"That why you set them on fire?"

"Ah, see, Marie: perfect example, thank you! I wondered if you'd found out about Marie yet. I mean, you're a dumbass, but it was just a matter of time, it was in all those damn newspapers." Through all of this, he's never stopped smiling: it's a great joke, and we're all in on it.

"Marie is the perfect example. She was a drunk fucking whore who made that retarded kid in the McDonald's ad look like a Nobel Prize winner, okay? But she still managed to control me. For years. Back home she was the best a guy like me could hope for. Everyone said so, you know? My family, my friends. My *mom.* 'Oh, she's a prize,' 'She's a keeper,' 'Best thing that ever happened to you.' Like I didn't know what that meant: 'You're not good enough for anyone except this fat, sloppy cunt.' For a while, they really got me believing it. So I put up with her shit, day after fucking day after fucking day. Then one night, I come home and she's hammered out of her goddamn mind, screaming about how I only want her to cook and clean. Fine, she says, she'll cook me dinner. She can barely stand. She's falling all over the kitchen, grabbing shit out of cabinets, sticking it on the stove." He giggles. "I should actually have smacked some fucking sense into her, y'know? If I had, cunt would still be alive. But I just walked away. And the dumb fucking whore passed out with the stove still on and put me through a federal indictment and five years of fucking bullshit. Even dead, that bitch was controlling me, you see what I mean? Then I came out here. Fucking paradise. It's all out in the open here. Back home, I was worthless cuz I couldn't get a girl. But out here, I see some rich, slick bastard with shiny hair and a beautiful chick on each arm? Hey, it's cool. He's no better than me: he's paying for it. I want those girls tomorrow, I can have 'em. This place shows pussy up for what it is: a commodity."

I know better than to interrupt someone this fucking crazy, but if he does not get to the point soon, I am going to go for that gun no matter how slow I am.

"So you see: I'm finally free. I don't want some other bitch fucking it up. I want this as far from my fat ass as fucking possible, okay? And you, as it happens, can do that for me. This is the deal: I tell you what I know, and you spin it so however it goes, they don't come near me."

"You had to hold me at gunpoint for this?"

"Motherfucker." He laughs. "Everyone knows it doesn't pay to get close to you. You're kind of an emerging market. So, y'know, of course I need a hedge."

"So, I do what you want or you kill me?"

"Hey, this is a good deal." He sounds genuinely offended. "But look, if you wanna be that way . . . Obviously I can't keep this gun on you twenty-four/seven. So, just in case"—he leans in, like that makes him think I'll listen closer—"I know why you're out here. I got it out of Gus one time, when he was drunk. Thought it might come in useful someday."

A shiver runs through me; he sees it.

There are things I'm not allowed to think about.

So I think about the deal: the only reason Barry would make this trade was if he was sure something led back to him. It's not the diary, he doesn't seem to care. So something else: something he was seen to do, something he gave her—

"Sure," I say. "I'm curious. But if I find out you're lying to me, it's right back on your doorstep."

"That's fine. Just remember it's not in my interest to lie, any more than it's in yours to betray me."

"So tell me: What am I covering up? What am I going to find that points to you?"

"The reason I know June was in trouble, capital-*T* kind of trouble, is that before she left, she asked me to get her a gun."

Hell.

Gotta hand it to Barry, he sees the angles. It's no secret he likes to shoot stuff. After fifty years of war, this country is drowning in hardware. One of the less savory aspects of the tourist trade: *barangs* pay well to go out in the woods and fire off AK-47s and grenade launchers. Sometimes the guys running the tours give them cows or goats to shoot at. Sometimes, I've heard, they give them people. Never tried to find out. Barry loves these excursions, and he's in tight with a couple of the guys who run them. Even someone new, like June, would know that if she wanted firepower, she could go to him. So if a gun came up or was found, someone would sooner or later look to Barry. His past would get dragged out, and someone with a badge and a low IQ would certainly assume he killed June.

"What kind of gun?"

"She was very specific about what she wanted—something small, that she could silence. Knew makes and models and everything. My guy didn't have exactly the thing, but he came pretty close."

"When?"

"Early August. I got it over a weekend, but she'd asked me a couple days earlier—maybe the fourth or fifth."

Interesting: Just a few days after she comes back from Koh Kong.

"She didn't say why she wanted it?"

"I really didn't ask."

"Do you know who she spent time with?"

"Other than us at the paper, I wouldn't know. She was closest to Two." Grin. "But I guess you've already asked him."

"Did she say anything to you about her past? Family?"

He snorts. "This is Cambo."

"The Khmer you saw her arguing with—was that real, or bullshit?"

"That was real. I don't know what it was about, I couldn't hear them. It wasn't a blowup-fight kind of argument, more a very intense discussion."

"How'd you come to see it?"

"Drank too much. Passed out, woke up."

"Who was he?"

"I don't know. But I've seen him around, somebody has to know him: middle-aged, pot belly, shitty wardrobe and expensive haircut. He had that look: he was ex-cop, ex-military, some shit."

"Why would June be arguing with someone like that?"

"That, my friend, is your job to figure out, not mine. Unless you have more questions, I'm done with this shit."

Exhausted, I shake my head.

"Then I'll be going. I'll pretend this never happened, but we have a deal. If you really need to talk, then come to me in the office, say you gotta buy me that drink you owe me. I'll find you someplace quiet." He pauses, breathes deep. "Please, don't follow me. Don't make me do something neither of us will regret."

I pull the makings from my pocket; start rolling another joint. He backs away, into the darkness of the stairwell, the gun still pointed at me.

Then he's gone.

———————

Moon's risen by the time I leave: nearly full, throwing long shadows in front of me as I walk. Brain full of hornets. Barry lies, but if his story isn't true, why would he talk at all? Where's he trying to lead me?

It's the Khmer he saw June arguing with that bothers me most. Military, Barry said, or police. June was working the heroin story—maybe the guy was a source? Feels like a long shot that one of those guys would talk, and I can't see them going to an American intern. Definitely not a woman.

The cops who hang around foreigners have another agenda. Mostly they're looking for work: You pay a few bucks, buy a few drinks, get your own pet policeman. He'll buy your coke, fix your traffic tickets, make trouble for your enemies. I don't like to think what would get June within miles of a guy like that—but if she's buying guns off Barry, she's in deep. And I still don't know what started it. A con gone wrong?

I can probably find out. There's a particularly unpleasant police lieutenant who hangs around the Heart, Pisit Samnang. Lots of bent cops out there, but Sam's a rare breed: works with foreigners because he likes to fuck with us. He'll jump through hoops for you, and you think you own him—then one day you realize he owns you. The kids from the paper stay miles away from him, even talking to the guy is enough to get you fired—but if June was playing around with the police, Samnang would probably know. I won't go to him unless I'm desperate, but I'm not sure that's very far off.

By the time I've climbed the stairs to my room, I can barely stand up—but June is so loud in my head, she's practically screaming. Again, I open the journals.

I can't sleep. When I close my eyes, all I see is the girl in the photograph.

It was taken in Kabul, in the early nineties. The Taliban hadn't come to power yet. Gus says they called that period the war of warlords. The country was in the process of regressing from the twentieth century to the seventh, where it would remain for the foreseeable future, and this was the image that captured it.

It won't come out of my head . . . so I will put it here:

The girl is lying in the street, surrounded by a crowd of people who appear to be cheering. She's crying, but you can still tell that she's beautiful. Her hand is to her neck. It's not a gory image at all: only when you look closely do you see the blood on her hands, the pool of red spreading under the feet of the crowd. What you see is the faces: the unholy joy of the onlookers, the sorrow of the girl in her last moments, as she realizes all she's about to lose.

The caption is "Girl killed by her family for being pregnant out of wedlock."

Gus says it should have won the Pulitzer. It was short-listed, but got edged out by something more America-centric. The Cold War was ending, no one wanted to be reminded about Afghanistan falling apart.

You've guessed who the photographer was, of course. Gus says he was great, once upon a time: the guy everyone looked up to. William Keller would go places other people wouldn't dare. He knew how to keep his mouth shut, he didn't judge his sources, and he could get along with anyone. He was patient, waiting days, weeks, for the right opportunity . . . and when it came, he got right up close.

I'm pretty sure Gus was trying to tell me something . . . about being a journalist, or living out here? I don't know. I wonder if he suspected why I want to go to Koh Kong, after all. . . .

He has a whole book of Keller's old stuff hidden away in his apartment. There's a series of pictures of the girl in the street: the crowd cheering and chanting, a woman in a burka who I think must be her mother, waving the bloody knife in the air.

Scenes from a village in the countryside, where a man beats a boy to death with a metal pipe for talking to a different militia.

In the hills with mud-caked warriors in sandals made of old tires, cigarettes welded into their faces until they died. They all died.

"Afghanistan changed him," Gus says.

I think he was trying to tell me something with that, too.

Some days I wake up crying, and I don't understand why. Other days I stand on my balcony, and the shining river and the palace roofs and the wet grass and the palms in the distance are all so beautiful I think I won't actually be able to stand it, that my heart will burst and I will die right there. I don't understand that, either.

I thought that by coming here, I could be someone different. It seems I was right . . . but I don't know who she is.

W I L L

It's spring in Kabul, and roses bloom outside the empty windows of the old villa where we'd meet. A hidden castle in a secret garden: its walls cracked and overgrown, reminders of this city's bright days, before the Russians came. Warm air blows through the sun-bleached sheets we've strung to hide us from the world. I'm waking from a doze with the soft weight of her head on my chest, her arm thrown over me, and I reach down to take her face in my hand—

"Fatima, baby, you wouldn't believe what I dreamed."

She smiles up at me: "Are we home?"

"Soon."

And her lips light me up, her mouth sweet and warm and my whole body is on fire with her—

Something's wrong.

"I have something to tell you," she says. "A surprise."

"Baby, you know I hate surprises."

"This is a good one. We are leaving soon?"

"Just two weeks, that's all I need. Everything will be ready."

You're dreaming. She's gone—

she's gone, and I'm alone in the villa, looking at the cobwebs spun in dusty corners and the sheet flapping in the wind, but it's as if I can still feel her presence: she's here, invisible, but she's lying on top of me, her weight—

her body

—bearing down on my chest and I can't breathe, she's crushing me, cold and heavy as lead, cold hands on my face, cold lips on mine, pulling the air from my lungs into her dead mouth—

And then I'm running: running through the street, body on fire and brain trailing ash, until I get to her house and I see it all again: the men shouting, the cheers, the bloody knife in the air—

This is where I live: forever and ever. This moment when I want so much to run to her, to cradle her and kiss her and pull her away, but there's nothing I can do, she is seconds from death and they're pouring gasoline and they'll kill me if I go to her so I don't, I stand frozen, a statue, a cheap and unconvincing replica of humanity, set here as a memorial—

I do the only thing I know how:

I raise my camera.

———————

Broken glass everywhere.

Torn paper, ash. Shelves overturned, shattered chair. Blood on the sheets from the cuts on my hands.

What the hell happened?

It's red behind my eyes and all I want is a shot, but there's none, I'm clean and I light another goddamn cigarette.

It almost helps.

Bats outside the windows, rattling out of the eaves of the museum. Nearly night.

Scan the wreckage, trying to remember. Yesterday was a million years ago. I left Two sleeping, came home, still puzzling over Barry's story. Then the journals. Sitting at the desk as the sky went gray, then blue, poring over the pages trying to listen for her voice. There was something important, violent—I can't remember.

Look again around the ruined bedroom.

I know what happened.

There are rules. Things I don't think, names I never say. I have to guard my thoughts: it takes so little for the past to drag me back. But last night, somehow, I let my guard down—

Enough.

There are rules.

I go to the kitchen, make coffee. I know from the state of the place there won't be any booze—I'll be lucky to find a fucking aspirin.

To the shower. I step into the lukewarm water, let it chill me. Bandages for my hands. I've got to hurry, it's getting dark already.

I'm so close to June, but for tonight she'll have to wait. I have a job to do, and hell to pay if it goes wrong.

———————

When I come downstairs, Gus is waiting. "Nice look. What's that about?"

I'm dressed in new khaki cargo pants and a brown T-shirt, sunglasses slung at the neck. Lightly scuffed knockoff Skechers. Camera stuffed in a big gray camping backpack. Hopefully the outfit says tourist. I've bought cover-up at the grocery store and put a ton on my face. Far from perfect, but the bruises don't stand out so much. I'd like to not be noticed.

"Work to do." I reach into the backpack, pull out a carry bag: June's journals, her photographs, the sheaf of her photocopied news stories. I've been carrying them around with me, but I don't want them on this job.

"Can you put these somewhere safe? Preferably not in your apartment—always a chance someone might come looking."

"Brilliant," he mutters, but he takes the bag, slouching back to set it on his coffee table. "I thought we were getting out of the missing-girl business. Did you learn anything from the sister?"

"Not much." I can't even begin to think how to summarize that meeting for Gus. "Got any Dexedrine?"

He sighs as he fishes a prescription bottle out from between the sofa cushions. Holds it without giving it to me. "You remember last night?"

"Course I do."

"What do you remember?"

"Do you know anything about a Khmer guy June was hanging out wi—"

"Fuck that shit, and fuck her. You know what I mean." His eyes flash. "I saw your room."

"Bad dreams."

"Mrs. Mun will shit when she sees that, I'll have to iron things out—"

"Do what you gotta do."

I turn to go and he shoves his way out onto the landing, putting himself between me and the stairs. "That is not the point! You're off the deep end here—"

"You threw me in."

"And *mano de dios* I am sorry now, but—"

"But what?"

We stand inches apart, hands trembling.

"Do what you're good at," he says. "Walk away."

I walk west all the way to Monivong, then south—don't want to risk getting a driver who knows me. Grab a moto out of the crowd, head for the Russian Market.

Narrow halls, jammed with tourists in every shade of the rainbow. I slip inside, let my body take their rhythm: someone drawn and distracted by the million things on display, traditional clothes and scarves and souvenirs and jewelry. I look and fondle and wander.

I let myself disappear.

Stroll through the stalls until I spot the guy Senn has picked out for me: youngish, blond—a backpacker type with bleached-out hair and the too-skinny look that suggests both exercise and chemical assistance. The gay mafia never lets you down. He's standing at one of the long counters, browsing through stacks of ripped-off American DVDs. I let myself drift down the hall until I'm standing next to him. Hands shuffle nameless films, not looking at the covers.

"What'ja see today?" I ask.

"Went to some temples, mate, pissed about." Aussie, then.

"Anything you like?"

"There was this one place, it had an elephant. That was cool."

Everyone loves the elephant: damn thing is on more drugs than me. I lean in to pick up a stack of CDs and set my ancient *Rough Guide* on the counter. "Take that when you go. It's your front end." Twenty crisp $100 bills, carefully stuck between the pages.

"Okay." He sets a hotel-room key next to it. I pick it up.

"Get yourself a plane ticket. For tomorrow: noon at the latest, early morning is better. Don't go back to the hotel until after the party. Once it's over, get out quick as you can. The rest of your money will be under the door of my room; grab it and go. If you gotta sleep, do it in a different neighborhood—or better, just get the hell out of here."

He nods. "Bali's brilliant now."

"Good. You leave the lights on?"

"Like the man said."

I turn to go.

"Seeya, mate," he says.

"If you do, we're in trouble."

———————

The Crane Hotel is across town, a bit away from the usual tourist hangouts. A big 1950s building, now run-down and scummy, it's favored by the discreet. The lobby is cupboard-sized, done in white glossy tiles and pale blue paint. Looks like a bathroom. Smells a bit like one, too. The proprietor, a squat Cambodian dressed in various shades of nylon, is chewing some mix of betel and tobacco. He doesn't look up from his paper when I come in.

"You wan' room?" He chomps down on the wad in his cheek. "Ve'y quiet."

"Yeah. Two nights. I'll pay now."

He spares me a sideways glance as I hand him some bills. "You wan' company?" he murmurs, looking at his fingernails like they might be fakes. "I know nice girls."

"I'm all set, thanks."

"Wan' boy? Ve'y young, ve'y clean."

"Just me and Mary Jane."

"End of hall, turn left, all the way to end, left again."

I nod and walk down the hall. I don't go to the room I've just bought, but to the one the Aussie gave me the key for.

It's tiny, just big enough for a double bed and a little table in a corner. Another near the bed with a lamp on it; fluorescent tubes in the ceiling. That's the main reason for choosing this place: the ceilings are high, and the pasteboard walls they've thrown in between the rooms don't go all the way up. At the top are bracketed air conditioners, surrounded by a patchwork of boards and drywall, occasionally broken by tin ventilation grills. Standing on the table, I can hold my camera up for a view down into the neighboring room.

I take a few test shots, checking the light. The fluorescents next door are off, the lamp on—it's almost too dark. But we don't need A-1 material, just recognizable faces. I check the shots, then take a few more. I can't see what I'm shooting, so I have to figure out how to angle the camera to get the bed and as much of the room as possible—then figure it out again for the doorway. I shoot and erase until I'm sure I can get it right later, in the dark. Here's hoping Charlie can last a couple minutes. When I'm satisfied, I get out the muzzle and put it on the camera. It's totally quiet, but bulky, and I won't be able to see the screen or use the controls when I'm shooting. I take a few more shots, unmuzzle the camera to check them, then put it back. I do it again, and again—until I'm sure.

When I'm ready, I kill the light and sit on the bed. Take my shoes off, then pull a couple Dexedrine from my pocket and swallow them dry. Wouldn't do to fall asleep now. I could have a long wait.

In the dark, time moves slow. I can't risk a light. Alone with my thoughts—not where I want to be. I keep going back to June. There was something else in the journals, something important. I'm trying to remember—but it's lost in the fog

in Kabul

and there are bad dreams there, shapeless figures waiting for me to say their names and let them in. To chase them off, I think about the beer I'll have when I'm done. About the river, the lights of the river, glittering off the water in the night

dark shapes moving beneath

Channi's smile as she hands me a frosted mug; her frown as she talks about her past.

She's a puzzle. Good Cambodian girls don't work in bars. Not at night, not with foreigners. They don't read your palms. But she's not dancing in a bikini, either—won't be what everything here wants her to be. Playing all sides: a Mormon and a waitress and, maybe, a girlfriend. Not good, not bad, but a little of both. I try to picture her face, and her eyes ask me how I got here. I don't have an answer.

I get edgier as the night goes on. Two or three times I hear footsteps in the hall and climb up on the table—but they always die away. Then, a little past two thirty, someone reaches the door next to mine and stops. I'm ready. Start taking quick bursts as soon as I hear the key in the lock. I try to hit the shutter just as their voices get clearer—my best chance for a face shot. Sound of giggling. I shoot again and again until I hear the door close, then change the angle to catch more of the room. I'm breathing deep and quiet. There's a clink, like glasses—hopefully the Aussie's sober enough to spike Charlie's drink. The less he remembers, the better we all are. I aim the camera through the lattice and shoot again, maybe another face shot. The drinking doesn't last long, quickly replaced by the sounds of lips, buttons, zippers.

There's a thud, and a voice I don't know says, "I turn light off."

I catch my breath.

"Leave it on," the Aussie says. "I want to look at you." There's a moan. I guess he's being persuasive.

I angle the camera on the voices: standing by the door, then back as they settle on the bed. They're taking their time. Good. I shoot a couple more bursts, checking the glowing dial on my watch.

To time myself, I imagine what they're doing, a selection of positions and actions. Now on all fours, now leaning on the wall. I imagine the sound of the shutter inside the casing: snap snap snap. Reaching for each other—

Snap snap.

After maybe five minutes of this, I think I have enough to risk checking the camera, so I step down and carefully pull off the muzzle, shielding the light of the screen with a thin blanket.

Lots of motion blur, it's inevitable. I got a recognizable angle on Charlie in the door, and another when he's got the Aussie's face in his crotch, but you can't quite see what's happening. Most of the shots of actual sex are muddy: reaching arms, the burled shape of a spine; dark spaces between, where hands and mouths and cocks touch just beyond the reach of light and lens. The Aussie biting Charlie's nipple. A couple that are almost the money shot, the boy on the bed with Charlie riding cowgirl—face turned away, but he'd be hard to mistake if you knew him.

Not enough to quit yet. There's a better picture somewhere.

The sounds from the next room are getting louder, more frantic. Not much time left. I double-check the settings and muffle again. As I get up on the stool, I hear more footsteps in the hall.

A moan from next door.

Snap snap snap.

The footsteps pause, just outside. *Why—*

Snap snap.

A key clicks in a lock. Their room.

I freeze, not even breathing. The boys don't notice, absorbed in their two-man ballet. My finger twitches.

Snap snap snap.

I hear a door opening and a shout—low, breathless, choked with fear and surprise. It ends in a wet-sounding thud. A splash, like water. Snap snap snap, even as another cry begins and ends in the sound of flesh on flesh. A sob, a gasp, a crash of glass. Something patters against the wall I'm standing behind, and I bite my lip so I don't start screaming. I can smell it, like a butcher's shop but a hundred times stronger.

Another thud.

It's happened in a second. I need to move but my body won't respond. I'm frozen, imagining what's on the other side of the wall. It's worse than seeing, and my stomach rises. Don't throw up.

Move!

Legs won't move.

Only thing I can do:

Snap snap snap.

My head is pounding, my mind screaming at me: run.

They'll see you.

Will they come here? Should go to the door, get behind it—shit, there's a hammer in my bag, maybe I can sandbag one of them and get out. *And then? Away? How?*

Thunk thunk thunk.

Snap snap snap.

Metal clatters to the ground, then silence.

Whoever they are, they don't bother closing the door, and I hold my breath as they step into the hall. They're walking fast, not running. No hurry. Their footsteps go down the hall and around the corner.

My body is mine again. I pivot the camera around the room, trying to catch every possible angle. Then I get down.

Got to get out of here. Right now. I stuff the camera in the bag. Shoes. What have I touched? I wipe everything I can think of with the corner of a sheet, still in the dark. Silence outside—I might only have seconds. No hesitation. Open the door and step out into the hall like nothing's wrong. Wipe the knob with my shirt, drop the key on the floor. The other room is lit up, the door hanging open. The glimpse I get as I pass makes my stomach boil.

Don't throw up—

I hear a voice around the corner: a question, loud and frantic. A door opens. I keep going, trying to match the fast, relaxed pace of those retreating footsteps. More steps now, down that other hall: Running. I don't look back.

I'm not going for the exit: the building could be watched. Instead, I head around the corner to my own room. As I put my key in the lock, I hear a man's shout from the hall I was just in, then a woman's scream that goes on and on and on. The key won't fit. It's not working. My heart's beating faster and faster.

Key's upside down. I curse, turn it, and slip into the room just as doors around me start opening.

There will be panic now. Guests will be rushing to grab their bags and get out before the police come. If I stay calm, I can slip out with them, unnoticed.

Then what?

I had a joint tucked in my pocket for afterward, and now I fumble it out and light up. Takes about fifteen tries. A few quick pulls to steady the speed raging in my blood.

Only then do I take the muzzle off the camera and glance at what I've done.

Christ, I need a fix.

D I A R Y

July 20

Midnight.

I'm invisible, on an invisible street, the kind you walk past a hundred times before you realize it is your destination: that up ahead, where the road appears to peter out, is a hidden path to a place you'll never have a name for.

I am not sure how I got here. What draws me, night after night, down these pitch-black alleys . . . around the knots of men gambling on the pavement by candlelight . . . past the cramped kitchens visible through glowing windows, where women in pajamas still sweat over camp stoves?

I am a collector—like Benjamin's backwards-facing angel, who from such discarded fabrics wove the whole of the twentieth century. I hoard these nights, store them away in the drawers of memory. I will make from them something astonishing. . . .

I am a liar: I do it because this is when she comes to me.

Stand me anywhere in the pitch black, and I can feel it, tugging under my ribs: a golden wire, strung across the night, connecting me to her. She draws, I follow. And sometimes, walking midnight streets and gazing in through lighted windows, I think I see her: This is the life we almost had, together. When it was just her and me it was hideaways, boltholes, tiny rooms like these, where our breath burned in each other's nostrils, where we cooked off rings plugged into the wall and the smell soaked into our clothes and never left. We smothered each other.

I remember waking to the feeling of her nails on my back, gently tracing hieroglyphs of dream, and she talked to me for hours and hours—though there is little left that I can recall.

I say this as though it happened often . . . as though I had many memories of her. Perhaps it was once, twice? I don't know. The rest of the time it was Father's house: far-off views, mist on treetops. Mother used to joke about those huge windows: she said it was so he'd see them coming.

His world, not ours. She became distant and cold, a figure down a lonely hall in a glittering dress. All that space seemed to make her afraid.

Of the things from my childhood I know are true, there is little more than this.

WILL

On a bike, city sliding by. I look back: Am I being followed? In dark streets, there's no way to tell. One arm around the driver, I fumble the phone out of my pocket, break it open, and toss the pieces into the night. Pop another of Gus's Dexedrine. Try to keep breathing.

I came out of the hotel with the crowd; grabbed the first moto I could find. The drivers saw what was happening: five times the fee to get me to Martini's. Not too many places crowded at this hour of the morning, but the taxi-girl clubs are still going. I hand him his money before we've even stopped.

Martini's isn't packed, but there are still bodies at the tables: middle-aged men, the ones who can't quite commit, nursing drinks as they try to find something to talk about with girls in cutoff shorts and bra tops, pretending they're here for more than a commercial exchange.

I make a beeline for the bar, wary of my incongruous backpack and roadkill eyes. I stand out. Get a drink and down it, always watching the door. No one suspicious comes in, so I head for the bathroom and change my shirt and pants for the spares in my bag. Slip out the back, down an alley, listening for footsteps, or bike engines gunning.

Nothing.

I walk a long way to another big street, flag a moto, and stumble over what to tell him. I can't go home. Can't go to the river, or the Heart: places someone looking for me would go. But I need people around: another nightclub. Can't think of a name, not sure where I am, what time it is—late or early, who can tell?

"Dancing. Take me to dancing. With girls."

The driver nods.

What went wrong? Were we set up? But if someone was onto us, why didn't they know I was there? It doesn't make sense. I've been try-ing to flush a tail, but there's no point: if the guys who got Charlie and the Aussie knew about me, they'd have killed me in the hotel.

My hands won't stop shaking.

We pull up to a club I don't recognize: run-down, set back from the road behind a fence. A dirtier, less prosperous version of the semi-brothel I just left. I offer the driver another 250 riel to make a call on his mobile. Senn's phone is off, so I send a message:

GET OUT.

I take another Dexedrine and head for the bar. Buy a drink from the girls, then another. They ignore me: they can see there's no busi-ness there.

Whatever happened, this town isn't safe. I still have the other half of the Aussie's money—enough for a plane ticket. I could go, grab the next flight to anywhere—

"Airports kill me."

I look up, half expecting to see June leaning over me, trying to open me up with those cold, inquisitive eyes—

"Do you like what you've found of me so far?"

Get out of my head, June. This is it: I'm in too deep, and so are you, but you're on your own now. Gus has your books, he can try to find you, if—

Fuck.

Gus.

I grab the arm of the girl behind the bar and shout in Khmer, "I need your phone."

Seven rings and a heart attack later, Gus picks up. "The fuck?" he groans.

"Where are you?"

"In bed. What fucking time do you call this?"

"Never mind. Just get out of the house—now. Meg with you?"

"No." His voice is different: alert, waiting.

"Go see her. Or a hooker, whatever. But first there's something I need you to bring me."

———

At 6:00 a.m. the Central Market is already heating up. Shops are opening, traders carting in cookware and vegetables and garment-store seconds. I take the chance to buy another change of clothes, then head for the butchers' section.

The air is heavy with the sugary smell of animal blood. Under the huge modernist dome, a hundred stone tables drip red as the day's flesh is hacked and sawed and hung on hooks.

After last night, this is not comforting.

Plenty of customers already—restaurant buyers, procuring for the afternoon menu. I wind through the aisles to one wide, white counter where a fellow in a stained apron is stringing up sausages. Gus stands watching, a sour look on his face and my carry bag slung over his shoulder.

"Sometimes I'm sorry I know you," he says, handing me the bag.

"Me too." I pause, looking through it. Everything's there. "Were you followed?" He shakes his head. "If nothing happened last night, I think you're clear. As long as I get out of town for a while." It's lame, and he knows it. "I'll call you if I'm coming back."

"Better still, don't."

———————

Look for a cab. Should check again I'm not being tailed. I don't: Even if Gus did lead someone to me, I'd be too tired to do anything about it now.

Outside the dome, the drivers gather, singing their old tune—
"Where you go?

"Mister!"   "Mister?"

"Anywhere you like—"

I mutter profanities in Khmer and they step back. A few feet from the scrum there's a battered, white Toyota four-door, with a guy leaning on the hood: thin, rectangular face, long coke nails on his pinkies.

He'll do.

Push through the crowd until I'm standing in front of him. "How much to take me to Koh Kong?"

He quotes a price. It's good, but I come back lower; they get suspicious if you don't. Plus it gives me a minute to suss him out. He speaks Khmer with a heavy, backwoods accent, but doesn't look like a farmer. I'm guessing at some point he was a fighter, and not for the army. Good: outsiders got no one to tell tales to.

When he makes his third offer, I take it, with a nod.

"You need to get anything?" he asks.

Shake my head. "Let's go." Koh Kong is four hours at least, over rough road—but I don't want to hang around.

I should be running. Instead, I'm following June. If I need to lie low, Koh Kong seems as good a place as any.

Might as well die someplace with a view.

For the first half hour or so, I look out the window, chain-smoking to keep my eyes open, watching the sun push higher in the sky. The driver—his name is Phann—is going on about how he started fighting for the KR as a kid, got hooked on yaba and meth:

"—my whole life. For ten years, I can't work, because of the drugs. But I needed them, for the pain. My family died, in the work camps, you know, everybody died there, so they took me and made me a soldier . . ."

Everyone over thirty has stories like these. I'm struggling to stay awake, at least long enough to make sure we're heading in the right direction. We merge onto the southwest highway, and in seconds the dark takes me.

D I A R Y

Sihanoukville.

The guys at the paper hate this place. I came expecting a sewer or an abattoir, or at least some grimy, run-down port city—Cambodian for Long Beach, and hot as hell. But it's the riverside, writ large. Acres and acres of sprawling entertainment: open-air restaurants and beckoning girls and music everywhere, a different tune from every bar and outdoor stage, Thai radio pop and gamelan and the Greatest Hits of the Eagles, over and over again until it's one big song. A market jammed with stalls and counters and carts selling every kind of food imaginable. And (of course) brothels, all along Victory Hill, where the women in the street grind and beckon to cars full of men, and the 60-year-old sex tourists walk hand-in-hand with their 14-year-old conquests with no shame. . . .

You'd think the guys would like it, but perhaps it's too naked for them.

Sihanoukville lives in constant danger of being devoured by the jungle. Trees and vines wrap the houses, flow into the streets and over the hills where creepers climb the bridges and telephone poles, and flowers find purchase on iron gates and billboard scaffolds. Over it all, the heat: damp and stifling, scented with rot like an orchid greenhouse. The afternoon rains just make it hotter. If the jungle doesn't tear this city down, the heat may melt it. Sihanoukville doesn't care. It floats above . . . it lives, breathes, eats, dances, has sex. At night its streets crawl with urgent life, looking for release.

If it stopped moving for an hour Cambodia would swallow it whole. . . .

Our hotel is on the edge, almost in the jungle, a pink cinder-block palace strangled by creepers and bougainvillea. Inside is clean enough, but totally Motel 5. It's achingly hot. Still, I'm glad for time alone to write. I couldn't on the trip down, not with the boy right there, sitting next to me in the back of the car, smirking and making jokes . . . he thinks I asked for this assignment because he's irresistible.

Sure, he's a pain . . . but I don't understand why just the sight of him makes me want to vomit, these days. It's got so bad, I almost tried to get out of this trip. Of course I didn't. Getting to Koh Kong meant coming here first, covering the election with the boy, letting him try to put his hand in mine in the car and smiling as I took it away. . . .

I don't mind. I am on the trail of something extraordinary.

Even at 3 a.m. the night is alive with the buzzing of locusts and mosquitos, the shrieking of bats and complaining of frogs. On and on, calling to each other in the dark. A different music, this, from a different city—hidden city, shadow city—give me a note and I could open my window, tear free the bars and vanish into your chorus. . . .

Soon, there will be no dark places left in the world.

WILL

Wake up soaked in sweat.

Was I followed? Is it safe?

I look around, panicked, head spinning: I feel sick. The sun is high and hot, beating through the car windows. I've been sleeping with my backpack clutched in my arms, and I rip it open with the sudden terror of a junkie checking his stash: June's diaries are still there. Her photos in neat packets, taped shut. Camera, muffler, extra lens, memory cards. Wadded-up clothes, soaked with sweat. Cigarettes: crushed.

I roll the window down. Hot outside—we're not going fast enough for a breeze. A narrow dirt road, hemmed in on both sides by hills covered in thorny shrub and cell-phone aerials. Ugly. From the terrain, I guess we're about halfway to Koh Kong—could be two hours left, or three, depending on the crossings.

I light a crooked smoke and try to think through the buzzing in my head.

I'm well past anything making sense. June and Kara—who are

they, what are they doing here? Number Two and Barry—what are they hiding? And what about Dead Charlie and his dad and Gabriel, and the war still coming—

They churn in my mind like gears in some huge machine, I'm trying to make them fit together—

Could the killers have been after me and got Charlie and the Aussie by mistake? No: I was in the wrong room. Did Gabriel double-cross me? But Gabriel didn't know the details of the plan. Senn? His dad is in customs—he might even know the Sihanoukville customs guys June wrote about, who got arrested after the Sydney heroin bust. Is that where this is going?

—I can't see it, never quite, the gears keep spinning and each time they almost fit they fall apart again, and the engine rumbles on—

Something is wrong with my head.

We jolt to a stop: a line of dust-caked cars runs down to where a little stream cuts across the track. The first is getting chained onto a rust-chewed barge barely big enough to carry it. The barge-men power up a row of little motors, creeping across the water. We could be here days.

"You wan' Coke, something?" Phann asks.

"Sure. And aspirin."

"I think you wan' food."

I nod—can't remember when I last ate. "Anything in a package."

He cuts the engine and stalks off to a dingy lean-to offering candy and snacks and sodas. I catch myself peering out the back window, looking for men with machetes.

Think about something else.

"Something else" always seems to mean June. I root through the bag, find the journal where she talks about going south.

Maybe it's a long shot, following her. I can't tell anymore. June seemed so sure something was going on in Koh Kong—but she visited in early August and came back just fine. She didn't disappear until weeks later. Still, trouble could have followed her back: it was just after that she got the gun. Or maybe she found something in Koh Kong and kept it quiet, then slipped back on the sly, telling everyone she was in Siem Reap? Expected a quick trip, left her luggage behind. Possible.

I haven't read all the journals yet, but some things are starting to come clear. Before her trip the entries are dateless, packed with minutia, full of interposed fragments or scraps of conversation you have to read around to follow the story—but they make sense. Somewhere along the line, that changes.

She goes south first, to Sihanoukville, to cover the elections with Number Two. That's a weird trip. She's not sleeping. Maybe it's the heat, maybe nerves. She wanders the city until late—then stays up writing, filling page after page with scrawled monologues. Something's eating at her. Time and again she returns to the same images: devouring, infection, decay. Something bubbling under the surface, waiting to emerge:

> *In the night, the cut on my leg starts burning again*
> *. . . think I need a doctor?*
> *. . . still not healing, despite my midnight efforts—wear long skirts so no one sees . . .*

> *. . . something like a mouth, wide and white-lipped and ugly. Angry red tentacles . . . climbing up my leg . . . think it's going to start talking soon.*

> *. . . I've got a little bit of this place inside me.*

There's something in my head, something I'm not thinking of—something I've seen, in the journals? Can't remember.

I feel someone watching me, jerk up in sudden panic—

Just Phann, coming back. He gets in and hands me a Coke, a

single-serving Tylenol, and three Tiger Tails. Packets all sealed. I tear into them, suddenly ravenous.

The sense of being watched stays with me. Cars behind us now; the driver of the first one has a shifty look. I turn away, fast. My mind won't settle.

After Sihanoukville, June's diary gets worse. There's a chaos, a frantic energy to her writing. More and more things seem to be blacked out or obscured, entries written on top of each other so they're nearly illegible.

I pull up the stories she did about Koh Kong for the paper.

DESPITE PROMISES, LITTLE DEVELOPMENT IN KOH KONG

By Jun Saito

KOH KONG—Lon Chmmol's tiny boat is one of only two vessels offering "ecological tours" of the magnificent mangrove swamps that surround the town of Koh Kong and the island of the same name. The boat is barely big enough for three people, with a plank for a seat and no life vests—Mr. Lon says there are none available in town.

When he does have passengers, he pilots over the swells at breakneck speeds, and the wake of each passing fishing boat threatens to spill them into the surf. But most of the time, he says, no one is interested in tours. He has no way to advertise his services, and for most of the week he makes a meager living driving a taxi around town.

"I would like to show [tourists] the region, the beauty," he says. "But no one comes."

It goes on over three issues. No jobs, locals barely hanging on, cutting the trees for fuel and taking payoffs from timber smugglers, and dynamiting the water to catch fish. A country eating its own future. Too bad the photos are crap—

It would have been me with her.

I'd have been desperate to get out of town; Gus would have humored me. The thought makes me shiver.

June talked to everybody: the Ministry of Environment, the governor, local shop owners and tour guides. A few quotes from Wendy Koenig, country director for Global Partners Cambodia—the NGO that got broken into. No mention of the guy June described, Luke. If she found out something about them, it's not here.

I go back to the journal.

It's the same: the wind-whipped town, the sea, the sea, the beauty of the sea, the open boat where—

. . . all around the water is the lightest blue imaginable, and in the distance it blends with the blue of the sky until the whole world seems painted on the inside of a globe of glass, and at its center a tiny boat and its three tiny occupants, gazing up . . .

She wanders hidden coves and secret islands in the mangroves, a regular smuggler's tour, to distant floating villages—

. . . fantastic concoctions of piers, sheds and shacks that bob on makeshift pontoons of plastic tubs and barrels, and between them a web of streets nailed together from planks, old boat parts and driftwood, swaying and shifting with the waves . . .

It's like June's words are echoing in my head as I read. Try to focus—

My mind is moving too fast, running away from me, and that great machine still churning with June and Bunny and Senn and Charlie—

. . . they have boats in hidden coves, and ride the waves after nightfall, not doing anything yet but listening to the dark . . .

Sweat streaming into my eyes. I wipe it away. The car is moving now, fast, uphill, and bouncing through potholes, and each jolt sends a current like electricity through my head. June is sitting to eat, her back against a tree—

. . . when I notice I'm surrounded by legions of tiny ants: on the dirt beneath me, on the tree I'm leaning against . . . precise, military columns, around my feet and up over my arms and under my clothes, my face . . .

—crawling over me, how the hell did they get in the car—

. . . not just one of them, they're everywhere, all through the swamps, I couldn't believe it at first, but true, a whole network, just waiting to come alive . . .

. . . soak everything in poison, (tons of it) till it chokes you, but you will never even slow them in their determination to carry it all underground . . .

. . . the whole country is slipping away a bit at a time, sinking . . .

I heave myself to the open window and vomit something tiger-striped onto the dizzying grass.

Shit, I think, *there goes the Tylenol.*

It begins to dawn on me that I have a fever, that I'm hallucinating, but there's nothing I can do except hang on as the car crests the hill and dives into the nuclear green of the valley, through mist and days of rain, and then plunges into the sea, and I'm struggling with the seat belt and look over to Phann for help, except he's not Phann anymore: he's the Aussie, head lolling and chest sliced near in two, and when he opens his mouth, little silver fishes swim out.

"You put me here," he says. From the backseat, dead Charlie reaches around to finger the Aussie's bloody nipple.

I throw myself at the door, scrabbling with the lock as the car fills with water until finally, finally we hit bottom and it shudders open. They've built a life-sized replica of Kabul down here—*See, that's touristic investment*—and I'm swimming through the ruins of streets I once walked. I can hear Charlie and the Aussie gurgling as they come after me. They've got the others with them now: Joost, who got a bullet right under his Kevlar and died there in the street, and Tom cut in half when his jeep took an RPG, and the mujahideen boys fluttering like deadly eels with machetes in their teeth, Bunny paddling along behind them with flipper hands.

Up on the surface, there's a boat—June's boat, she's out for her tour, and I'm supposed to be with her; if I can just reach her, I'll be safe, they won't get me, and I break the surface and grab the rough plank side to pull myself up, but it's not June at all.

It's Fatima, throat cut red and dress black as grave earth, and she grabs me with fingers that slide between my ribs like knives, and—

   I could swear this part is real

   —back in some tiny, dingy room she's leaning over me, whispering in my ear:

"She'll make you wish I'd torn you apart."

DIARY

July 23

IN SIHANOUKVILLE, TENSIONS
HIGH AS VOTE NEARS

By Jun Saito and Sok Narit

Additional reporting by Christopher Grimsby-Roylott

SIHANOUKVILLE—"I do not plan to vote this year," says Leang, as he takes a break from stocking the coolers of his small fish shop in Sihanoukville's central market. "I am afraid of what will happen. If it is like last time, it is us who will suffer." Like many other business owners, Mr. Leang did not want his full name used for fear of reprisals.

With Cambodia's third parliamentary election only days away, the mood in this southern port town is tense, with many voters saying they will stay away from the polls altogether. Opposition party leaders and watchdog groups have accused the ruling Cambodian People's Party of carrying out a vigorous campaign of intimidation with the aim of keeping its leader, Prime Minister Hun Sen, in power. Though most of the incidents they cite have occurred in villages and rural areas, the heavy hand of the CPP is also feared here in downtown Sihanoukville. Several merchants said CPP campaigners have come to their neighborhoods with dark warnings about the consequences of voting for the wrong party.

"They say if the opposition takes seats [in Parliament], it will be dangerous for Cambodia's future," said Sovanny, who runs a small wicker furniture shop. "The message is clear." Others cited veiled threats against their businesses or homes. And a legal case is still pending against five members of the Sam Rainsy Party, who were charged with assault after a violent incident in a Prey Nob suburb. The defendants claim they were investigating charges of vote buying by the ruling party when they were attacked by hired thugs. (See story, p 7.)

But for many, staying away from the polls is less about intimidation than simple fear over what will happen if the opposition is successful.

"Hun Sen does not like to lose," one prominent local businessman said. "We saw what happened last time [in 1998], when an opposition party made gains in the election: he removed them by force. This time, you have two big opposition parties, not one, and they are strong, especially in the cities. They might do well, and if they do, no one knows what will happen."

Everyone is nervous: The elections are a bomb waiting to go off. Back in Phnom Penh I thought it was just the old White Men, the thrill seekers, scheming about what could go wrong, but it's more than that: something almost *has* to go wrong. The whole country smells of gasoline. . . .

And so I am making my preparations. I got a letter from Indonesia, there's a school there that could take me. I have to run, I can't face the darkness that is breaking free down here, it could sweep me away in its jaws as if I never existed. . . .

I am so afraid.

But lying here with the night music drifting in my window, I hear that voice speaking to me out of the dark . . . and I want to *see*. Almost more than I care what happens next. Is this what the boys feel—what the photographer felt, all those years ago?

Has it already got me?

WILL

It feels like years, but finally, the madness begins to pass. Perhaps I sleep. When the hands grab me again, they're just mosquito netting. The sunken city a cheap hotel room. I'm awake—more or less.

It's day.

New pack of cigarettes on the nightstand. Light one and my head clears a bit.

No memory of where I am—nothing since the car. The room tells me little: walls of white tile, pink fluorescents. One window, less than a foot square and well above head height, speckled with dust and dead mosquitoes. A little bath with a clapboard door, smelling of stagnant water. A TV is bolted to the ceiling, like in a hospital. The local news is on, volume low: cops and crime scenes. Looks bloody; must ask someone.

I struggle my way out of the mosquito net, careful not to touch it with the ash: that's a bad end. Check my bag. Everything's there. My ex-junkie driver found God, I guess. I make a note to keep him around if he wants the pay. Count my cash and think wistfully of the envelope of money I left with the Aussie.

There's a knock on the door, and I crack it on the chain: Phann, looking unconcerned, scratching at his ear with those long fingernails. I let him in.

"Thank you," I say, staggering back to the bed.

"No problem." He stands there.

"I've got plenty of work for you here, if you want it," I say, in Khmer.

He nods. "You speak Khmer well."

"How long have I been out?"

"About a day."

"Jesus." I hand him some cash. "That's for the ride, and four days' work. I'll give you more if we stay longer. And this is for supplies. I need a new cell phone. And some antibiotics." He nods. "And some grass, if you can find it."

I half expect him to argue, but he just nods again. Good enough.

"Get the stuff, then see if you can find a guy in town named Lon Chmmol. The Dane should know him. Tell him we want to rent his boat for a tour of the swamps. As soon as possible."

Phann nods again and disappears.

I lie on the bed and smoke. After a while, the hotel guys bring me penicillin and some food. It's simple stuff, rice and fish soup, but when I've finished I'm able to stand without my knees buckling.

I stare at my camera awhile—wondering about Charlie, and what he was doing in my hallucination. I don't want to look, but if there's a clue to what happened, it's here. Finally I switch the thing on. Scroll past the screwing around, the cramped hotel room brown and orange in the low light, bodies pressed together, a haze of movement—

Next photo: two men entering. They're dressed in tank tops and camo pants. No effort at concealment. The first is dark—zoom in on a square face, broad nose, mouth a sullen line. Cheeks spotted and rough with acne, or scars. Can't guess his age, but not old.

Next: they crowd in. The second is a kid—might be sixteen, eighteen. The machetes are coming up.

Next: a blur of motion.

Next: Charlie rising from the bed, his face bisected by a yellow blade. They went for him first.

Next: falling. A smudge on the edge of the frame, maybe the Aussie trying to get away. Then he's down, too.

Next, next, next. Blades slash the air in glowing curves. Orange walls speckled with brown—then splattered, then soaked. The face of the older killer: quiet, calm as he raises his weapon. The younger's is never clear, but the glimpses I get look like joy. Like ecstasy.

Next photo: the bed a splatter of blood, a pile of meat. The figures stooping. They leave in a blur.

Last photo: the door hanging open.

Not much past what I knew already. Machetes suggest a vengeance thing, but these men have clearly done this before. A contract hit, made ugly to send a message. It would help if I could ID them, but there's no one I can show these to. Still, they might be useful at some point. I make a slit in the inner sole of one of my sneakers and cram the memory card inside.

Then I get up. I need a drink. Maybe a dozen.

The Dane has been in Koh Kong forever. Married a girl from here, years ago, and stayed. His guesthouse is the biggest building in town: two floors, wood-frame. Most of the front is a huge balcony, strewn with plants, looking over a mess of palms and flowers with names like fruit drinks. It's a thin town, thin and tough, and the Dane has to pull just about every foreigner who comes through to make ends meet.

But there are compromises. Four of them are sitting on the deck now: fat reptiles in polyester print shirts. They've got a kid with them, a tiny girl in a dirty pink dress, cradling a naked plastic baby doll. She's being passed around the circle, taking turns sitting on each one's lap.

I grab a bottle of vodka from the bar, and go looking for the Dane before I start looking for needles. Find him hiding in the kitchen.

"Germans. They disgust me," he snarls. "But what can I do? Trade is bad enough already." I hold out the vodka, and he takes a long chug. "I saw your fella, Phann. Came around looking for Lon. He's taking a bunch of Koreans to Sihanoukville tomorrow, but I can find you another boat."

"I want Lon."

"Then you have to wait until Sunday to go out."

"I'll keep busy."

"Good, good." He glances at the camera slung over my shoulder—an attempt to look like I'm here for work. "You taking pictures?"

"Yeah. Pretty trees and shit. Could be some money in it."

"There was a girl down here from the paper. A couple months back. Japanese name."

"June." Though I don't mean it to, it comes out heavy, like a prayer or invocation.

"That's right." He settles his arms across his massive chest. "Interesting girl. She did a nice story."

"I never met her." Try to sound casual this time. I'm sure I fail, but he bites.

"Well, she was all right, I think. Not the kind who sees just what people tell her, you know? She was looking for what was really going on in this place, if you see what I mean? The real thing, the story behind the story."

I have no idea what he's talking about, but I nod along, encouraging. "She find anything?"

"She was asking about smuggling. I know it goes on, but I don't know much about these things. You know, for a businessman, it is better not to know. But I told her to get Lon to take her to some of the Cham villages out in the mangroves, Koh Sraluav and those. They are very poor. People out there, they might have stories."

I take another swig of vodka, pass the bottle back to him. "Word is she ran off somewhere," I say, as he drinks. "Disappeared." What can I say—I like to bury the lede.

He gets a funny look and hands the bottle back. "Well, this is Cambodia," he says, like that explains everything.

I stagger back to the hotel; the world isn't spinning yet, but the tilt light is on. Maybe vodka wasn't such a great idea. The Dane drank a good whack of it, at least, while I quizzed him about Luke and Wendy and their NGO. They've been at it almost a year, and for an organization that's essentially a funding broker, they seem pretty hands-on. Luke is out in the swamp all the time with the locals, gathering info: Which areas should the government protect, which should it develop? Where are the openings for private investors? And he's secretive. Not surprising: that stuff can cause resentment. People start thinking the government's going to fence off the forests, take away their work— especially if their work is already not quite legal. The Dane thinks it's all some kind of World Bank plot, but he said most people here are so poor, any kind of development sounds good to them. But someone's always left out—I'd like to find out who.

The hallway by my room is unlit. I lean against the wall to open my door—

Listening to the dark.

Stumble inside, lock tight behind me.

Sitting on my pillow: a secondhand cell phone—no ID necessary— and a plastic bag stuffed with half an ounce of tarry, black grass. Well done, Phann. I think I like him better than Khieu.

I'm looking longingly at the bed, but despite the drink and the pills, I can feel the fever still clinging to me: a restless, hectic energy that won't let me sit still. Start to roll a joint while I call Gus.

He perks right up when he hears it's me.

"I don't know what trouble you're in, but it brought friends." Yesterday's anger all blown away: now there's *news*: "Two bodies in one night, and one of them is another FUNCINPEC official: the third guy from His Highness, gunned down outside his office . . . seems like the old one-eyed dog is getting serious about the competition."

"What's the other one?"

"Oh, that one was personal. You remember that singer, the one supposed to be Hok Lundy's mistress? She got hit with acid in the street. Didn't make it. They figure it was probably the wife, but . . ."

"There's more."

"Eh?"

"The son of a police colonel got hacked to bits in a room in the Crane Hotel, along with an Australian backpacker."

"I didn't hear about that."

"Would have looked like a hate crime, or a personal beef. Given that he was found with his boyfriend's cock in his mouth, boyfriend not attached, I'm guessing Daddy kept it quiet."

"You didn't see that on the news," Gus says carefully.

"I got a little too close."

"How close?"

"About five inches."

"*Hijo de puta.*"

"That's two dead people who were close to high-ranking cops. Start looking, I bet you'll find more."

"Right." He pauses, and I can almost see him rolling his fingers into fists as he thinks. Old fighter's habit. I know what he's thinking: men in uniform with brown packages on their shoulders. "I assume General Peng didn't like the look of his cell."

"He still in lockup?"

"No, he's out. What about the FUNCINPEC guy?"

"Could be separate. Peng kills Van and the singer, Hun Sen takes out Bunny and your official, for different reasons. What's he saying?"

"Hun Sen? He's claiming the murders are part of a conspiracy to discredit him."

"That's not so far from what you said the other day. Maybe it's all Peng: taking on the cops and trying to pressure the PM at the same time."

Gus whistles. "Then this is going to be a coup: it's too big for a turf war. Hun Sen won't like being pressed. Someone else doing that much killing in his city makes him look weak. He'll have to prove he's still in charge. One way or another, there'll be a show of force. Tanks in the fucking streets."

I can smell it, coming over the wire: the smell of bloody murder, of demonstrations, the crack of police batons—and just over the horizon the riots, the city in flames. I should be there, in the smoke, shutter clicking, waiting for the crash or the flash or the pain before it goes dark—

Try to control my breathing, to fight the excitement creeping up my spine—

From the shadows, the dead Aussie smiles at me. *"Give it a go, eh, mate? Wat'cha got to lose?"*

I see the rest, crowding in behind him. Feel sick. Shut my eyes, light the joint, inhale. When I open them, the corner is empty and so am I. The thrill is gone.

"You still there?" Gus says, distant.

I don't have an answer.

———————

"Wheels within wheels," that's what Gus would say. He's right about one thing: this is too big for just a turf war. Maybe Peng really thinks he can move himself into the big chair—but it's hard to picture. I keep seeing him in the back of that police car, eye swollen shut, leaking blood. Seems more like he's desperate to me. But why? Could Hok Lundy have him in that tight a corner? It doesn't feel like Cambodian politics as usual: people die, sure, but that's just PR. In the end, these things get worked out. A guy like Peng doesn't go all in.

Unless there's someone we haven't seen yet: an outside player, pushing at this thing, stirring up trouble. But what for?

Sometimes simple answers are best.

Simple like Charlie?

He had a target on his back all along. Gabriel wanted him photographed because of his dad's position in the police: it was clear from the start that it was tied up somehow with the heroin trade, the big bust at Peng's house. Gabriel thought Charlie's dad could tell him something, maybe do something for him if properly motivated, and Charlie was a weak spot. But if Gabriel could see a vulnerability, others could, too. So when Peng decides to strike back at the cops, who does he go after? Not the bosses, yet: the weak links. Hok Lundy's mistress. A police colonel's gay son. The guys who did it could be military, easy. They'd have been watching for hours, maybe days. When Charlie ditched his guards and his thug friends and went to that crappy hotel with a boy, he was a perfect target.

And I put him there.

From the shadows, he grins.

"Better lucky than smart," says a voice behind me.

Bunny.

"You'd know, asshole," I say.

Stagger to my feet. The Aussie is leaning against the door, dripping blood on my backpack. Shove past him, out into the dark hall, and slam the door on the whole fucking lot of them.

———————

The night clerk has off-brand vodka in little miniatures. It's rotten stuff, from some Muslim Central Asian country with no business making it. Tastes enough like lighter fluid that I'm scared to smoke while I'm drinking, but it does the trick. I take them back to the room and empty one after another, pausing for joints. When the dead show up, I pitch bottles at them. Get Charlie square in the eye, and he actually winces before disappearing in a fit of pique, which is fucking hi-larious.

Open the next and toast his health. Poor, lonely, dead Charlie. Sure, he was the kind of guy who'd fire automatic weapons into crowds for fun, but he didn't get much choice in the matter. He never went looking for this shit; his family was playing blood poker long before he was born. Of any of us, he has the best excuse.

"You're not one of us," Joost mutters in my ear. *"Not yet."* He always was a dour fucker, even before I got him killed. The Aussie cackles and steals the spliff out of my hand.

I shouldn't even be here. I should be in some suburb of Hoboken with a car and a brat and a family photo studio; an idea for a coffee-table book I'll never finish. But I screwed that up. Wanted to see the world—went too far. You scratch the surface, and faster than you'd think, you're out here in the swamps with Charlie and his friends.

You cross that line, it always ends in death. I learned that long ago.

So why am I doing it again?

D I A R Y

July 25

Sihanoukville.

Shit.

I still can't sleep. Can't hardly think.

At first I thought it was the heat, settling over me like a blanket, heavy and wet, so I made the hotel boys bring me a fan . . . but it doesn't help: when it hums I can't hear the music.

I can't sleep, so I write. Even after these endless days, I never seem to stop: the lights go out and my head is crowded with the past, old memories pushing their way in with the voices of bats and frogs and night-born insects. In lieu of exorcism, I have this diary.

I have told you most of what I remember of my mother, but there is still the final thing, the most important. The night she left. I was standing outside in the rain, watching through a window. I remember I had gone out there because I heard voices, but when I recall the scene, now, I hear nothing. All I see is my mother's face: she is screaming at my father, cheeks red and eyes swollen with tears. I cannot see him: I remember his presence, the feel of him in the air, the smell of his breath—but I do not have any memory in which I can recall his face until after she was gone.

Only years later did I begin to understand the story, to piece together the clues: phone conversations I wasn't meant to overhear, whispered talk among the men. The little hints I could squeeze out of my sister, each one earned by days of painstaking interrogation: laying barbs, setting snares, waiting for her guard to slip just enough that one might catch on her and drag some truth out with it.

They say Mother married Father for his money. She, herself, never spoke of it, except obliquely.

"You don't get to know where a path leads before you take it," she told me. Perhaps it was in that little room, I can't remember now. "Sometimes the path will seem terrible, but when you walk it, it is no different than any other."

I don't know what Father was in it for. Once, listening through the door to the men who watched outside my room at night, I heard one say Father was under a spell, that Mother was a white witch. The other said she was just a whore, and it made an aging man feel good to have a beautiful, young blonde on his arm.

I had different guards after that. I never heard those two again.

The general wisdom was that Father was desperate for an heir, and if there is any story I believe, it would be that. Father, after all, valued strength, fearlessness and cunning, and the foul names they call my mother suggest she was all these things. She was the kind of woman he would choose to give him the son he craved . . . but the son never came, and in those years of waiting, whatever my parents had began to rot away. There was talk of a miscarriage, maybe several. I know everyone was excited when my mother finally got pregnant: twins, a boy and a girl. Everything was going to be OK.

I don't know what happened to my brother. There was just me: scrawny, white and hideous. For years I did my best with what I had, but it was never enough.

WILL

Saturday afternoon I grab Phann from the hotel, and we go looking for Luke's office.

The town feels flat and empty, a studio set after hours. No one in sight. Overcast sky, two roads lined with gray shacks. Swirling dust; it hasn't rained here in a while. Flashes of color where laundry flutters in the breeze, no one tending it.

We hike around for forty minutes, Phann asking directions. My body is stiff and shattered, my head hollowed out from another night fighting something I can't remember. I should really try not to drink today.

Everything has hurt so long I hardly notice anymore.

Eventually we find Cambodia EcoCare, Luke's local partner. It's nothing, just a room on the second floor of an apartment building, but a Khmer woman answers when we knock. Western-dressed, a bit overdone—probably from Phnom Penh. Surprised to have visitors.

The reception room: a desk piled with binders and dusty stacks of paper; a single poster on the whitewashed walls, hideous memento of some long-forgotten environmental campaign. Through a second door there's a glimpse of some equally abandoned-looking cubicles. We seem to be alone.

You can never tell with these outfits: an unused office could mean they're not doing quite what they say they are—or just that they save their energy for the field, where it counts.

Phann says we're out here to shoot the area's environmental glories. I try to look blank, which isn't hard. I barely speak English right now, much less Khmer. He says we want to talk to Luke, and the woman says he's out of town today—probably in Phnom Penh, not that she'd know, he's very busy. Yes, he'll be back soon, but he spends most of his time on-site in the mangroves. No, she doesn't know when he'll get in.

"How's the assessment going?" I ask, perching myself on the windowsill and reaching for a cigarette. Phann translates.

"You'll have to talk to Luke about that." She glares at me until I put the cigarette back in my pocket.

Phann solemnly explains that I'm on a special assignment for the *New York Times,* and her eyes get a bit big. Impressed—or worried? I can't tell. One more point for my new hustler. The woman still isn't sure Luke will ever be free, but our royal status means we can get his mobile number. She keeps glaring until the door shuts behind us. I say nothing to Phann on the stairs, but as we cross the empty street outside, I stop to light my cigarette, glance up. Are the blinds above us twitching? Or is it just me, with the jitters? If something is going on down here, I wonder how much these folks know about it.

Hard to imagine anything happening in this town.

I try calling Luke's mobile a couple times, get a "switched off" message.

We don't have a boat until tomorrow—not sure I could handle the trip yet, anyway, not if it's as rough as June described.

I leave Phann to his own devices and walk down the main street, toward the beach. Just a brownish strip of sand with a rickety excuse for a pier. Deserted. The Gulf is choppy, waves dark and metallic. A shudder runs through me.

I could go back. If I'm right about Charlie, and I just put him in a convenient place to get killed, then no one is after me. I could give Gabriel his pictures—maybe suss out how he got his info.

Am I just trying to avoid tomorrow: getting in a boat, crossing this black water?

But something about the horizon tugs at me. This place makes no sense. I want to know what June was looking for down here. Maybe Steve can tell me something, if he ever—

Hell.

I haven't told him how to find me since I ditched my phone. Meant to call last night, but—

Don't think about it.

I send him a text and consider heading back to the Dane's for a cup of coffee, but as soon as I've stood up, the phone rings.

"Where the fuck have you been, Keller?"

"Better you don't know."

From his voice, I know it's bad. I hope he's not about to ask after a dead Australian backpacker. That could get awkward.

"I got a name for your girl." I wait for it: watch the waves as they beat against the pier, wonder what he knows. "You're gonna have to get straight with me, Will. People are about to get very interested in this."

"Who've you told?"

"I asked around, like you wanted. Turned out that got a lot more attention than I expected. You want the rest, you tell me what you know."

"I told you, I don't know anything." Struggling to remember three days ago's lies. "The girl's story started unraveling, she's out of town, we—"

"Stop pissing about, mate. This girl isn't vacationing at Angkor Wat, an' you know it. So where is she?"

I have to give him something; too tired to work the angles. "I don't know. She said she was going to Angkor, that's the truth, but it was nearly three weeks ago now. She never came back. Just vanished—"

"Christ," he mutters. Then, in a different voice: "You should have let her."

I wait for him to tell me something new. Clouds churn overhead.

Eventually, he sighs. "So, she vanished . . . you didn't think to tell the police, the family, the embassy?"

I'm thinking fast. "Police out here? Are you kidding?"

"And where are you now? Siem Reap?"

"Yeah." As good a lie as any. "I needed to get away from Phnom Penh awhile."

"Why's that?"

"I don't know if you noticed, it's got a bit dangerous."

"Last I checked, you weren't FUNCINPEC."

I stare out at the water, doors opening in my head that I'd rather keep shut.

"I was friends with Heng Bunly. The Radio Ranariddh guy. I didn't think anyone was coming after me or anything, I just needed out."

Steve's quiet a second. "Sorry for your loss," he says—close enough to serious that you could believe it, if you wanted to. He's still suspicious, but I'm hoping he's not going to push it.

My head is spinning; sit down on the pier. "Who is she, Steve?"

"She really is called June, but her name's not Saito. It's Koroshi. The other one you described sounds like her older sister, Karasu Koroshi."

Oh, fuck me. "*That* Koroshi?"

"His only children."

I expected bad, but nothing like this.

Ryu Koroshi: don of dons to the American spin-off of the yakuza.

He must be in his seventies now and has never been indicted, never even charged—but if half the stories about him were true, he'd be the devil. I'm guessing they're not, though: no one knows anything about a guy like that. It's safer not to.

Now I know way too much.

"The girls got records?"

"Karasu's a clotheshorse, hangs out with celebrities but steers clear of coke. Nothing on her except Versace and a few parking tickets. June had some trouble, but since she was a juvenile, it's hard to say. I think the Feds tried to use it to leverage the dad, but they got nowhere."

"She's not a juvenile now. Where's she been the last five years?"

"Funny you should ask. See, my FBI buddy recognized her description right off and said someone was fucking about with me. Got real excited when I told him I'd seen June myself. Seeing as she's been dead for five years."

Huh. "She never said anything about being dead."

"The things people forget to mention, eh?"

"So how'd it happen?"

"LA classic, mate. Driving drunk in the hills at four a.m. Took 'em almost a week to find her. By then, the critters had been at her pretty good."

"Still, there'd be DNA—"

"DNA needs a comparison. I don't know the details, but I'd be fairly surprised if a member of the Koroshi family stepped forward to give a sample. Most likely they ID'd the body and that was that. Or maybe your Feds cooked the whole thing up: give the girl a new life if she'll inform. My mate wasn't close enough to know that stuff."

I can't think anymore—this whole thing is too far out of control. I need a drink. The only saving grace is that Steve doesn't know Kara is here.

I can only guess at the kind of hell to pay if she finds out the FBI knows about her sister. "I suppose it's way too late to keep this quiet."

"No chance. Out of my jurisdiction, and my pay grade."

"How long do I have?"

"Dunno. If the Feds extracted her, then lost her, they could be on their way up your ass already. If they really thought she was dead, there's no telling how long it'll take that ball to start rolling. Weeks, maybe longer?"

"Any way you can buy me some time?"

"Sorry." He doesn't sound sorry at all. Eventually: "You know you're not going to find her, right? If something happened, it happened a long time ago. And if she doesn't want to be found—"

"I know all that," I snap.

"Just don't get your hopes up, mate."

"I haven't got any hopes." I hang up.

The waves hit the shore and draw back. A shadow moves out on the water, and for a moment I think I see a shape—like a boat, with a figure in it, waving to me. Then it's gone.

———

The back balcony at the Dane's. Bottle of vodka—two-thirds left—and June, spread out on the table in front of me.

June Koroshi. I turn the name over in my mouth, seeing how it tastes.

Sharp, like a penny.

What would Ryu Koroshi's daughter want in Cambodia? I bet it's not a Pulitzer. More important: What did she want in Koh Kong? June Saito could have been down here chasing some teenage fantasy of being a reporter; June Koroshi had a reason.

I look again at the journals, the news articles, the photographs: Are they all a blind? Some carefully constructed code, meant to hide June's real mission?

I can't believe it.

It's not that no one could be that meticulous, that painstaking—no. I can't believe it because I saw something in those journals. For a moment, I thought I knew her.

I go back through the pages I've flagged. Words take on new meanings: June's idealism rings strange and frantic; her family dramas loom large. The way she talks about her mother leaving—I should have asked Steve what happened.

It must take a special kind of guts to walk away from Ryu Koroshi.

June writes about running away, about feeling haunted, and somehow I still believe it. Sounds like she had plenty to run from. Maybe she really wanted to be someone different.

DIARY

July 27

ELECTION FIGHT NOT
OVER, EXPERTS WARN

By Augustín Franco

PHNOM PENH—As the country celebrates what is being called Cambodia's smoothest election ever, some poll-watchers are warning that a new conflict could be just around the corner.

"The Cambodian People's Party still does not have the votes to form a government," said Thomas Stockmann, head of the independent political research consultancy Poll-Watch Cambodia. "It's simple math: one of the opposition parties will have to form a coalition with the CPP, or Cambodia will be left without a government." After months of campaigning for major political reforms, Stockmann said, it was unrealistic to expect either opposition group to join a coalition without demanding substantial concessions from the former ruling party.

Other analysts agreed that the election results could set the stage for a more severe political crisis.

"Both opposition parties still believe the election was unfair, based on the campaign of intimidation that preceded it," said Mu Keo, head of the Cambodian Center for Political Rights. "They believe they have popular support, so they will ask more than the CPP is willing to give." The negotiations could leave the country leaderless for weeks, she added. "The longer this situation lasts, the more dangerous the political environment will become. . . ."

The polls closed, and I'm keyed up, restless. I've been waiting, holding my breath, but nothing happened and now I'm gasping, starved for air, dragging myself through Cambo streets at night, looking for my fix. (Ha.)

Clever won't help me now.

There's Koh Kong, but that's a day or an eternity away, and I want it now . . . so I've come here. Victory Hill. The streets were nearly deserted when I arrived: prowled by a handful of foreign men, aloof and nervous, never looking straight at what they'd come to buy. The women lounged in doorways trying to be seductive, but I could tell they were edgy too. They all noticed me. The men peeked at me sideways, the girls stared and didn't try to hide it. They could see I was *half,* and it made them curious: Why was I here? Spy or client or competition? I was asking myself the same question. The first place that didn't look completely over-the-top, I crept inside.

It's just a bar: seedy, crumbling, smelling of jasmine air freshener, and the girls all in the back, waiting; sparkling on their stools, waiting; screaming with laughter louder than boys and throwing ice cubes at each other . . . waiting. They're different, in here—not the tired statues that stalk the streets. And again, just like that night in the

Heart, some shameful part of me is jealous: they may be faking, but it's a fakery more real than I have ever been.

For years, I have waited. Even with my looks, I had offers, but not the ones I wanted. I could always see the pity in their eyes or the predator behind their smile, and I was never willing to pretend. I told myself I was waiting for something right and true . . . but I never found it. I made up reasons. I told myself that bodies meant little to me, but that wasn't true, either.

I was always afraid.

Afraid of the terrible darkness that might be down that road; afraid of what I might find out. Here, where all flesh is used and dying, clawing its way back toward the earth, I see no further reason for fear.

I am not who I thought I was at all.

WILL

OCTOBER 12

Up before dawn. In the dark, the hotel room looks like the cold storage in a morgue and smells about the same. I dress fast, roll a joint without turning on the lights. Make it strong: take the edge off what comes next.

Phann is waiting for me in the lobby, and we walk to the marina in silence. Lon is already there, unhitching a rowboat with a little motor on the back. June was right: it's a toy for paddling in the duck pond. I feel dizzy just looking at it. At least I know she's wasn't going Jayson Blair on the details.

Phann goes through his spiel: we saw June's stories in the paper, we want to visit some of the same places she did, take pictures. Promote some tourism, that's us. Lon smiles and nods. He's another one—nearly as skinny as Phann, though it looks to be from hunger rather than years of speed. Square face, phony enthusiasm. He's making his own little speech about how bad tourism is here, and I recognize a few lines June quoted in her story. Like all hustlers, he's got his part down pat.

He sees me tuning out and waves to the boat. "Come, I show. Come, come."

I put one foot in, and the boat bobs and shifts. My stomach does a backflip. Lon smiles and I crouch, gingerly, holding the seat for balance. He and Phann step on like it's nothing.

I've never liked crossing water.

In the predawn quiet, the motor sounds like distant gunfire. The sky is the color of a bruise, the sea gray and greasy. I touch the water with my hand, expecting a chill, but it's blood warm.

Even in the shallows the Gulf is choppy. Once we're out, Lon guns the engine and we're flying, clanging and jolting over the low swells. I breathe deep, trying to keep my heart somewhere around my chest.

Phann doesn't look much happier than I do. He tries to light a smoke, but the wind tears his flame away. I'm clinging to the side and wondering how long this is going to take.

It's not light yet, but it's coming. Behind us the town is retreating fast, already just a shadow. In the opposite direction: nothing. No sign of a destination, just gray sea blending into gray sky like a Sugimoto picture. It looks smooth and still out there—riding over it is anything but, and my knuckles are broken-china white on the boat's edge.

"Mr. Lon says there are no life vests in town."

I can't swim, either.

Too soon, the land is gone in the haze: we are very small and very alone. I picture the little craft pitching over, dropping us out into the warm, gray nothing. We'll disappear—like we were never here at all.

I think of June's photographs. Some might have been taken in this very spot, but how could you tell?

I could tell.

Thinking about something other than the water helps get my breathing under control.

I still can't see the sun, but the sky has gone a shade of gray that suggests it's there at last, behind the clouds. Take out my camera, set the

ISO. June used a low-light film, to get that grain in daytime. Black-and-white mode, autofocus off. What do you do to photograph nothing?

I point at the sky, at my shoe. At random. Snap snap.

On the screen they're just blurs, occasionally flecked with light or dark.

———————

By the time we reach the island the sky's gone cloudy blue, the water turquoise, the trees bitter green. I feel better. Photogs love black and white, but the world is more comfortable in color.

Lon brings the boat to a crawl as we enter the mangroves, and I start to remember why I'm out here. The swamps are a maze. Trees spread their roots underwater and emerge in tangles of trunk and leaf. Between them, the surface is dotted with projecting stumps—the rest hidden below, ready to catch on hulls and motors. Someone who knew these channels could hide just about anything in here.

I remember I'm supposed to be taking pictures. Look for anything that might anchor a shot: a quiet pool, a hidden cove. A few snaps, fiddling with the settings, trying to catch how the light slips between the leaves. I look for the fish and birds June described, but all I see are trees and more trees, their branches hanging down like curtains.

Now it's full light, I try Luke's mobile again: same message.

"The first village is close now," Lon says to Phann, who dutifully translates for me. He's good at this game. I guess you don't survive as a KR soldier without learning to lie.

We round a bend and see a sagging wooden pier projecting out into the water. Behind it the trees grow thick and tall, making a dark tunnel into the woods. I change my aperture and get the pier in frame. Not too close: the foreground is green and lush, framing the path like a stage set. There's something. In an hour it'll be too bright, but the sun's still low enough to pull it off. I take some more shots as we pull up. Climb out of the boat, onto damp boards. Walk to the end and turn around for the reverse, using the pier now to frame the marshes: the road to wonderland. Not bad. I should come out here earlier, for dawn—

Except I'm not really looking for art.

I edge back, back, widening the view, gesturing to the others to stay behind me. A white bird that looks like a heron flies down, and I catch it standing in the water. It's looking for prey, peering into the shallows with black eyes. Seeing nothing, it flies off. I stay still, watching the swamp move through the lens. I'm hanging on to the light, waiting for something: for the right play of sun or gust of wind. My knees start to ache. The moment passes, and I stand up.

"Let's go," I say.

———————

The village is good for a shooter, got to give it that. Tidy little Cambodian peasant houses on stilts—snap, snap. Women sweeping the dirt in wide, smooth circles, drying fish on racks of thin branches. Teenage girls in T-shirts with *kromahs* wrapped around their hips like skirts, bare feet the color of chocolate pressing gently into coffee soil. Snap.

Most of the men are gone—fishing, maybe—but Lon chats up a couple of women, and shortly we're confronted by a middle-aged fellow with a scratty mustache and hair pomaded like Travolta. Also wearing a *kromah*-skirt, but with a white button-down shirt and a suit jacket. He waves us up to one of the houses and crouches on the porch to talk. Phann gives his speech again, with Lon chiming in on the choruses. Pair of ravens, the two of them.

I play my part: ask about tourism. What is there to see? Where can people go? The headman knows how to complain. The people are poor, the fish catches are shrinking. They need help from the government; the government should be taking care of them.

I ask about the NGO. "Very good, very good," he keeps saying, in English, then lapsing into Khmer for another funding request. Luke and his crew have made this guy feel important. *He* understands the need to save the wetlands—but people are poor, you see, and it's hard for them to think about the future when they worry about putting rice on the table. He looks at me, like, *What would you do?*

I ask about the poor: How do they get by? He says fishing and charcoal burning, like those are a living. I ask if he thinks any of them are involved in smuggling. No, no, there's nothing like that here. He knows everything that goes on in his village.

I nod. "Of course."

"You shouldn't ask about these things."

"I'm sorry. I didn't mean to offend."

He nods. But his eyes aren't the eyes of a man who's insulted. They're the eyes of a man who's afraid.

———————

I call Luke's mobile again; this time it rings.

"Hello?" Clear, American voice. I say some of who I am, and some of what I want. I tell him I'd like to look around the areas he's assessing.

"It's a difficult time," he says.

"I won't be trouble. I just, y'know, figured you could show me the best spots to take pictures, the stuff people would come to see."

"If you want to know about our recommendations, you should really talk to the main office."

"They sent me to you. Look, I'm out here now, in Chroy Chambun. Really, I'm just shooting around, I'd love a little advice."

He hesitates, then comes back sounding friendly again. "All right. Come to Koh Sraluav this afternoon. You got a guide, yeah? From town? He should know where it is. Ask around, the guys will know where to find me."

"Thanks."

The line goes dead.

———————

I was hoping to poke around on my own, but no such luck. The head-man insists on guiding us, and we spend an hour hiking from one sacred spring and secret lagoon to another. Snap snap snap: Playing at shooting keeps me from dying of boredom.

I'm not going to ask about smuggling again. I don't know what to ask, so I keep snapping and lathering on bug repellent. I've had den-gue three times already; they say it gets worse every time. If that's true, the next one kills me.

Finally I say we have to move on; our guide looks relieved.

I consider heading straight to Koh Sraluav, just in case Luke decides to vanish before afternoon. But if he really wanted to avoid me, it would be easy just to send me on a wild-goose chase. If I have to, I'll stake out his office.

It's another nervous, jolting boat ride to the floating fishing town June wrote about. Its plank streets creak and shift as I step out of the boat. Below, the water is dark and ominous. Village kids run back and forth, shrieking and spraying each other with water pistols. No shade except a few lean-tos—don't think I could even fit under them. Tiny women sit there, actually mending fucking fishing nets. Who knew?

Keep the questions basic: What makes life hard for you? How are the catches? It draws less attention, but I'm learning nothing.

I wander around for a bit, and the children follow me. The older girls are giggling—I guess I'm a sight. My shirt is soaked with sweat, and some grandmother offers to douse me with water. I turn her down: Who knows where that comes from? Some of them ooh and aah over my white skin. One hangs back, and I hear her talking to her friend: "He looks like he's made of bones."

It's getting time to head out, but I ask to use a bathroom first. They offer me the one in the headman's house, which is a whole new mind fuck: a big room that looks like a beachfront bar, complete with neon beer signs and a pool table. I puzzle over that—how the hell did they get it out here?—then go into the toilet. A cupboard of clean planks painted sky blue, with a hole looking straight down into the water. I congratulate myself for not letting them get me wet.

When I step out, she's standing by the pool table: the one who said I looked like bones. She's a teenager, very brown, with the perfect skin and huge eyes those poverty photogs love. The light from the door is hitting her face and I raise my camera. She steps back into the shadows, looking down, and I lower it.

"Where from?" she says, in English.

"America."

"You know girl, American?"

I just stand there. For a moment I wonder if she's propositioning me, hoping for a quick buck before I head out. Then I look at her downcast face and realize what she means.

"Yes," I say, in Khmer. She looks up, surprised. "I think she's in trouble."

The girl nods. "She asked questions," she says, in her own language. "Bad questions."

"About what?"

"About the people in the boats. You be careful."

"What people in boats?"

"The other Americans. The ones who come at night."

The room sways under me. Outside, something bangs shut. The girl casts a frightened glance over her shoulder—then she's gone.

———————

Koh Sraluav is up the coast from the main town, best accessed by boat. June called it the filthiest place she'd ever seen, and I guess she'd seen a few. The main street is lined with heaps of rotting garbage and smells like a slaughterhouse. The people are all ribs and eyeballs; they stare at us like we might be good to eat. Even Phann and Lon look put off. The Chams who live here are pretty much despised by other Cambodians, and I suppose this is both effect and cause.

Phann hasn't asked any questions, the whole place is too dire. But there's no need: word has spread, and two men are sauntering up the road to meet us. One is a wizened, chain-smoking headman out of a Steve McCurry book; the other must be Luke. He smiles and waves, and a shiver runs through me.

He's Asian American, Chinese maybe, but tall, five-ten or eleven. Late twenties, early thirties, and handsome in a well-used sort of way, dressed in cargo pants and ventilated walking shoes and a loose white linen shirt.

He's all wrong.

If he'd been out here ten years, I might believe the hard, creased face; the empty, faintly yellowing eyes. But he's too young, and just arrived. This is not a guy who went to Yale or SOAS, who grew up in temperature-controlled rooms drinking eight glasses of water a day and learning to share his toys. This guy is from that other world. Even in the midday heat he has his sleeves rolled down—covering tattoos or track marks, or both? When he smiles at me and sticks out one carefully manicured hand, I can see where a couple of his teeth are a shade whiter than the others: fake, and recent.

"Luke Ho, project manager." Half-friendly, but he's daring me to contradict him. Prison, then.

"Will Keller. Thanks for seeing me on short notice."

"No problem, man. You know, we just have a lot of work to do here."

"With the assessment, yeah. How's that coming?"

That smile again: *Do not fuck with me.* "Yeah, man, so like I said, I can't talk about any of the details of that stuff. You understand. It's touchy, y'know—the wrong thing gets out, people get real upset. I'm sure you've heard." He's watching to see if I react. What have I heard? I just nod along. "So, anyway, if you want to know anything about the specific sites, the report, I gotta defer you to head office. I'm sorry, it's just policy, y'know? But I'm happy to have my man here show you around—"

He claps the headman on the back, and the fellow staggers like he might go down. After a moment he recovers and turns bloodshot eyes on me, chewing air with toothless gums. I'm not sure he could show me to the nearest hut.

"It's a beautiful place," Luke says. Again, it sounds like a threat.

"He reminds me of the men who used to hang around Father's businesses. . . ."

You knew right away, didn't you, June? You saw Luke Ho at his office, and you clocked him for a dealer and a thug. But you played it cool, writing about his sexy smile and his Frodo hair, and made it your business to figure out what he was up to. . . .

"No worries, man," I say, slipping into a reflection of Luke's too-friendly tone. "I'm not here to get in your way. I just saw those stories in the paper, thought, 'Hey, this is a place people are gonna be into.' Wanna get to know it, get the edge on the competition, y'know?"

"Too true, man, too true. It's great out here, more people should see it." We're grinning at each other so hard my cheeks ache. "Come up to the house, I'll tell you what you're gonna be looking at."

As he turns away, I make a tiny gesture to Phann, a finger across the lips. He nods.

No, we're not going to ask this guy any questions. Not today. We're going to shut our mouths, take our pictures, avoid anything he tells us to avoid, and go back to our hotel. That's the smart move, and from here on in I'm going to need to be smart.

———————

In the boat, heading back down the coast. Can't stop my hands from shaking.

I've got a head full of crazy, wild elation, like I've dodged a bullet or jumped from a crashing car. Now they've seen me, they know my name: Now there's nowhere safe.

The sky is still bright, but getting overcast again. We're flanking the island, heading home. Sea blue, streaked with purple.

The great machine that haunted my fever dreams is starting to come together, gears clicking into place—

"*. . . they have boats in hidden coves and ride the waves after night-fall . . .*"

I have a guess what's going on here—but it doesn't tell me what happened to June. I don't know what comes next.

Up ahead, a spit of land juts out, silhouetted in the late-afternoon glare. It's somehow familiar. I pick up the camera, track the frame over the horizon. Soften the focus and I see it: *a flat, gray body of water, dark specks that might be trees visible in the distance.* Just like I've seen it before, in fuzzy black-and-white.

"Pull up to the shore," I say to Phann. He stares at me, then translates.

The boat nudges into the shallows, between thick stands of mangroves. Up ahead a patch of dark, silty earth rises toward the forest. Lon pushes up to it and waits.

I lean over and test the water: not deep. Start taking my boots off. Phann mimics me, but I shake my head. "I'll just be a minute."

The water is hot around my legs, the bottom sand and muck. Is this the place? I can't tell, but there's something—in my nostrils like lightning after rain. The earth tingles against my feet. For a second I think of land mines and my legs seize.

Come on, Will. No one would lay mines in a swamp. Come on . . .

left, right. That's it. The ground gets firm, and the sense of electricity in the air grows stronger. My fingers are tingling. Tiny insects whirl around me in stinging clouds. Up ahead, the trees close in. I look for a path: a shallow mud cliff, just a couple feet high, where the roots provide handholds. Pull myself up and stand a moment, letting my eyes adjust to the gloom.

A white spot in the dark: a cut branch. And another. A path has been cleared.

That electric feeling is almost overwhelming as I walk ahead. *It's here,* I think, *it's close,* and my eyes fall on a tree that grows in a low arch over the forest floor. Beneath, the ground is covered with fallen leaves and bark, but no plants: turned.

I get on my knees, brushing at the dirt with my fingers. It comes away loose, and then I'm digging, pulling up the soil in great handfuls. I don't have to go far: only a couple inches down, they start to come clear.

Bones, brown and muddy looking in the black earth. They're so small. Smaller than a whole person anyway. You think you'd be able to look at a skeleton and see that it's a man or a woman, but of course you can't, it's just bones.

I wonder if I just found her.

———————

Back at the boat. I wash the last of the dirt from my fingers and climb aboard. Lon hands me an old shirt to clean my feet, and I wave to him: *Down the coast, go.* He starts the engine.

"What was it, boss?" Phann asks.

"I had to take a piss."

He raises his eyebrows, but doesn't say anything.

———————

Alone at last, in the hotel. I call Vy. She doesn't answer. I call again. And again.

Eventually she picks up. "What exactly do you want?" Enunciating every word. She sounds French, so she's pissed.

"I'm out west, and I need your help."

"Forget it, Will, I'm not playing any of your games—"

"Vy, there's a girl missing. A twenty-three-year-old reporter. And I need that friend of yours: the one who does bones."

For a moment she's got nothing to say.

———————

There was more yelling—always is, with Vy—but she said she'd come. She sees an angle; trouble is, I don't know what. Can't think about it now, anyway. The afternoon buzz is wearing off, and I can feel the exhaustion creeping in.

I have to fortify my room. Bottles of vodka. Bed against the door. TV on, loud, so I won't hear their voices.

It's not the living I'm worried about: it's the dead. They'll all be coming for me tonight.

If I'm lucky, June won't be with them.

D I A R Y

... can soak their determination ANNOUNCEMENT: the 25-year plan to save Cambodia from EVERYTHING while somewhere and

she's back she's back she's back she's come for me
the chorus to carry it all underground and in the air-conditioned boardroom the man from the ministry points to his slides goes silent,

the night is everything in poison till it chokes you, but you will never even slow them in lost because we are out of balance . . .

run, run, it won't do you any good
while skinny men in shorts lean over sides of their narrow boats to drag them in

. . . Earth feels what they are doing and moves, mud gathers where there are no trees and slides down slowly into outside maybe just over

choking the fish that feed the people and the bombing into the muck on the edge of the water, tearing up the tree roots the sea

The whole country is slipping away a bit at a time brings the last of their corpses to the surface in great waves of bone and meat, but fewer every year . . .

. . . can I hear you calling when there is no darkness left?

W I L L

OCTOBER 14

Sun burning my eyelids.

Something stings my face.

"Jesus, Will. What have you been doing?"

The voice gets my eyes open: Vy.

She's the kind of tall, classic blonde you see in cigarette ads from the early sixties. I always forget how stunning she is. Now she's standing over me, all in white, practically glowing in the morning sun. The look on her face is the same one guys on a ten stretch in Rikers get from their wives. Phann hovers behind her, solemnly smoking.

Look around: the room is a wasteland of shattered glass, torn paper, decaying trays of hotel food, roaches and cigarette butts. The bed frame is upturned against the door: they've had to push it aside to get in. I'm in the corner, in some kind of nest made of the mattress and the bedclothes. I'm smeared with blood from my cut-up hands and feet, and I appear to be naked.

"Thought you couldn't make it until Tuesday."

Vy lifts an eyebrow. Guess that means it's Tuesday. "Get dressed." She stalks out.

Phann rests the cigarette in his mouth and sticks out a hand to help me up: supremely unconcerned. He hands me my boots.

"Thanks."

He shrugs, reaches behind his ear, and produces a joint. "I think you need it."

Viola.

She used to be a lot of fun.

Now she dolls herself up in white chiffon and linen like something out of colonial Indochina, but she's still the high priestess of destruction. Her dad's a Nobel Prize–winning novelist; her mom was *the* star of 1960s French cinema. (I never read her dad's books, which drove her mad; it was her mom who first introduced her to smack.) She was born beautiful, empty, and damned. She came to Cambodia looking for Colonel Kurtz with a needle hanging out of her arm. When we met, it was all playtime. But things changed. She got the fear, cleaned herself up. Left Cambo in the mud while she climbed the ladder. Country director, regional coordinator, UN talking head. Start your own foundation so your jet-setting pals can give to a good cause. She spends more time in Paris than Phnom Penh now: visits here are strictly pity trips. She's the only one who can't see the cliff coming up ahead.

What Vy doesn't know is how much she still hates herself.

It's just after noon by the time I make it to the Dane's. I'm hungry as hell and my head is pounding, but I feel surprisingly solid. Guessing

I did most of the damage in the first twelve hours, then slept for the next thirty.

I remember nothing.

I ask the Dane for a vodka tonic and whatever food he can get me in the next five minutes. Vy is waiting on the back balcony, smoking Gauloises and reading some magazine with a big-eyed child on the cover. With that much money, I guess you don't mind being a cliché.

"Thanks for coming." I collapse into my chair. She doesn't speak. "Where's Bones?"

"She's waiting in the hotel." No expression. British accent now: she's keeping her cool.

"Until you decide I'm on the level."

She lifts her chin with practiced indifference, but her eyes grab me, electric green. "Well, what am I supposed to think? You call me out of the blue and tell me you've found—"

"Not here." I hold up a hand. "Get the professor, we'll talk on the way."

She's looking at my drink, lips pursed. "You sure you're in shape—"

"I'm fine. An—" *And you don't get to tell me what to do anymore.* "Anesthetic. You know I don't like boats."

She's looking to delay, tries another tack. "You should call the police."

"Sure, once I have a clue what I'm looking at."

"And how will you explain how you found it?"

"I'll think of something."

"Well, you had better at least tell *me*."

I let that hang in the air. Finally: "You know how I found it."

She looks at me, first angry, then scared, then like she's about to cry. She settles on angry. "No, Will, I don't." Razor blades on glass. "It's one thing to jump on every city shooting and say you have a nose for trouble, but this"—it comes out "zis," her fingers tangling a web of air—"this is unreal."

There's the angle: she's looking for a fight. I thought she'd be tired of those, but some people never get enough. I'd hate to see her in the ring.

"You know better," I say. Give her a minute to remember.

There's a moment I think she's going to walk out, that it's too much: I can see all the old stuff flooding through her head and nothing I can do to stop it. I have to let it play out.

I'm thinking of the day we first met: in the FCC a million years ago, smelling of opium and grinning at each other over cocktails like kids psyching themselves up to shoplift *Playboy*s from the corner mart. We had fun.

Try not to think about that: none of it was real, anyway.

She stays seated, so I figure I have a chance.

"I didn't call for old times' sake," I say, once everything that could possibly happen hasn't. "I'm working."

"Really? It looks like you're having a psychotic break. Or possibly just doing your best Burroughs impression."

Grin. "Wanna play William Tell?"

"And you're drunk."

"Not yet. What, you gonna arrest me?" I stick out my arms, wrists up like I'm waiting for the cuffs. Spill some vodka. She has a good long look, running her eyes from wrist to biceps, then back to my face.

"Let's go, then," she sighs.

———————

Vy's forensic scientist is named Bun My. She cuts up corpses for just about everybody—National Museum, Antiquities Ministry, United Nations. Plenty of work in Cambo if you're an expert in human remains. Folks still find mass graves from the Khmer Rouge days on a pretty regular basis. Bun My isn't the best around, but she's good enough, she owes Vy a lot of favors, and she's not in too deep with the cops. She's small as a child, but there's no way the boat takes five, so we have to leave Phann behind. That worries me some: I've got to like the old fighter, and I figure he'd be good to have if things get rough.

I don't mention that to Vy.

It's already hot by the time Lon pulls out onto the blue, and no one is saying much. We just hide under our hats and wait. I've poured some vodka into a water bottle, so the boat's stuttering and jerking is manageable—still, the ride seems to take hours.

When we reach the spot, Lon cuts the motor and we drag the boat to rest. Vy's in jeans now, but still rolls them up over her swamp boots to clear the muck. Bun My jumps straight out, not worrying about her clothes. She's wearing the same khaki outfit and sandals they issue all dirt hounds with their master's degree.

She looks puzzled. "How you find this?"

I settle on something close to the truth. "The person I'm looking for took a photograph of this spot. I recognized it and wanted to look around." It's believable enough—if you haven't seen the photograph. Bun nods; Vy frowns.

Lon starts to follow, but I motion for him to stay with the boat. The rest of us go into the woods.

I shoved the dirt back over the bones before I left, but it's easy enough to see where. Bun goes right in, clearing with tiny, careful fingers. Vy and I watch—I'm wishing again we had Phann with us.

"Wait here," I say.

"Where are you going?"

"I want to see where this path leads." Better not to be surprised. Vy glares, and I turn away before she can say anything.

———————

The strange, nervous energy that filled the place on my last visit is gone, but the narrow track through the woods still makes my heart pump faster. I don't see any marks that look recent—but I'm not much of an outdoorsman. Mostly, I'm worried about who I might find on the other end.

I've pushed through a few hundred meters of brush when the ground starts to rise. The path twists up a muddy little cliff, and then I'm standing on the edge of a wide dirt track. Large enough for a truck, and used often: green grass sprouts between brown wheel ruts. A logging trail?

Wherever this leads, I don't think I'll get there on foot. But someone has been moving something through these woods. Someone who leaves bodies behind?

"It's not her," says Vy, voice like rock candy.

"Are you sure?" I'm looking at Bun, who looks back at Vy and says something in French.

"The bones are male, probably forty or—late forties, early fifties," Vy translates. "About five foot six, likely Asian, though she can't be certain. He has several old wounds, stabs and one gunshot. The bones are all cut up, marks all over, so no clear cause of death. Not much else she can tell without a lab, but it's definitely not June."

For some reason, the news doesn't surprise me. I'm relieved—then not. How convenient would it be to have it all end here? A simple story, another Cambo casualty. I push the thought away.

"Fine," I say. "Finish putting them back, and let's get out of here. I'll think of something to tell the police."

Vy looks down at Bun, who chatters something else in French. She's looking back and forth from Vy to me, excited.

"What?"

They're both looking at me now, Vy's eyes wide and bright.

"There's something else," Vy says. "You said the ground looked turned up when you got here."

I nod. "There was nothing growing there. Soil was soft."

"Even in this climate, it would take months for a body to go completely to bone. Maybe a year. Long enough for ground cover to grow back, certainly."

Of course it would. Idiot. Well, what do I know about this stuff? I've seen people go into the ground; not usually around when they come out. "So it's a reburial," I say hopefully. "Body was moved from somewhere else."

But there are other explanations, ones I like less, and I see them all flicking over Vy's face: that these bones have been here much longer, and I found them because I knew where to look. Better still, I put them here.

"Are you sure they're all from the same person? Only one body in there, right?"

Vy turns to look at Bun, who nods. Back to me: "How did you find this, Will?"

"I told you." Vy is staring, hard, but Bun is talking again, trying to get her attention, gesturing with her hand like with a knife.

"What's she saying?"

"What do you think she's saying?"

"Fuck's sake, Vy, just tell me!" I'm screaming.

She takes a step back, wary. "She can't say much without a microscope, but she thinks some of the marks on the bones are . . ." Bun nods, Vy sucks air. "Are marks like you would have from someone cleaning the flesh off. With a knife, maybe, or—" She shudders.

Bun looks at her expectantly. *"Ou des dents,"* she repeats, spreading her lips wide and biting down.

Vy's eyes: open wounds.

"Cover them," I croak. "We're getting out of here."

———————

In Vy's room at the Dane's. I'm well into a fresh bottle of vodka; she's chain-smoking on the bed.

The sun was still high as we made our way back, but it felt like midnight all the way. No one said a word. I kept trying to figure it: Maybe a whole corpse would have been too easy to identify? Or the murder could have happened a long time ago, and the killer moved the bones? Better: someone uninvolved found the bones and reburied them rather than deal with them. There were plenty of stories of cannibalism from the KR years: someone found an old grave and didn't want the hassle of police and reporters and historians, so they dumped the bones in the swamp. There: that's simple, believable.

But then how did June know? That photo exists for a reason.

At the docks I paid Lon—a little too much, but nothing remarkable. Trying to buy silence usually just gets you noticed. Hopefully he thinks I went to show my friends the beautiful lagoon I found the other day.

Alone now, it takes us some time to get our voices back. When we do, I tell Vy almost everything—glossing over the details of why I was staking out the Aussie and Charlie. She's not impressed.

"And Bun doesn't know how old the bones are?" I ask, for the eighth or ninth time.

Vy shakes her head.

"If we had them in a proper lab, she could tell you how long they've been in the ground, whether they spent all that time in one place, whether they were buried with a body or separate. All sorts of things." She drops her lashes and looks at me. "But we don't."

"Shit. We'll go back and take a couple. Just the little ones, enough for her to look at. They won't even be missed—" I'm cut off by a shoe flying past my head.

"What the hell is wrong with you?" Her face looks like someone grabbed it in the middle and twisted. "Do you understand nothing?"

"What do you mean?" I'm drawing a blank. I can handle people, but around Vy it breaks down fast.

"That body was a person, and he's dead. Something horrible happened to him. You can't just leave him lying out there because it might inconvenience you." She's crying now; it makes her ugly. "That man, whoever he is, deserves an investigation, deserves some justice!"

Is she serious? It must show in my face, because she screams again ("This is not a joke!"), grabs another of her shoes, and tosses it at me. This time her aim is pretty good, but I see it coming and knock it out of the air. She reaches down for something else and I pitch the vodka bottle over her head. It smashes against the wall, showering her with glass, and she freezes. Then I'm around the bed, reaching for her. Block a kick to the groin and catch her fist halfway to my face. She plants the other one in my solar plexus, and I grab that, too. Let her struggle: she's not moving me anywhere. I think she expects me to scream or hit her, and when I don't, she finally goes limp, looking at the floor.

"Listen to yourself," I say, soft as I can manage. "You think we're in Paris? Where do you think we are?"

Vy looks me in the eye and spits. "In hell."

I don't move. "You want to go to the police? It's as likely as anything the police did this. Or if not them, then the army, or someone else connected to the government. They'll move in and cover it up and say nothing ever happened, just some silly tourists having a scare over . . . dog bones. The best chance that skeleton has of getting a name would be if it turns out to be three thousand years old. But it's not, is it?" I drop her arms. Wipe my face. Light a cigarette.

Vy's still looking at the broken glass at her feet. "No one ever says no to you, do they?"

"Everyone I've asked for an insurance policy."

"What would you be worth?" She's not laughing. "You're a parasite. You use everybody—just to get to the next score. Even when it's not the drugs, or the money, you play with people, so I guess you must enjoy it."

"And you just like rolling in the mud." She slaps me, hard enough I drop my cigarette. It smolders on the bedclothes, and I pick it up before we have to call the fire department, too.

Her look says everything about where she's running, and what from.

"Gimme three days before you go anywhere with this," I say.

"Fuck you."

"Please."

"Oh, who am I going to tell?" She laughs now, long and low. Tosses herself back on the bed. For a second I see the Vy I knew. This is hell—and she can't stand to be too far away.

"Now the pleasantries are past"—I lean over her—"there's one more thing I need from you."

———

By the time we're done making faces at each other, the exhaustion has come back, and I can barely stand up. Vy and Bun are on their way up to Phnom Penh, and I'm staggering back to my room, thinking wistfully of all the pretty bottles of vodka pining away in the Dane's closet. Sorry, ladies, another night.

I find Phann sitting in his car outside the hotel, listening to the radio. Give him the rest of his cash, and some extra, and tell him I'm done. He should go back east. He pockets the money, then he reaches under the dash and pulls out a gun. Some kind of automatic: silver, greasy looking. Big. I have a half second of fear, but he holds it out to me, butt first.

"Never touch the stuff." He just sits there, looking at me like he knows better. "I'm a journalist," I say, in Khmer. "If I take that, I won't be one anymore."

Phann doesn't move. "You not journalist now," he says, in English. "You detective. Need protection."

"No thanks."

Phann shrugs and puts the gun back in the car. "There's nothing so important it's worth dying for," he says, just kind of conversationally. "I learned that a long time ago."

"I learned the opposite."

"May all the devas protect you from harm."

———————

Back in the room. Phann talked the hotel guys into not kicking me out, and they've reconstructed the bed while I was gone. I sit on it and smoke my way through the last of my gear. Look at the floor for a while, then change it up and look at the ceiling. The tiles make a nice pattern. The ones in the walls, too. Everything adds up.

About a thousand years ago, in another life, I had an uncle who tried to teach me chess. I could never get it. Trying to think five moves ahead—I lost and lost. Eventually I stopped playing. All I remember of the game is the feeling I have now: I'm in the dark and I can't see what's coming.

If I'm even halfway right about what Luke's up to, sticking my nose in his business is going to be instantly fatal. Taking my suspicions to Kara could be just as bad. Time is running out before the Feds show up—and I've got no moves left to make. A pawn against an army.

That's when I hear the click.

I roll off the bed, feeling in the dark for the metal poles that hold up the mosquito netting. Pull one out of its socket and grab the net in the other hand. The door bangs open and men rush in. I get the first one right in the eye with the end of the pole and toss the net in the face of the second, but there's a third in the doorway with a gun pointed right at me, and I freeze.

A moment of relief as I realize there are no machetes.

The first guy grabs the pole out of my hands. The world goes red as he brings it down on the bridge of my nose. The room spins, hands grab me—

Then nothing, for a long while.

DIARY

August 1

I feel awake, for what must be the first time in days. I'm still a bit groggy, which I guess is from the medications. . . . I don't know what all they've done to me. But it's good to write again (in my right mind, that is, haha).

The hospital is some kind of colonial gothic—a big gloomy ward, divided by curtains on rails, which they mostly keep closed, but up above I can see the arches in the ceiling, and the edges of high fan lights. It's all super clean and smells vaguely of bleach. The nurses have been in and out since I woke, asking me things in Cambodian that I can't possibly understand, so I just do my best to smile. I'm not really sure that helps much. They wanted to give me a drip, and I could see from the bottle it was just saline, but I remembered my training: no needles. So I mimed drinking, and they brought me some kind of Tang-product. It's amazing we have any astronauts left alive, if this is what we give them.

There was a doctor who came to see me sometime in the afternoon. He was absolutely tiny, in a perfect white coat and spectacles, and spoke a little English. He told me my leg had got infected. It must have been that cut, the one from the car on my first week. It never did heal, and I guess wading around in the swamps aggravated it. The doctor seemed very concerned.

"Bad cut," he kept saying. "Why?"

I told him a dozen times that a car had hit me, but he just kept shaking his head, looking worried and vaguely accusatory. "Very bad," he said. Gus called to shout at me, too. He said he had half a mind to send me home (which I managed not to laugh at) and if I wasn't more careful, and this is a dangerous place, and etc. Apparently I gave him a scare. I think he was ready to drive all the way down to Sihanoukville just to yell at me in person, but I managed to convince him I was sorry, and would take better care of myself, and would have his story ready soon . . . eventually he seemed to calm down. Sok came by, and says that tomorrow we can finish the drive home—ideally without me having a seizure in the passenger seat this time.

And now I have a real story. I'll tell Gus—in due time. Once I have all the pieces in place. Then I won't be faking anymore.

Funny, though . . . I was so messed up, with working and not sleeping and being sick—well, I don't even remember a lot of it. But one thing I do remember was this feeling of being watched. It started in Sihanoukville, I think, with the insomnia—I would doze and then wake up, sure someone else had just been in the room with me: hearing the rustle of curtains, the sound of the door closing. The sense of another body, somewhere, nearby. Once or twice, I could swear I smelled perfume in the air. In Koh Kong, it was worse. I thought—well, I can't even tell you what I thought.

I feel mostly fine now, sitting up in bed eating hospital food with a liberal mixture of crow. But the funny thing . . . that feeling of being watched has never really gone away. . . .

WILL

OCTOBER 14–15

I'm coughing, shaking icy water from my eyes. Shivers run through me like electric shocks and I try to curl up, but I can't: pain in my wrists where they pull against—what? Tape, maybe? Ankles strapped to the legs of a hard chair.

Naked, wet, freezing.

My face burns. Nose blocked, trying to breathe, to brace myself: if I'm alive, it's because they want something from me. I know what comes next and my mind is screaming, *just one more beer, one more screw, one more fix, one more cigarette—they have to give me that at least, a last smoke—*

Beneath that, silence.

I have to piss, so I do. One less thing they can use against me.

"Jesus Christ, you grow up in a barn?"

Pain runs through my face—

—please god no no no just give me a cigarette i'll tell you anything—

—I'm guessing rubber hose. Sparks, rainbows of blue and pink and yellow, resolving into a single, bright light.

"You piss when we tell you. Do that again and we'll cut it off."

It's Luke. He sounds less cheery now. I can't see him past the light. Shut my eyes.

I can hear other people in the room, moving. Muffled footsteps, no echoes: a shack or a shed?

More pain.

—*godgodmakeitstoppleaseanything*—

I've come off the junk three times. I can do pain.

"Eyes open. You rest when we tell you. We can cut your eyelids off, too, y'know." I let my head loll and do as told. Dirt floor. Faintly, the sound of frogs—still in the woods, then. I look back into the light before they figure out what I'm doing.

"Answer my questions, tell the truth, and you'll get out of here just fine." That's a lie. He says it like he's asking me to fasten my seat belt in the event of a water landing. And I still love him for it, mind screaming, *yes, please, anything*—"Lie, or stall me, and we'll start cutting." That's the truth.

"Okay." It comes out like slush, but I guess he knows what I mean.

"What's your name?"

"Will. Keller." Pain again. "Can . . . check, been here . . . years." He hits me three more times. Pain like liquid, filling me up from the face down until I'm a bottle of fire and *god, jesus, just make it fucking stop*—

"Don't answer any question not asked of you."

I wait.

"Who sent you looking for us?"

"I wasn't looking for you." The hose in the face again.

—*pleasepleaseanything*—

"I'm telling you what you want to know," I shout.

They hit me some more. My face burns and burns and I feel the pain spread through my body, like it's burning away the cold. Things come into focus: I guess that's adrenaline.

—*stoppleasejuststop*—

It isn't going to stop.

"Hit me again and you won't get any answers," I mutter. Another blow, now across the thighs. "You might as well start cutting."

"Really?" I feel a hand grab my balls.

"Fuck yourself." The hand squeezes and twists. I go ahead and scream.

Everything red—

Black.

Some while later, when I'm able to think again, I notice I've vomited on myself. The seat feels wet underneath me. I'm sobbing. This is worse than cold turkey—worse than anything.

"Who sent you?"

I'm desperate, trying to think of an answer that will satisfy them— but there's nothing. Game over. These aren't subtle guys: this isn't going to last much longer. I breathe into a pain that's tearing through every nerve—turn my head and spit on the floor.

Best I could do.

Something cold grabs my cock, and I look down. Having trouble seeing—a pair of bolt cutters.

"Cutting off your cock is worse than cutting off your balls, you know. Thing about cutting someone's balls off is, they don't mind so much, after. The urges are gone, y'know? But cut off a guy's cock? He spends the rest of his life thinking about what he's missing. Now, who sent you?"

I shrug.

When I was maybe fifteen, sixteen, my buddies and I would drive out at night to what was probably once a wheat field, though by our time it was just a couple acres of flat, dusty earth, sprinkled with dandelions and switchgrass and rape. We'd chalk a line down the middle, and two guys would pull their cars up on opposite ends and drive at each other. No strategy. No planning. The first one to swerve lost.

I was very, very good at that game.

Mutilation is a cheap threat to a dead man, and as I sit there, silent, Luke finally realizes it. He holds the bolt cutters to my cock as long as he can, making these menacing grunting noises. But it's over: he wants what I know more than I want anything from him.

The only thing I'll bargain for is a fucking cigarette.

And like that, it really is over. The door opens. A new voice: American, smooth. This guy did go to Yale.

"All right, amateur hour is over. Clean him up, give him something to eat—we got any candy? Give him some sugar. And get some lights in here, for God's sake. Not much of a criminal mastermind if you trip in the dark and break your damn neck." He's still muttering as he goes out.

Not over: now it's actually started.

———

The first thing I see is Phann. He's taped to another chair a few feet away, shirt off, covered in cigarette burns. His face is purple, neck black and bloody, clearly dead. My chest starts heaving.

Not again.

He was okay. He should have got out. I should have—

Another bucket of water hits me in the face. Focus on the cold as it sluices away blood and urine and vomit. Then someone is drying me off with a wadded-up shirt. I try not to look up.

These guys really are amateurs: if they'd kept Phann alive, they could have used him to get me to talk. Guess I don't look like the type.

Luke has left, but the others are still there. Two are Cambodians, dressed in nondescript garment-factory seconds. The third is bigger and has the same thug look about him as Luke—guessing he's another American. They cut the tape on my arms and legs, and let me get dressed, my whole body screaming as I try to move. I can't see out of my left eye.

We're in a small shack, some kind of waypoint. A few crates in a corner, empty; some folding chairs, a camp stove, and a couple fishing boxes full of supplies: cereal, candy bars, Nescafé, water bottles. The American tapes my hands again, but in front of me this time. One of the Khmers hands me a Snickers and I tear into it, too hungry to care that it's probably my last meal. They start boiling water.

Now a fourth guy comes in, I guess the one who stopped the interrogation before. Mid-fifties, Han Chinese features, but everything in his bearing says *American*. In a tan summer suit, he looks ready for martinis on the Vineyard. He makes two coffees; hands me one. "I apologize for my associates. They see all this stuff about Guantánamo on TV, and they think that's how it's supposed to be done. That's why we're going to lose the war on terror . . . just like we lost the war on drugs." New England accent—not Boston, could really be a Yale man. There's a trace of hesitation there: not another accent, just the space where one was erased.

He pulls out some expensive European cigarettes; offers the pack. I take two.

"Why don't you tell me a story?"

I don't see anything to lose by the truth. "Name's William Keller. I'm a photographer, I've been here for nine years. Before that, a selection of other shitholes. I have no interest in you people or what you're doing, I'm down here looking for a missing girl. She used to be an intern at my newspaper. Name's June Saito. Twenty-three years old, skinny, blond, half-Asian. You'd know her if you saw her."

He hears the question in my words and smiles. "If you think you'd like to run this, I can always get Luke back in here. You were doing very well with him."

"No thanks." I manage a crooked smile, too, but I know he sees through it, to the terror freezing my spine at the mention of Luke.

He knows I'll say anything just to keep him in the room. "June went up to Angkor—or that's what she told us—and never came back. I figured she ran off with a boy and it would be an easy buck, but I was wrong. I found out she'd been down here—got a bug up her ass about that break-in at Luke's office. I thought maybe she'd come down again without telling anyone, to try to get a scoop, so I followed. That's when things got hairy. As soon as I saw your boy, I knew something was going on and it was out of my pay grade. I was gonna get out of town, but as I was headed back, I stopped in the mangroves. A spot I recognized from a photo June had taken. I thought I'd look around, and I found a body."

Did Yale's eyebrows rise, just the tiniest bit?

"I had a friend come down, we checked it out on the sly. Wasn't June. I didn't know what else I could do, I was set to go back to Phnom Penh. That's when you fellas grabbed me."

He keeps looking at me. I give him a second. This is the tough part. "So Peng didn't send you?"

"General Peng? He's the guy you're trying to put out of a job?"

"Clever."

"I saw him once. Your buddies were stuffing him in a police van."

He nods. "So. Just another white man in the wrong place at the wrong time."

"It happens to us a lot."

"The thing you don't understand is that everywhere outside your hotel room is the wrong place. You should have gone home."

I don't rise to that. He's starting to stand, though, so it's now or never. "I guess you know I'm telling the truth, and now you're going to kill me and dump me in the swamp. But that's not your best play."

Yale raises his eyebrows. "Why not?"

"For a start, killing Americans causes problems. People notice."

Yale just smiles down at me. "Not you, Mr. Keller. I checked on you. All those years out here, running away from whatever it was that made your home unbearable. A bad marriage. A nasty uncle who fiddled with you. Something you did that you just can't live with."

"What are you, my analyst?"

His voice is melting sugar. "I've seen plenty like you. You grow up in America and it hurts you, it hurts you so much. So you come out here, into the real world." Suddenly, he's hard, harder than Luke could ever be. "In the real world, you're not special. You have a drug problem. Who knows what kind of trouble you might get yourself in, looking for a fix? So you'll be found somewhere with a gun in your jeans and a needle in your arm." He shrugs. "Even your friends, if you have any left, will hear what happened and nod their heads sadly. 'It's too bad,' they'll say. 'But we saw it coming.' You'll be a cautionary tale they trot out at parties: 'I knew a guy who died in Cambodia. Addict. So sad.'"

"That doesn't solve your problem." He looks at me, curious now. "I'm not the only one. You've also got an American girl who's gone missing, probably dead. That may not be your doing—I'm coming to think it's not—but it's connected to you by circumstance. If I can find that connection, others will, too. First the paper, then the girl's family. They've got money; they'll keep looking. Especially if I disappear. You'll get one nose after another poking into your business down here, and I don't think you can kill 'em all.

"But if I go back and spin a tale about how I think June went up to Siem Reap, met a boy, and left the country, you're in the clear. I get to stay alive. I get paid by my client and get out of here. Like I said, I don't care what you do. You already know I can keep my mouth shut."

He's weighing this, not bothering to hide the fact. Or he's toying with me. An idea begins to dawn: it's a hell of a gamble. Then I see Yale's hand move absently across his pocket, fingers brushing whatever he's got in there, and I know I've only got seconds.

"You might still decide it's easier to kill me and worry about the rest later. But I have something I think you want. Something I came across looking for the girl."

Now his eyes get narrow. "And what might that be?"

"Photographs. Not here, they're with a friend in Phnom Penh. She'll trade you the card for me."

"Photographs of what?"

Deep breath. "A few days ago, two Cambodian guys took out a kid named Van Chennarith. Broke into his hotel room and took him apart with machetes."

Van's name turns on the electricity. They're all looking at me now. The two Khmers, who had been sitting scratching their arms, are practically vibrating. Yale is staring at me intensely, suspiciously: Have I blown it?

Straight down the line. "I've got photos of the whole thing. Blood, faces, and all. I gave them to a friend, as insurance. Now I'm guessing you're still working with Van's dad, but maybe not—maybe you ordered the hit yourselves. I don't care. Either way, I figure maybe you want those pictures."

Yale pulls out a knife. He puts the tip under my good eye. "If this is a lie, I will take your eyes before I kill you."

I stop breathing.

He laughs. "Mercenaries. I have a soft spot for mercenaries. And, yes, I would like very much to have those pictures." He slices through the duct tape on my hands. From another pocket, he pulls my cell phone.

"Set up the trade. I'll give you a location."

It has to be done carefully. As soon as I hear her voice, I start talking.

"Viola, it's me."

"Will. What—"

"Never mind, Vy, never mind. I'm okay." I don't sound okay. Keep going. "Remember I said I might need you to bring me that memory card I gave you?"

"Of course. Where are you?" That's my girl.

"I'll give you GPS coordinates." I look up at Yale, who's writing down the numbers on a piece of paper. He nods slightly. "Rent a car and come out to meet me. Alone. You're going to give the card to some friends of mine, and I'm going to come back to Phnom Penh with you, all right?"

"I understand."

"Make sure you follow my instructions exactly. Remember: alone. If these guys see more than one person, I'm in trouble." Glance at Yale, squinting down at me. "Call this phone fifteen minutes before you arrive. If I don't answer, don't come. Once you've seen I'm okay, give the guys the card and we'll go home."

She doesn't hesitate. "Okay, Will. I'm coming."

D I A R Y

August 3

It's good to be home—though it feels funny to call my cage "home." Still, it feels more like home than a lot of places that better deserved the name. I finished the first part of the story in the car, and handed it to Gus: peace offering. He seems to have grudgingly accepted that I was being foolish, but not irresponsible, and offered some gruff words about taking better care of myself. I pinky swore, and came up to get changed.

Tonight: drinks with the guys. Everything back to normal.

. . .

3 a.m.—

The bedroom is empty. I've looked everywhere: The balcony, the stairwell . . . is it just nerves?

But something woke me. A rustle from the house—footsteps on the stairs?

From the bed I can see everything, moonlight in the balcony door, pale squares on the ceiling. I don't know why I'm afraid.

—downstairs—rattling locks

Is someone here?

That smell again—perfume, thick in the hot night air. God, it's everywhere!

And I know it. . . . It's on the tip of my mind, where I've smelled it before, a thousand dollars an ounce, scent mixing with the smell of blood . . .

She's found me.

WILL

OCTOBER 15

The spot Yale picks for the trade is perfect, considering he's planning to kill both me and Vy there. A narrow stretch of dirt track, about an hour's drive north of wherever we were. Probably near the Thai border. Tall grass on either side, posted with the bright-colored signs the NGOs put up to warn of land mines.

Nowhere to sneak up from, nowhere to run.

I laugh when I see it, and Yale and Luke both look at me. We're in one car: me and Luke in the back, Yale up front and one of the Khmers driving. The other Khmer is following us in a second car, with two more of their Chinese American thugs.

"This reminds me of someplace I used to come when I was a kid," I say.

Luke glares. Yale smiles.

They made me tell them how I wound up with the pictures. I considered making up a more plausible story than the truth, but decided against it. Yale would be watching my eyes, not doing lit crit. I felt bad about Gabriel: they'll kill him if they get the chance, just in case he knows anything. But he'd have done the same for me. They didn't talk to me much after that, just scurried around getting ready for the trade.

We're early, so the guys can scope the area. Luke has my digital camera, and he's made me show him how to use it, so he can check the photos. It's just starting to get dark when the call comes in. Yale hands me the phone, lets me answer it.

"Hey."

"Will, are you okay?" She sounds breathless, scared—perfect.

"Yeah, Vy, I'm fine." As instructed, I talk her through the last directions to the meeting point.

"Just do what they tell you, and it'll all be fine."

"Okay," she almost sobs.

"Vy?"

"Yes?"

"I'm sorry." I hang up. That's it, then.

One of Yale's guys comes over and whispers to him: presumably they've had someone watching her.

Yale nods. "Your friend has done well. She must care about you a great deal."

"We've had our moments."

He smiles, and it looks genuine. Guess he likes this part. "What will you do when you get back home?"

"Get stoned and go to Martini's."

That makes him laugh. "A man who knows what he wants!" He turns in his seat to look at me. "But I meant America."

"Oh." It's been a long time since that was home. "CBGBs. Ever been?"

He smiles again. "I saw Guns N' Roses there in 1987. Amazing." The sick fucker is loving this. Like a cat playing with its food.

"Awesome. I'd have given a finger to be at that concert." We both laugh. "Iggy Pop, that's what I'm gonna do. Iggy at CB's. After, get some of those honey peanuts. Go up to St. Mark's, go to the Holiday Cocktail Lounge, if they haven't torn it down for a fuckin' Starbucks. Drink till I pass out on the street."

"I wish you luck with that."

"Unless you need help here." I smile back. "Luke's good at what he does, but he doesn't really blend in, y'know. I know the territory. You could use a guy like me."

Luke's glaring like he's ready to go for the bolt cutters again, but Yale's still smiling. Why get riled? I'll be dead in ten minutes anyway.

"I could at that," he says. "But I think perhaps it's better for us all if you go on back home. Rediscover American life, and stop thinking about all the bad things that happen out here at the edge of the world."

"Maybe you're right."

He looks at his watch. "Get up," he says, his voice sharp again. "It's time."

It's full dark now, the moon obscured by heavy clouds. Car headlights cut tunnels through the black. Luke and I stand out front—him a bit behind me, piece rammed into my back. Yale next to us, the two thugs behind him. The Khmers are still in the cars.

It's a warm night, and the air has that near-sea-level fug. We stand there awhile, Luke shifting from leg to leg.

"Where the fuck—"

"She'll be here," Yale says, his voice calm. We wait some more. The moths and mosquitoes do a flying-circus act in the lights. Finally, just when I'm getting worried Luke's going to shoot me and be done with it, another pair of glowing lamps starts to flicker over the track.

The lights blend with ours, making a yellow corridor between the three vehicles. She's in some ancient sixties-era Renault, must have been sitting in someone's garage since before the war. It stops about thirty feet from us, and she steps out.

Tall, dark, and gorgeous in severe black pantsuit. Her heels look unsteady on the dirt, and the men with their fingers on the triggers relax a bit at the sight of her.

"Turn off the lights first, remember?" Luke shouts.

"Sorry," she shouts back, and starts to do it, then stops, looking confused. "I've got the card." She holds it high in her left hand—nervous, scattered.

Brilliant.

"Are you okay, Will?"

"The lights," Luke says, taking his gun off me and pointing it at her.

"I'm fine," I say. "Sorry about the mess."

"I'll take it out of your salary," she replies.

Luke and Yale have just about enough time to register something's wrong when a faint pop echoes from somewhere in the bowels of that old car. Luke's head rocks back and he crumples to the ground.

Already I'm moving, grabbing Yale's arm with my duct-taped hands and spinning him like a shield against the guys behind me. They look confused. As we hit the floor I see one of them fall. Gunfire, loud: she's shooting now, too.

Yale struggling on the ground, hand at my face—

I lean on his arm, pulling as hard as I can until I hear something creak and pop. One of the cars behind us revs up—then stops with the sound of bullets punching through glass.

Yale yanks his good arm free. I don't see the blade, but I hear the click of it snapping open. Roll away—not fast enough. Burning across my upper arm.

More gunfire: Yale stays low, bracing himself for another lunge at me. I spin on the ground and kick out at him. He scuttles back, forced to use his good arm to move, and I feint again. He brings the knife around, slashing my leg, but now his face is in reach: plant my heel in his jaw and he goes limp. Then I'm on him, pinning down his knife arm and hammering him with my elbows.

The shooting stops. I look up.

Kara is walking down the lighted path, flanked on one side by Miss Eyre, her bodyguard from the hotel, and on the other by a tiny Japanese man, both carrying rifles. I see the holes in the Renault's hood, and I get the logic of the ancient car: it's a rear-engine, and they've converted the passenger seat and trunk into a sniper's nest.

The yakuza works fast.

Back in the hotel, I'd made Vy promise to take Kara the memory card as soon as she got to Phnom Penh. I needed to know where the Koroshis stood: they could have been behind the smuggling ring themselves and would kill me for learning too much, but I didn't think they'd go after a public figure like Vy. When Luke and Yale took me, Kara became my best shot. I already knew she'd play along when I called. I guess she isn't in on the smuggling—but I don't know if I've saved myself or just bought a few more hours.

Just this second, it doesn't matter.

Yale is still dazed, but his eyes go wide when he sees Kara standing over us, cutting my hands free.

"Mr. Chua," she says. "Pleased to meet you in person." Then something in Japanese; all I catch is the name, but her face makes the meaning pretty clear: Ryu Koroshi sends his regards. Yale makes a noise like a chicken getting its neck wrung, looking from her to me and back.

"Welcome to the motherfucking jungle," I say, and break his jaw.

Maybe I like chess after all. At least when I can play with the queen in my pocket.

D I A R Y

August 9

. . . crying, again . . . a last indulgence: the luxury of tears scalding my face

. . . soiled and torn, barely even a person . . .

. . . time, I will remember. I will keep all the pain, the shame, the fumbling fingers and the sickness inside me: I want it. I would not let it go. It's just a path, and now I am walking it, it's no different from any other. I let him use me, thoughtless as a child or an animal—and why not? It didn't matter. I'm ready.

I'm not waiting for anything anymore.

WILL

OCTOBER 15–30

The road north is a mess of ruts and holes, but that doesn't stop Kara's driver from taking it at sixty-plus. He can't weigh more than 110, and he's wrestling with the Range Rover's huge steering wheel like it's a wild animal. Out the front window, rocks and stumps and potholes loom up in the headlights, some big enough to send us crashing into the trees. A sharp twist of the wheel and they vanish again in the dark.

"Relax." Kara's voice comes from the blackness behind me. "Mr. Keihatsu knows what he's doing."

We've been driving like this for hours, hurtling up this midnight highway at speeds that make my teeth chatter, Dexedrine and nerves keeping me awake. No one says much. Once I tried to turn the radio on—Keihatsu reached over and shut it off.

Kara hasn't said where we're going. I wonder if she's taking me somewhere just to dig a hole. If so, she went to a lot of trouble. Clutched to my chest is the backpack I retrieved from the trunk of Mr. Chua's car. Inside, I can feel the rectangular shapes of June's diaries. Kara hasn't searched it, but she might, anytime.

If she has the books, will she decide she doesn't need me?

After the gunfight in the tall grass, there were a few minutes of hurried cleanup: arranging corpses and planting guns so it looked like the Cambodian drivers and the American thugs had shot each other. Keihatsu took a quick look at the cuts on my arm and leg and pronounced me not about to die. Miss Eyre slapped some tape patches over the Renault, Kara tied up Chua and stuck him in the hood, and we got out of there. We drove in the dark for about half an hour, until we came to a grimy little roadside restaurant and garage. Miss Eyre drove away in the Renault, while the rest of us piled into this huge black machine. Headed north.

On the rare moments when the moon breaks through the clouds, I can make out Chua sitting behind Keihatsu, slumped against the door, his face a chiaroscuro of bruises. Behind me, in the mirror, Kara's is serene: as empty of expression as a model's in a magazine. Then the clouds close again, and all I see is the red glow of her cigarette.

Every time she stubs one out I hold my breath, waiting to feel steel wire sinking into my throat. It doesn't come.

I scan dark skies for any sign of a horizon. How long has this night gone on? Has to get light sometime.

Waiting seems to take forever.

Eventually, though, the outlines of treetops become visible against the clouds, black slowly warming to green and charcoal gray. The road in front of us gets longer and longer, until we're driving down a narrow country lane rather than careening through the dark. Then we pull out of the woods onto a patch of asphalt in front of a large building, and Keihatsu brings the Range Rover to a halt.

We're in the parking lot of a not-very-expensive hotel: a health-resort kind of place, where wealthy Khmers and Thais go for relaxation. All at once I know where we are, and I look at Kara in the mirror. "Battambang?"

"I thought we could use some R and R."

As soon as we get to the suite, it starts.

Ashen morning light is breaking through the windows as Keihatsu gestures Chua to a leather armchair, then pulls another up across from it. They sit leaning forward, so close they're almost touching, speaking Mandarin in low, empty voices. There's something tense and repellent about the sight of them, like mating scorpions.

Kara turns and whispers, "We can take it from here."

"I want to see."

She doesn't smile, but the expression on her face might be approval. I realize this is how she wanted it. I'm just another part of her math. Chua doesn't know what's between us: he thinks I'm one of hers, and he knows that even half-dead I'm a better fighter than he is. Two on one, he might still try something, even given how terrified he is of Kara. Three on one, he knows he's got no chance.

Once he's broken, the math will change.

I want a drink, but Kara's eyes hold me in place. She hands me a cigarette. I'm too unsteady to light it, so she does it for me.

When I see Chua slump down in his chair, I know it's done. He's lost. Kara takes my hand and guides me into the hall. I try to stay solid as I face her, but my vision is blurring with exhaustion.

"He made the smart move," she says. "Interrogators are pragmatists. Chua's operation doesn't even know there's an enemy. When they find out, they'll get rid of loose ends, and he's one of them. If he cooperates, we protect him. Maybe Keihatsu even finds him some work."

"His boss won't like that."

"If he's too scared to flip, he can still hope for a clean death," she says, like she's discussing the TV schedule. "A body to send home to the family. He knows if he doesn't talk, it'll be as bad for him as anything his boss would do." She looks me up and down like she's seeing me for the first time, and I feel my muscles tense—

But Kara just smiles her tiger smile and hands me a room key. "Get some rest. I'll send a doctor to look at you."

———————

Bedroom—kill the lights.

Can barely stand, but have to do one thing: stash the journals. Too tired for anything fancy—under the mattress. Hard for anyone to find them with me passed out on top.

So much speed, it might take me a while to—

———————

Vague impressions of doctors coming and going.

"Don't touch the bandages, it needs time to heal."

My left eye is bad, they think I might lose it. Days half-blind in a halo of gauze. Sitting in the dark, drinking juice and eating soup from room service and licking my wounds. Sky News on television, nothing in my head.

Waiting for whatever happens next.

When I'm strong enough to stand, I hide the journals again: better this time. Even that's more than I can manage. Make it almost back to my door before I collapse. They find me later, in the hall—

"What are you doing out of bed? You need rest."

Darkness again.

———————

I wake to see Kara looking down at me, her expression unreadable. "Time to get up, lazybones. We're having lunch."

She helps me out of bed and I get a breath of her scent, jasmine and cordite. She's taller, in five-inch Louboutins: not pretending to be a tourist anymore. She looks ready for breakfast at fucking Tiffany's. I take in the view as she opens the window, revealing a balcony I never knew was there. On it, two chairs and a table laid with crisp white linen. Trays of miso soup, prawn-and-seaweed salad, fresh sushi, ice-cold bottles of Asahi.

A cleaver-faced Japanese man pours my beer as I sit. Kara raises her glass, and we drink together.

Tastes like heaven.

———————————

By our third lunch together—oysters on the half shell, probably flown in by helicopter; chicken Caesar salad, Sapphire martinis—we're tired of talking about how nice the weather is in Battambang. I don't know what Kara wants from me, but I'm going to make the most of it.

"When are you going to tell me who Luke and Chua were moving heroin for?"

Surprisingly, I get an answer.

"I don't suppose the names of West Coast triad overlords mean much to you?"

"Nah."

"Well, it was one of the major ones. He got tired of dealing with the Mexicans, and decided to reopen the Eastern Pipeline." It makes more than a little sense: the Golden Triangle, where Burma, Laos, and Thailand meet, used to be the biggest source of heroin for the US. After the Burmese bought out Khun Sa in the early nineties, the flow dropped to a trickle. If the triads could start it up again, they could carve away the Mexicans' territory with a better product.

"So Cambo is just the tip of the iceberg," I say.

"Oh, yes. This was a sophisticated operation. They saw how the South American cocaine cartels worked and figured they could start the same thing up here. They were playing a long game, working Burma, Thailand, Laos, Vietnam . . ."

She lets it sink in: how very much I should be dead. I think about it as I freshen my drink.

"I don't understand why you're telling me this."

She doesn't answer, just swirls her glass like she's enjoying herself. Her eyes say: *You're mine.*

―――――――――

The rest of the story comes in bits and pieces. While we hide up here drinking martinis, Kara's guys are crawling the country. Every day brings some new update. One morning, she tells me they've found a bunch of customized boats hidden in a Cambodian port: tugs and trawlers with cleverly disguised compartments, the kind that could carry tons of product through US customs undetected. Another day, they've turned up two more aid organizations with plants in them: guys like Luke, scouting out the kind of desperate, isolated communities where refining and smuggling would seem like good business to the locals.

Turns out the Koh Kong governor really did order the break-in at Luke's office: not because of the damn assessment, but because he guessed about the smuggling and wanted his cut. He thought he was dealing with a few rogues, not a major international operation. Chua got him straightened out somehow, and that blew over.

Mostly, the triads had been able to co-opt or bully existing outfits into working with them. But here, General Peng and his army buddies weren't interested in new partners. So Chua and the other lieutenant in charge, a guy Kara called Tan, got the bright idea to turn the police against the army. Hok Lundy went for it: saw a chance to expand his operation and get Peng out of his way. Maybe he thought he'd be prime minister someday. He came up with the idea of using the international advisers as cat's paws: he knew a hand-picked police unit to root out the drug runners in the security services would appeal to guys like Steve. The police could harass the competition and everyone would think it was just standard foreign interference—really, they were figuring out how to take over. When the Sydney bust made waves, Hok Lundy just blamed the Australians, made some payoffs, and everyone calmed down.

Peng didn't see the trouble coming until he wound up in the back of a police van. Then he struck back hard, taking out officers, friends and family members of task force officials—including Charlie. But he was in a vise: his bloody payback made Hun Sen look weak, and that couldn't stand, not with the political deadlock.

Now Kara's seen an opening, and she's taking it. I don't ask what her endgame is—figure the yakuza has its own reasons to worry about the triads getting too much power.

I worry about what comes next.

Do I ever get to leave this hotel? It's packed with Japanese now—a tour bus full of young, middle-income couples from Kobe, looking for peace and quiet and natural healing. Their stories check out, long as you don't look them in the eye. I can't get from my room to the elevator without one of them latching onto me, wanting to talk in broken English about how beautiful the backcountry is.

I don't see much of Keihatsu—I think mostly he babysits Chua, whose leash is even shorter than mine. But Kara is always around. She keeps me close. At any hour, Miss Eyre or one of Kara's crew of young, female "personal assistants" might show up to summon me to the suite. There are usually drinks, and always questions. Kara pumps me on Cambodian politics, on various officials and their roles, on who's who in the criminal underworld. Other times she just appears, unannounced. I might wake to find her working at the desk next to my bed, or sitting on my balcony to watch the sunset. On these occasions, she says nothing at all.

It frightens me that I am becoming used to her presence.

One thing we never talk about. Kara is taking apart Chua's organization piece by piece, but there's been no sign of her sister. Chua says he never saw her: I believe him. It's possible Luke killed her without telling his boss and dumped her body in the water somewhere, but it doesn't seem likely: they were all too disciplined for that.

One day, Kara asks for details about the body in the mangroves. She seems particularly interested in the marks Bun My found on the bones: "I'd like to see them."

"Lon can take you there."

"Lon?"

"The boatman. He'll remember." I'm not hiding the bitterness in my voice. "It had to be him who told Luke what we were up to. Best guess, he was paid to report on who was moving around that bit of coast. He can take you right to the spot."

"Yes."

I catch her look and realize what I've done, but it's too late.

———————

In the dream, I'm back in Koh Kong. It's just before dawn, the main street empty and black. I walk down to the marina. For a little while, Phann walks with me, still in silence.

This always happens at the beginning.

I find Lon tying up his boat. When he sees me, his eyes go white and he starts to babble, then turns like he's going to run. I show him Phann's pistol and he stands still, not sure whether to look at my eyes or the gun.

"Relax," I say. "We're just going to the island." I start up the little engine, guiding us out of the harbor.

The sea is charcoal, the sky is ash. Clouds like mountain ranges hang overhead. The land recedes behind us.

"Just to the island?" Lon asks.

"Yeah."

"What you want see?"

I don't answer. Finally, we come far enough out that we see nothing at all: dark water extending to a dark horizon. I cut the motor and we sit there awhile, both of us waiting for light.

"You have to answer for Phann," I say at last. He starts to protest, to say he doesn't know what I'm talking about. I cut him off. "You sold us out to Luke, and Phann ended up dead." He doesn't say anything, just stares straight ahead, his head hanging slightly. I'm undoing my belt. "He wasn't a good guy; he probably had it coming. But I liked him. And I got him into this, so I can't let it go."

He nods slightly, still looking out at the horizon. I loop the belt over his neck and pull the buckle tight. It's slow work, choking a man. He claws at the leather a little—not much. His eyes never leave that thin line in the distance. The sky does its magic thing, changing from ugly gray to brilliant blue so subtly that you can't quite say when it happened. Finally, it's done. I stand up, carefully, and lay the body back against the motor. Lash him down with the belt. I have Mr. Chua's knife in my pocket, and I use it to make two deep slashes in his abdomen, so the sea will keep him.

I expect to feel something, but I don't. I have plenty of blood on my hands already. Doing it myself doesn't feel any different.

There's a dark shape in the distance now. I wait, standing, as it grows closer. After a while it pulls up next to us: a small commercial tug. Keihatsu waves down at me from the deck and lowers a rope. I climb up.

When I'm standing next to him, I pull Phann's gun from my waistband and empty the clip into the bottom of the little boat. It fills with water shockingly fast, and in less than a minute it's gone, along with the body, down into that warm, gray nothing. Keihatsu laughs and claps me on the back. Job well done. You made your bones, kid. Come on, she's waiting.

I put the gun back in my belt. When I turn around, though, I see who's driving.

It's Dead Charlie.

Behind him, the whole damned crew: the Aussie and Bunny, and the dead Afghans, and more. They fill the boat there are so many. Lon clambers over the side to join them, seawater pouring from his sliced-up guts.

"Where are we going?" I ask.

"Just to the island," says Charlie. "She's waiting."

"Who's waiting?"

He just laughs and spins the wheel. The boat starts to sink.

I claw my way out of the sheets, gasping for air.

Light a cigarette. I can't drink anything—still expecting to wake up, my lungs full of warm water. It takes a while to believe I'm really in my hotel room, and not out there, sinking slowly into the Gulf.

Walking through the hotel lobby, backpack slung over my shoulder.

This is a test.

No one stops me as I head for the door. I'm outside and halfway to the row of motodops when I feel someone at my elbow—recognize the driver of the tour bus.

"Sir, I hope we have not offended you with our presence in your hotel. As an honored guest, I offer you free ride in our tours limousine."

"No thanks. I prefer the bike."

Big smile, deep bow.

"Of course, sir."

One moto has nosed out of the pack and pulled up in front of me. I ignore him, slinging myself up behind the third guy in line and telling him to take me downtown. There's a bar I know from before, in an old Khmer house overlooking the Sangker River.

I don't see anyone following us on the ride down, but when I arrive, Miss Eyre is sitting at a table in the corner. She doesn't move as I find a space and order a drink. She doesn't even seem to be watching.

I know better.

I'm not getting out today—but that's not why I came here. It's afternoon, and getting on to hot. I order an Angkor. Drink it; order another. From my table on the balcony, I watch the Sangker creeping by below, sticky and slow as maple syrup. Clouds of midges and mosquitoes whirl over its surface. Finish the second beer.

It takes a half dozen of them for the girls in this hick town to start looking good—but the state I'm in, I don't mind the extra work. One keeps looking over at me: skinny as a twig, with a lopsided face and misplaced incisors that jut out like fangs. When she smiles, she looks half-jackal, and she smiles a lot—but she's the best of the bunch. I wave to her and she comes up to my table.

"What's your name?"

"Theary." In Khmer, it means "helper."

"Would you like to have a drink with me, Theary?"

———————

It's 3:00 a.m. by the time Theary totters out of my room. Good God, how she can bend—like fucking climbing ivy. I fumble through the glasses on the end table until I find one with some booze left in it—suck it through a twisty straw and hope to sleep, too tired to dream.

I must doze off, because when I open my eyes, Keihatsu is standing over me.

"Miss Koroshi requires your presence. Please put clothes on."

We march downstairs and he bundles me into the back of the

Range Rover. After a few minutes, Kara shows up. She and Keihatsu get in front, and one of the assistants climbs in next to me.

I'm wondering if this is going to be my last ride. But it goes on and on—after a couple hours, I don't care enough to stay awake.

I open my eyes to see soldiers surrounding the car, and my chest seizes up: checkpoints are bad news at the best of times, and times now are pretty rough. I'm looking ahead for an exit, but there's none—they've got the road blocked with rolling barriers. My heart rate slows a bit as I realize this is a real security check, not just a bunch of thugs collecting tolls.

Only a bit, though.

The others seem unfazed, and we file out to let the soldiers search us, then the car, then us again.

All around is broad, flat countryside; tall grass and rows of palms. Where are we? We left Battambang going north, then turned east—we're past Siem Reap, most likely, but how far? Finally the soldiers seem satisfied and let us go. About 500 meters past the checkpoint, we turn off the road onto a narrow, well-paved lane, its entrance guarded by more soldiers, who make us go through the whole search business again. This happens about four more times before our destination appears: a mansion in shades of Pepto-Bismol, with pagoda tops in neon green, surrounded by heavy security walls and Jersey barriers.

Inside, a carefully manicured drive leads up to a grand main entrance, bordered by hedges trimmed like Christmas-tree ornaments. The *ancien régime* grandeur is spoiled by a pair of jeeps with mounted .50 cals lurking behind the topiary, inconspicuous as a gunshot wound on a wedding dress.

"They always this nervous?" I ask.

No one answers. Black-jacket security guys appear to usher us inside, down a bunch of hallways and into a courtyard that would go well at Versailles, if Louis had been into disco. We sit drinking iced tea for another half hour, until two men in suits come out and join us. The first is tall and angular, with a drawn, hungry kind of face. Reminds me a bit of Phann. Context being what it is, it takes me a second to recognize him as the prime minister.

Kara stands and bows deep, Japanese-style. Hun Sen gives her a brief Cambodian *nop,* then takes her arm. They walk around the courtyard, chatting like old friends.

The second man, a little fellow with a round face, sits next to me and offers a hand-rolled Russian cigarette from a gold case.

"Such is the life of a factotum," he says, in faintly accented English. "Always in attendance. Still, it is good to have you and your friends here. We can bring this stupidity to an end quickly." I nod like I know what he's talking about. "Everyone thinks we are fools out here, just gangsters taking all the profit we can. But it's not so. We are serious about change, but you know, with all our country has been through, it is difficult to move on." He leans toward me. "Why should we want Americans using us to traffic their drugs? Everyone knows the days of smuggling won't last."

"Drugs last."

The fellow laughs, gestures toward his boss. "His Excellency has bigger plans for this country. All our projections indicate that within two decades, the Western nations will give up the drug war. The cost is too high, and the benefits of legalizing and localizing the trade are too great. By 2025, New York will be getting its heroin from Colorado, not Cambodia. You'll need the money for the real wars you'll be fighting. The cash crops of the next century won't be coca and poppies, they'll be rice and wheat." He smiles. "Banking, finance, development: these are things you can . . . sink your teeth into, you say?"

"In five years, Cambodia will be completely legitimate?"

He gives me a big, gold-toothed grin. "Five may be optimistic. Twenty. The prime minister would like to leave his children a country better than the one he saved from Pol Pot." He pauses, still smiling at me, reading my face as I look over at the mad dictator, standing there laughing with Kara. "You have trouble seeing such a human emotion on our leader? Perhaps you don't understand this place as well as you think."

Maybe I don't, at that.

No tanks in the streets, anyway. Assuming I get back alive, I get to tell Gus he was wrong.

———————

The next morning, there's a newspaper waiting on the table in my hotel room. Hok Lundy has died in a helicopter crash.

———————

Afternoon: long and hot. Nothing changes. The Sangker still creeps by below, sticky as maple syrup. The midges and mosquitoes go on with their dance. I sip my Angkor.

Battambang.

Two weeks now I've been up here, like a fly in amber. The world has stopped.

I'm on beer number five when Theary struts in, swaying on heels like circus stilts. She stops next to my chair, and I run my fingers up under the fringe of her daisy dukes. Get a little hard as I imagine her pulling her blue tank top over her head, brown nipples popping free above gently heaving ribs. I follow that thought with another, chase them with the rest of my beer.

"You gonna sit down?"

She smiles and runs her nails down my leg, slowly tracing magic words in Khmer. They do spells like that.

I give her hand a squeeze. "Did you bring them?" She nods. "Did anyone ask about them?"

"No."

Good. I still can't say why I've kept the journals secret all this time—why I moved them from hiding place to hiding place, why I smuggled them out for Theary to keep safe. Maybe I want the answers all to myself.

As I feel Kara's claws in me, maybe I just want something that's mine.

Theary leans in and whispers in my ear. She wants to go to the hotel, she's found a new position on the Internet and wants to try it out. She kisses me, breath sour under the sweetness of rum.

"Let's go," I say.

But as we walk away I glance back at the river, and for a second I think I see that shadow, waving silently to me out of the glare.

———

I wake up gasping.

Theary is still asleep. She grew up in a one-room house with four brothers and five sisters: nothing can wake her if she doesn't want it to.

She lies curled up like a dead spider, brittle and brown. Beneath her left shoulder blade, a patch of dark, rough skin extends halfway down her back: a birthmark of some kind, like a place where wings started to grow and gave up.

I reach between her legs, feel the roughness of her hair, the lingering dampness. Her eyes don't open, but she shifts her hips, spreading her thighs. She must have been dreaming of sex. Her hand comes down to move in sync with mine, and we slide our fingers back and forth, letting them grow wet. Carefully I kneel on the bed, bend down, and slide inside. Still, she keeps her eyes closed, and I wonder what she's imagining. Her fingers knot themselves in the sheets. As gently as I can, I place a hand alongside her face. She turns her head and her mouth finds it, working slightly against my palm as we move together in slow undulations, like the waves. She doesn't scream, but sighs, deeply, three times, and then we're done. For a moment I think she's going to open her eyes, say something—but she only reaches up and places a finger to my lips, then subsides back into the depths of whatever dream she was having.

I cross to the little window and have a final cigarette, looking out at the trees under a darkened sky.

When I'm done, I pull on a pair of jeans and go out into the hall.

The lights are dim. My feet make no sound on the oxblood carpet. I have to go all the way across the building and up to the top floor to get to Kara's room. I don't meet anyone.

Knock lightly on the door. After a moment, it opens and she's there. I've never known her to sleep. She's wearing some kind of transparent, black nightdress thing, giving me a good long look at a body men would go to war for. She might have just got out of bed, except her hair's perfect and she's carrying a machine pistol.

She doesn't say anything, just leaves the door open and turns around. I shut it behind me. The big coffee table in the main room of the suite is covered with papers, and she drops the gun there and goes back to sitting cross-legged on the couch, looking over them. I go to the bar. Pour myself a drink; she frowns.

"Want one?"

She doesn't seem to hear—but she did, and the answer is no.

"It's time."

She knows exactly what I mean. "It's no good. I've got dozens of guys scouring this country now."

"Lot of broken collarbones."

Kara's expression doesn't change. "No one's turned up anything. She walks out of your paper and off the face of the earth. I'm not spending the next two decades sticking posters on telephone poles. She's lost; that's the life we're in. The one she wanted to get away from." I'm surprised, again: so much bitterness in her voice. "On the remote chance she's alive, she's been drugged and sold into slavery, or she's gone up the Mekong to work on her collection of human skulls. But she's not going to be found."

"You don't have to help. There's no harm in letting me keep trying."

She gives me a surprisingly soft look, for a woman whose eyes are razors. "You've done your job, Will. You'll get paid, if that's what you're worried about. This is an operational area now, there's money to burn. You don't have to go on with some hopeless quest."

"You've paid me enough. I'll get my bonus if I find her, no more."

"Are you afraid to be in my debt?"

"Yeah." Simple enough to say, really.

She takes it a bit hard. "You don't have to be afraid of me." I raise an eyebrow. "Well, not much." She gets up and goes to the bar, which appears to have been imported straight from Sardi's, and starts making us manhattans. It takes a while: everything just so. Finally she hands one over, looks me up and down. "You're a decent guy to have around, Keller. More so when you're sober enough to stand, but not exclusively. Why don't you come back with me? I'd have plenty of uses for you in LA." The way she says it, I guess they might not all be professional. "And the drugs and arm candy are much higher quality." She smirks. "What do you say, Will? Come home."

"That speech ever work on June?"

For half a second I think the look on her face is fury: she barely seems human. Then she laughs, laughs so hard she spills her drink and has to sit down on the floor. I sit across from her.

"No," she says. "No, it never did."

When the manhattans are done, Kara grabs the rye from the counter and pours us two doses. We drink again.

"Why do you really want to find her?" she asks.

"What else have I got to do?"

She smiles. Refills our glasses and then looks at me, serious now, hard and icy like when she first came out of the surf. She's appraising me, and my skin grows cold as I wonder what she sees.

"You think you know something I don't," she says. "It's all over you."

I'm struggling to make my face blank.

"Keep it. But if you go hunting her, be careful." She's staring right down to the bottom of me now, and I feel the room falling away as June's words come out of Kara's mouth: "There are still dark places in the world."

Then she smiles again. Sips her drink.

We finish the bottle in silence, sitting there on the floor with the cries of bats outside the windows for music. When it's done, Kara goes back to her paperwork. She doesn't look at me as I get up. I can't help giving her a last glance from the door: wondering if I've slipped the trap, or if it's still closing silently all around me.

Then I go. June is waiting.

D I A R Y

August 10

I remember the Killing Fields.

There are so many things about my time here that I can't seem to get to—memories that elude me, as if I'd been sleepwalking—but that day is crystal clear. I stood on a path under giant palms, and on either side the earth fell away, leaving me walking along a raised hummock between pools clotted with bright green ferns and waterlilies. Farther down, they went from brown to blue as tentative fingers of water reached out to join the river. On the far shore, I could see the peaked roofs of Phnom Penh.

I remember watching red and yellow dragonflies wheel over the flowers. I wanted to learn their names, but there are no names here.

It is hard to recall what brought me. I think I was looking for history. I wanted a museum, filled with careful, scholarly descriptions of what happened and how it was discovered, of what was known and what unknown, and what still awaited knowing somewhere in the soil. I wanted an explanation. But there was only a tiny monument stacked with skulls, with a few panels in mock-English, decrying the brutality of the Khmer Rouge.

I remember looking at it, and thinking of my mother.

I have read all the books. No one who writes about this place manages to convey anything about it: Cambodia is the opposite of meaning. Yet our shelves are lined with dozens of volumes repeating the same pat phrases, carefully worded to make tautology sound like understanding. The brutality occurred because the regime was brutal. Even Pol Pot is an invention: a fake name placed over a fabricated history. The dragonflies are nameless because no one has ever named them—unless perhaps the namer lies beneath, and the flowers they feed on put roots over her bones. And what do parents tell their children at night, except tales of the ghosts waiting in the ground to come and get them. . . .

No. Let me say it another way . . . if there is a way to say it at all.

You and I, we live in a world of words. They give us shape, they bend time into an orderly line, progressing from "long, long ago" and "once upon a . . . ," up through "the modern era" and "now, today," and then on to "tomorrow," and "some day, when . . ." A great chain of history, forged of language.

I always knew who I was, and I knew that I was going somewhere.

Then I came here, where there is no history. No stories left, just skulls in nameless piles. No traditions, their keepers were murdered. No time, or if there is, it is not a river but the sea, vast and gray and on every side the same. Here I am neither measured against the past nor connected to the future, for past and future are interchangeable. Here, I am free.

I am beginning to understand who I really am.

So now it is time for you and I to say goodbye. You will never exist to look at these pages and laugh at your youthful follies. You were only a dream, and now is the time for me to wake up.

It's time to remember.

WILL

OCTOBER 31

In a van, headed back to Phnom Penh, courtesy of Koroshi International Inc. Unfortunately I'm out of drugs—nothing to put between me and the diaries:

> *Red lights . . . pillars of fire . . . they scuttle as he comes, the Bad Lieutenant, wreathed in smoke, his human face barely attached . . . the eyes don't work why he never blinks!*
>
> *He looks my way, must pretend to not know him but my leg burns for the sharp taste of his knife—*

I'll think I'm reading, then realize I'm actually rooting through my bag, searching for some lost shred of weed I can smoke to get it all out of my head.

June's story has no ending. It's not even clear where it stops: she's writing over the same pages again and again, like a Renaissance painter reusing old canvases. Not one picture over another, but dozens, interlocked: Maybe you like the figure you drew last week, so you just leave it, paint around it, incorporate it into the new work. Then do it again, and again—

Time itself is collapsing.

Now, awake and sober with nothing but time, I can finally trace the threads that eluded me before:

He is careless with me now. If I have let slip too many secrets, then so has he: lying naked and white, sex shriveled as a snail, veins in his arms swollen and black as bruises, while I draw my nails along his chest and fill my imagination with razorblades.

I know where he goes—I've wondered ever since that night so long ago (years, I think) when he thought no one was watching. I have photographed him, when he was too far gone to notice . . . developed them in secret in the office darkroom . . . and now I show him:

"Aren't they beautiful," I say, "portraits of you?" I'm picturing an art installation.

He screams, then threatens. . . .

Then he listens:

"I want to meet the man," I say, "your Bad Lieutenant. I have a proposition for him."

There were plots and conspiracies, but none of them made much difference: if it hadn't been this, it would have been something else.

She came here to get lost, and she did.

———————

The locks on Number Two's apartment were all made in China. Easy enough to get past, if you know the right guy. His name's Roen, and he's waiting in the hall while I check the stairs: no lights under the doors, no sound I can hear over the din outside. It's the king's birthday, and the whole damn city's out partying along the river. Everybody loves the king.

A round of firecrackers goes off down the way. The real fireworks won't start until later, and they'll go on for hours. All the activity is good for me. No one knows I'm here yet, and the longer that can go on, the better. Maybe I can get what I need from Two and get gone before I have to deal with any of the shit I've started. I could use some luck.

A nod down, and Roen goes to work. I light a cigarette.

Number Two may not know what happened to June—but he's the piece that connects all the others. No games this time: I just want him alone.

He'll be out drinking; I'll wait.

Getting dark fast, but Roen doesn't seem to mind. Voices from outside echo up the stairs; distant music. Finally he looks up at me: door's open. I hand him some bills and he counts them, nods.

"Enjoy the party," I say, and slip inside.

The apartment looks different: the dust and clutter somehow thicker. In the main room, the piles of papers are scattered, strewn everywhere. Two was looking for something, and in a hurry.

The bedroom is worse. Drawers pulled out, clothes rumpled over the bed. Wardrobe hanging open—half-empty, hangers on the floor. Jumbo suitcase in the closet, but no other bags.

On the frayed carpet by the foot of the bed: a .38 round, live.

I give the place a quick toss, check drawers and hidey-holes: no money, no drugs, no laptop, no phone charger. No sense waiting, then. Number Two is gone.

———————

Back on the river. Everything lit up for a carnival, paper lanterns on the buildings and streamers in the air. Dressed-up scum filling the cafés, prowling the street in hungry packs. Khmer couples, holding hands. Fireworks and a fug of marijuana smoke. I've given up trying to stay low: finding June means finding Two, and for that I need help. I've been scoping some of his haunts, just to make sure I'm not grabbing the wrong end of this thing. Howie hasn't seen him in days. He's not on the river. Eventually, I have no choice: call Gus.

He's drunk and genial, shouting over the noise of the crowd. "Keller? *Hijo de puta,* Keller! Where the fuck have you been? We thought you were on KR holiday!" He means it in the nicest way. But he'll be good and pissed at me when he sobers up. I talk fast.

"Nearly was. Long story, just got in—"

"Vy is fucking mental—have you seen her?"

"Later," I shout. "I'm looking for Number Two, you know where he's at?"

"Took a couple days off. Said he had a friend visiting, was going up to Siem Reap."

I've heard that one before. "Fuck Siem Reap, he split. Place is cleaned out."

"Are you fucking kidding me? I'm down another writer?"

"Don't think of it as losing a reporter. Think of it as gaining a headline." Applause in the background. "Where are you?"

"I'm by the palace. Some rock band is gonna play! Where are you?"

"Just up the street."

"I'll meet you at the FCC—"

"No, I'll see you at the house, later. I gotta think."

"Right."

I hang up and edge through the crowd, past the restaurants and their liquefied patrons—but as I reach the turnoff that goes to my house, a strange impulse hits me and I keep walking. I can hear the music now, from the stage down the street: feedback, gritty and grinding, like Lou Reed in the nineties, then bursting suddenly into chords. Before the revolution, Cambo had a scene, doing amazing psychedelic rock. The KR took out all the musicians, but some folks are bringing it back.

I wander farther down the river, until I see the stage clear. The front man is all stringy muscle, wearing low-slung jeans and a skin-tight yellow T-shirt that leaves half his abs exposed. Not Lou: Keith. He's got this old autumn-red-and-white electric guitar, and he's wrestling with it, and the chords he's making shiver through the crowd and out across the water into the dark. Along the river, everything has stopped: families standing rapt, motos pulled over, food vendors resting their knives to watch. Looking at what they've lost.

No: it's what they've managed to claw back.

June never saw this. If she had, maybe things would be different.

Headed back to the house. Three blocks from the river and it's gone quiet—the shouts and music just a hum in the background, punctuated by fireworks. No business here tonight: the park is empty, the tourist shops shut tight, plates of corrugated steel chained over the entrances.

I hear them before they come at me: a crackle of broken glass from the gutter. Turn: two of them, young. Baggy jeans and sports jerseys. Wool knit cap, aluminum baseball bat. Cambodian kids from the States, the ones who got deported after 9/11.

If these were locals, I'd be dead by now.

Most of these guys got pinched for small-time stuff, but fell into serious crime here pretty quick: only thing on their résumés.

I take a cigarette from my pocket. "Whaddaya want?"

"We come from heaven," says the one in the cap. "I guess you could say we're angels."

"Yeah, yeah. Spill."

"You took a job for our boss. Got paid 'n' everything. 'Cept the job never got done. So, we're hoping you have our boss's money. If not"—the guy with the bat steps forward—"we're here to remind you to get it. Soon."

Really? This is who he sends? I light the cigarette. "Why are you here again? I forget."

The kid with the bat takes a run at me. I step into him and lock his arm, spinning him fast and tossing him straight back at his buddy in the cap, who's fumbling around in his waistband. Aluminum clatters on gravel, and they go down in a heap.

Pick up the bat.

The first one is still trying to untangle himself when I put his lights out. The one in the cap makes another grab for his gun. I let him get it. As he tries to take the safety off, I ram the end of the bat into his nose. Now he's busy bleeding. Put my foot on his gun hand and he looks up at me: broken face and scared-rabbit eyes.

"Way I remember, that job got done. Not my fault someone decided to take a machete to the guy I'm following. But you can't blackmail the dead." I shift my weight; bones crunch under my foot. The kid screams. "I also seem to remember being owed something for the work done. Quite a bit. So why don't you tell Gabriel to start finding *my money*. Before someone sets fire to that rathole of his."

Crunch. Scream. Nod.

"And tell him to get better thugs."

———————————

I take the gun apart as I walk home, toss the pieces in the sewer drain. Gabriel's going to be a problem. He wants to get rough, I can play, but it's a headache I don't need.

In fact, my head is pounding as I unlock the garage gate. My eye aches and itches under its patch. The stairs make my ribs burn. By the time I get up three flights, everything hurts.

Finally, my room. A little dusty, but nothing new—except the two guys with guns. They're a recent addition.

"Was there a memo?" I say. "Keller's back, everybody go nuts?"

"We'd like to ask you a few questions." Black suits, sidearms poorly concealed in shoulder rigs: guess the Feds have arrived.

"You couldn't have phoned?"

"You're a hard man to find, Mr. Keller," the small, skinny one says.

"You found me in my bedroom." Silence. The big, fat one really wants to come back with something witty, but he can't—not without telling me how much he knows about where I've been and what I've been doing. So they just stand there, Laurel and Hardy, looking at their shoes.

"You want a beer?"

They blink. "No, thank you," Laurel says automatically.

Hardy glares at him. "You should take this seriously, Mr. Keller. We're working closely with Cambodian law enforcement. If you don't talk to us, we can get them involved."

I might actually laugh. Instead, I step forward, into the light: let them get a good look at what's left of my face.

"Are you trying to scare me? I'm happy to answer your questions, but I've had a long day, and I want a beer first." They don't answer, so I get one. Fridge is dead: it's warm.

"Have a seat," Laurel says.

"Where?"

He's sitting in the only chair.

Hardy looks like he might start beating up his partner any minute. *Another nice mess you've gotten me into.* "What can you tell us about Ju-on Koroshi?"

"Not a damn thing you don't already know. She's supposed to be dead, but she was here, maybe, except now she's gone missing and I haven't found her."

He looks angry: I think he was expecting denials. "What about the sister, Karasu Koroshi?"

"She's cute. I think she's single. You wanna get more specific?"

"If you're gonna make jokes—"

"Relax," Laurel steps in. "We mean, what's your relationship with her?"

"I work for her."

"Doing what?"

"I just told you I was looking for June, so take a wild stab in the dark."

Hardy decides to lose it. "Bullshit. You know something about the Koroshis' operation, and you better wise up and start giving us straight answers. Right now it's them we're interested in, but you start playing games and we may need to take a closer look at you."

"You're close enough to break into my room."

"Your landlady let us—" Laurel starts, but I run right over him: My turn to get pissed.

"Look, I'm answering your questions—never mind you guys showing up without badges or paperwork, or even telling me who you are. Now if you wanna get hostile, I'll start by asking what jurisdiction you have here, exactly?"

I half expect Hardy to go for the cuffs, but Laurel steps in again, playing good cop like he thinks he's got a talent for it. "Mr. Keller, we're liaisons for the US Drug Enforcement Administration, here to assist the local authorities. I'm Agent Klowper, this is Agent Schmidt. The Koroshis are . . . persons of interest in an ongoing investigation, and we just want to find out as much about why they're here as possible. Anything you can offer would be useful."

"Since you're here, you already know what I know. Someone answering June Koroshi's description was here, working under the alias June Saito. She had Kara Koroshi's number listed as her emergency contact. When she disappeared, Kara came out here and asked me to find her."

"You never reported her missing, to the embassy or the authorities."

"Hard to report a dead girl missing."

"About that," Laurel says. "Did Karasu say anything to you about what really happened to her sister five years ago?"

"Never. I assumed it was your buddies at the FBI, pulling her out so she could turn on the rest of the family."

I'm expecting Laurel to come back at me, but instead his eyes flick to Hardy: worried and puzzled. I don't like it at all.

"Did you ever meet the woman who called herself June Saito?"

"Once. Lots of people knew her better."

"And do you believe she really was Ju-on Koroshi?"

"She fits the description. I never met the original."

"Does Karasu believe it?"

Thinking now: that strange tone in Kara's voice when she talked about June.

"I could never hurt my sister."

"I can't say what she thinks. She's paying me to look for this girl, which certainly gives that impression."

"And have you found anything about what happened to . . . 'June Saito'?"

"If you want to know that, I'd prefer you talk to Miss Koroshi," I say—but I'm getting a nasty idea. "Though between you and me, it turns out June was involved with another reporter, an English kid named Christopher Grimsby-Roylott. Maybe romantic, maybe something else. I went to talk to him today, thinking he might know something about where she went. Seems he's also left town unexpectedly. So I wonder if you guys are in the right apartment."

They share another look.

"And Kara Koroshi had nothing to do with this?"

"Not to my knowledge. Why would she?"

"What happened to your face?"

"Motorcycle accident."

"And where have you been the past two weeks?"

"Siem Reap. Miss Koroshi was nice enough to pay for my accommodation while I recovered." Kara and I worked that story out ages ago: if they check, it'll pass. There's another long pause. I finish my beer and set the can on the floor.

Hardy's looking me up and down. "That's how you want it? Fine. But be prepared for us to get very, very interested in your business. And hope we don't find anything interesting."

"Sure you won't have a beer before you go?"

————————

When they're gone, I call Kara, telling her the same stuff I just told the cops about Number Two. Think about calling Steve as well, but it'll just go right back to the Americans. I have another warm beer, and another, till they're gone. Pick up one of my books and read a few pages, but it's not making any sense.

This town is trouble. Time to start thinking about getting out.

I'm in the middle of that when the cage door swings open.

I start looking for a weapon before I realize it's Vy. She's wearing some piece of couture that might be a shopping bag attached to a fishing net, if they were made from $1,000-a-yard silk. Street mud on her Blahniks. First thing out of her mouth:

"You never even told the police, did you? About the body?"

"Things got a little complicated—the torture, you know—"

She looks at my face and manages to be contemptuous even of that. For a moment she doesn't speak, just looks. Then: "I was thinking about that time you sneaked me out of Le Royal. Remember?"

"That was a laugh."

"You didn't actually care if I went down. You were just afraid I'd take your dealer with me, and you'd be out in the cold."

"Sounds like true love."

"Was it ever anything more?"

I don't know what she wants me to say, so I say nothing.

"You really are a monster. The funny thing is, you even act like one. But people fall for you, again and again. There's no reason for it, is there? You're exactly what you seem."

"Yes." Nothing else—she knows it all, she's always known. I'm the worst thing in the world. For a while, that was what she wanted. Now she thinks she's changed, and she wants to change me, too.

She's too icy to even slap me. She reaches into her bag and I tense, expecting a gun. She smiles, pulls out a cigarette, lights it. Stops smiling. "Two weeks. With that woman. And I thought you were dead." She takes a long drag, blows it out. "Next time, I let you die." She doesn't wait for me to respond, just turns and walks away.

Maybe she really has changed.

The grass by the palace is still a carnival—Khmers party all night— but the *barang* side is winding down as folks move on to more serious debauchery.

A few stragglers hang around the sidewalk tables at the Edge, but inside there's no one: Joe Strummer singing about death and glory to empty chairs. Channi does a kind of triple take as I walk in, and I feel something in my chest start fluttering. Decide it's the broken ribs.

"Your face—"

"Told you it would get worse." I sit down.

She hands me a beer, and the Khmer mother in her comes out. "You gone long time! Where . . . have you . . . been?"

"Working."

"You need a new job," she snaps, face stern. I smile, she smiles back. This is getting ridiculous.

"Can I have some peanuts?"

She hands me a bowl and I take one, letting the fat salt flakes sting my tongue. "See, I can chew again."

She takes a peanut from my bowl and sucks on it.

"I want to see you," I say. "Not here." She looks at me, waiting, and I pause, wondering what the hell is coming out of my mouth. What will happen next? Apparently, I keep talking. "There's a puppet show in the park tomorrow. For the king's birthday. It starts in the afternoon, before work. Will you go with me?"

She looks at me, appraising. "King birthday is very . . . important." Why do I get the idea she's been practicing? I raise an eyebrow, and she laughs. "I must celebrate my king birthday. I go with you."

"Great."

"I will wait for you without breathing," she says, in her own language.

For a while after that we don't say anything at all.

WILL

They're waiting for me in the morning.

First thing out my door, some middle-aged white guy who's been browsing the tourist shops starts moseying down the street after me. For the moment, I let him.

Head down to the river and harass the boat operators. Number Two's name gets no hits, so I cruise back to his apartment and ask the motodops on the corner about the guy with the long blond hair.

"He go yesterday," says one, broken smile and ancient Skynyrd T-shirt almost in ribbons. "He in car, late. Night." This guy is low even for a motodop—just singing for his supper? The others nod along like dashboard dolls. Leaving in a car doesn't sound like Siem Reap—you wouldn't go by road, unless you didn't want to leave a trail.

"Anyone know the driver, hear where they were headed?" That gets nothing. I pass around some bills and move on. If he's running, he's probably left the country by now.

I still need to talk to Steve—and I need to do it without my new friend along. I head back toward my apartment.

Time to see how fast Prik can drive.

———————

The restaurant is huge and empty, a converted house in the old prewar hotel district: two stories, wrought-iron balconies looking over wide, palm-lined streets. It's one of those NGO places that hires land-mine victims and elephantiasis sufferers, and the walls are covered with self-righteous pictures of kitchen staff with massive deformities, which is why no one actually eats here. That, or the ballistic quality of the dumplings.

I'm here for the privacy, not the food.

I've been waiting up top, and when I see the embassy car pull up, I come down the back stairs into the dining room. Steve is sitting facing the front door, talking on his phone. I wait for him to hang up, then sit down.

"Christ! Where'd you spring from?"

"We have a meeting."

His face gets even longer as realization comes. "You're an Australian master's student doing a paper on law enforcement cooperation?"

"Friend's girlfriend."

"Fuck." He stares at the table, lowering his voice in an empty room. "I can't be seen with you. You're a person of interest."

"Well, you haven't been seen with me yet." I let that hang a second. "So let's talk fast: What do they want?"

He shakes his head, working himself up to get angry. "I told you to stay out of it."

"All I want is the girl."

"Fuck's sake, why? The goodness of your heart?"

"Why not?" I grin.

He doesn't. "You don't have a heart."

Fine. My turn to lean in and stage-whisper. "Then don't fuck with me. What are they after?"

"Ask them, they don't share with me, I'm just a bushwhackin' cop."

"Some fucker actually said that, didn't he?"

He starts to nod, then glares again. "Don't get friendly with me, mate. You're fucking poison right now."

"Don't get caught up in the moment. Remember our long history together. Just for a start, I bet you didn't mention that you'd been having off-the-record meetings to brief Ryu Koroshi's daughter about the details of Australia's effort to fight smuggling in Cambodia."

I can almost see the steam coming out of his nostrils. His face is beet red. "You ready to go down with me?"

"I'm down already. Like you said. So it doesn't matter to me, does it?" I call over the waitress, order a beer.

Steve sulks. When the girl goes, he's calmed down enough to speak. "You got me in a spot right now, with all these fuckers breathing down my neck. Whole country's falling apart, and the Americans are sending in more black-suit, three-letter wank jobs every day to try and get a piece of it. But they won't be here forever." Real malice in his voice now. "I do this, you and I are through. And once this shit is over, I will bust your ass for everything I can, until I bust it off of this continent or into a Burmese prison."

"Good to know I can count on you, Officer. Now tell me what they want."

He looks enviously at my drink. "The Americans are clueless, and they don't give a crap about Cambodia: they just want Koroshi. There's something big happening back in the States, I don't know, fucking geologic plates realigning, and he's right in the middle of it. The girls are a mystery, no one knows why they're out here. Best guess, it's some kind of feint in a bigger game."

I shake my head. "They got it backwards. Koroshi's an oppor-tunist. He wouldn't be here at all except for June. Some West Coast triad boss had big plans for this place, June found out and tried to get involved. Koroshi came looking for her and saw the chance to screw over a rival." I smile. "See, there's something for your troubles. Use that knowledge carefully."

"I'll keep it in mind." I don't much like how he says it. "But there's more to this. Fucking *French Connection* shit. All those three-letters get their hands in things, they don't like it when the situations change. Koroshi's playing tough chess, and it could bring him down. And everyone who's close to him—which right now is a list that starts and ends with you."

Hah—wheels within wheels. "Koroshi can take care of himself. I told you, all I care about is finding the girl before they do." He's silent. "I tipped those DEA assholes to June's boyfriend from the paper. Just let me know if they find him. It's the fastest way to get me out of your hair."

"I could give you some advice, not that you'd take it." He sounds as tired as he is angry. "Girl, drugs, whatever. If you're half as smart as you think you are, you'll get out. Now, before they find some rea-son to stop you." He pauses. "It's Kabul, Will. Kabul all over again." I light a cigarette. "Oh, what does it matter? I'm talking to a dead man." He gets up and stalks out to his car.

I finish my beer in silence.

———

A drier kind of heat marks the beginning of November. The festi-val grounds are crowded—families with eager children buying cotton candy, watching the tumblers and pointing and shouting at the boats on the river, eating roast chickens from the hot carts. Young men in pompadoured gangs, shirts like peacock feathers. Gangsters parking their tricked-out bikes to laugh at the comedians or hear the gamelan players. Whores looking for a mark; pickpockets and beggars and hustlers with their stuff strung up on bamboo poles; hopeful young lovers dreaming this day will change their fortunes.

Nothing like a holiday.

Channi takes my hand in hers as we walk. She's eating a big blue ball of polyester something, and chattering in Khmer about some book she read. Like most Cambodian stories, it's a romance, all separated lovers swooning over each other from afar—along with monsters, bloody duels, and man-eating demons. Hallmark by way of Hieronymus Bosch. I can only understand about a quarter of what's going on.

"Stop, stop," I say, at last. "I don't know all these words."

"But you speak so well!" She squeezes my fingers.

"Only about some things." Drugs and deal making, violence, sex: my vocabulary is specialized.

"I can try to tell it in English, but it won't make any sense."

"No, go on. I like listening."

"I was just at the part where the uncle takes the girl to the temple, not knowing that her lover has become a monk and is making his pilgrimage at the same time. So they can be reunited, as long as the abbot can put the river spirit at peace." I'm watching the sun on the water, wondering if it's always looked like that. Did I just never notice? "Listen." She smacks my arm, carefully avoiding everything already broken. "You might learn something."

They've put up a big tent for the puppet show—they need the shade. It'll go on all night and well into the morning, but Channi has to be at the bar at five, so we'll only catch the first hour or so. That's still a lot of puppets. Inside, the crowd is sparse. It's hot. Channi's brought a blanket and a huge basket of food she made with her mother—"I gave good advice"—and she spreads it out on the ground and we sit down. There's two Cokes, carefully packed in plastic bags of ice and old pieces of packing-box foam, and I sip the cold drink gratefully as she sets all sorts of things I can't identify on the blanket.

I try to ask her about her family as she does it, but she shushes me ferociously, pointing at the show.

The puppets are elaborate contraptions of stiff leather and paint, operated with narrow sticks. Despite the bright colors, they're only seen as silhouettes cast on a white screen.

"You know story?" Channi whispers to me, in English.

"No idea."

"Is old story, like Angkor." She points at the big fellow with a head full of feathers. "He is prince and love beautiful girl. But demon steal her and take her to island."

"Is that the demon?"

"No, demon before!" I should have known. "That monkey god, prince friend. Prince is also god. So he and monkey go to island, to rescue girl from demon."

The tent seems to grow darker: I do know this story. On the screen, the shadow prince swings his arms, dancing some dance to get the monkey king to come with him. What lies does he tell, what screws does he turn, to drag his friend along on this suicide mission?

"What's wrong?" Channi asks, in her own language. Doesn't give me a chance to answer, just puts her hands to my face. "You live in a shadow. Will you tell me the story, someday?"

"I'm a lousy storyteller," I say, in English.

She doesn't laugh or look away. "But you will tell me." It's not a question.

"Yes. But not today."

———————

Channi leaves me in the field where the food vendors have set up, and we say good-bye wreathed in sweet-smelling meat smoke. Khmers don't do public displays of affection, so I'm surprised again when she stands on her toes and kisses my cheek before walking away. As the light hits her, I see her slim figure silhouetted through her dress. My face burns.

I don't know what's happening to me. I feel like someone dropped two hits of acid in my Coke. My head buzzes; the colored lights shift and burn, the paper lanterns dance in the red sun. I wander through the crowd, letting it all wash over me, the smoke and the incense and the far-off thrum of drum and gamelan.

But as the sun gets low, the feeling is replaced by another, a pins-and-needles sensation that starts in my thumbs and spreads quickly upward. Something's wrong. I buy a roast chicken and haggle with the seller, eyes roving. Scan the crowd.

To my left, a face: Khmer, young, nondescript clothes. Watching me close. Another to my right. I don't know them, but the list of people who want a piece of me is as long as my arm. The crowd is pressing in on all sides. Laughing faces, swaying lights. I try to push through. A little girl in a purple tank top swings her cotton candy like a mace. A string of firecrackers pops. Shove against the bodies. Cheers and explosions.

Corner of my eye: that hard face, coming closer. He knows he's been made, but he's not backing off. He's not here to watch—or to talk.

I edge deeper into the press, blood pumping. The crowd surges and I think of stampedes, people crushed on their feet in the O-Bon celebrations, angry mobs beating thieves to death. I can't risk a fight, not here. I'm moving as fast as I can, waiting for the bright feeling of a knife in the back. On the river, Roman candles split the air as the boats go by. A burst of static from an amplifier. I see something glint through the crowd, a flash of blond hair. I shove my way toward it but there are too many people—they're gathered in front of a giant screen showing one of the king's movies from the sixties.

As I turn, one of those shadows is right behind me, just feet away, glaring over the heads of a family pushing between us: a little girl up on her father's shoulders, boy laughing, waving a toy gun.

I can't get lost in this crowd—too tall. I wedge my way around two young men of Senn's crew. They give me little waves and I grin back at them as I push on. Make a break around the side of the screen. The FCC isn't far now; it'll be packed with foreigners. Cover. I dash past the food sellers. Don't look back. Don't think how close they are. Footsteps, coming hard. I tear around the front and dive into the ornate colonial lobby.

The place is heaving, tables crowded with drunk journalists. As I reach the midpoint of the stairs, I glance down, see my shadows pushing in the front door, looking for me. Hurry up and into the hall, pass the bathrooms and the storage closet. I put my shoulder to the door at the end, and it busts open onto a first-floor balcony. Below, empty green fields, the museum in the distance. I take a deep breath and go over the railing, clinging to the rotting wood, white paint peeling away under my fingers. Hang low, praying the grass is soft.

Falling takes forever. The balcony drifts away like the stern of a ship pulling out of harbor, and for a moment I think I see someone with blond hair framed in the hallway door.

Pain shoots up my leg and I'm rolling through the grass. I ignore the sting, running as fast as I can across the park to the corner by my house. Prik is still there, lounging on his bike, my first luck in days.

I almost scream as I run up, "Norodom Street, now! Don't be followed." He guns the starter, and then we're racing like skiers, dodging motos and sliding between fruit carts, and I'm looking over my shoulder at nothing but dust.

Channi, I think, *they saw me with Channi.*

———————

I can't go back, I'll lead them right to her. I huddle in the bathroom stall at the InterCon, whispering every prayer I once knew, as Gus's phone rings on and on. *Pick up, goddamn you, pick up.*

Seven rings. Eight. It cuts off. Dial again.

Two. She's got to be safe in a bar full of expats.

Three. They could have got to her already.

Four.

Five. Click.

"The fuck, man, where are you?"

"Gus, listen, I need a favor."

"Don't you always? What are you doing, I've got guys in suits running all over me! Did I mention—" He breaks off. Fuck, fuck.

"Listen, please, it's not me, just help—I need help. There's a girl, works at the new bar across from the FCC. Name's Chantrea, Channi, Channi! Find her. Watch out for her, call—call some of the guys you train with, get them in, but watch her. Keep her safe."

"All right," he says, cautious. "I'll make sure they meet deadline." They're listening. "You okay?"

"Just do this one thing for me. For God's sake, keep her safe." I think I'm crying—

I can't do this again. I won't survive.

I have no choice.

"I'll make sure," Gus says. "You look after yourself."

I hang up, breathing hard, bang my head slowly against the side of the stall. Look down at the message that's appeared on my phone.

Unknown number.

CHRISTOPHER G-R STAYING AT GRAND ANGKOR HOTEL, SIEM REAP, STREET 17. ONE NIGHT.

Good to have friends in high places.

W I L L

November 1–2

Spray hits my face as the fast boat races over the water.

I barely remember getting here. Caught the last boat on a Saturday, and the cabin was half-empty. An old couple leaning back and trying to sleep. Crew of strung-out backpackers. Two Asian men in suits. Everyone looking at their books, at the floor, at the fancy food in molded-plastic trays. Still, I couldn't take the eyes, so I came up to the deck.

Every few minutes I take the phone out and look at the messages, just to make sure they're still there.

SAFE: HAVE EYES ON. G. Every time I read it, my breath stops all over again. But my pulse is pounding, on and on and on: it hasn't slowed in hours.

CHRISTOPHER G-R STAYING AT GRAND ANGKOR HOTEL.

When I put the phone away, the drumming eats at me until I have to look again. I don't know how this happened—how it got its fingers in me so fast. I should go back. Find Channi, convince her to come with me, get the hell out of this country before it's too late for both of us—

I can't—and it is like being torn apart.

Gus saw this coming. *"Try not to let it get to you."* I didn't listen.

The moonlit river ripples, bound by marsh trees dripping moss. Beyond, pools and half-flooded fields: water country. I look for temples shaped like demons.

And in their shadows, June.

———————

The Grand Angkor Hotel is a ramshackle guesthouse on a back street. Old, wood-frame, two stories. A tiny garden out front, fenced in by partitions splashed with green Heineken ads: no one there. Little whitewashed houses to the left, tall grass to the right.

Past eleven when I arrive. I make the moto drop me at the head of the street and walk down. New backpack over my shoulder, stuffed with beer cans for weight. I don't have much of a plan. No one makes a break for it as I come up the drive and into the lobby, so I get a room.

I don't go to it.

Up the stairs; a landing, rough brown boards. A military-style cot lying in the corner. Roach corpses. Real wooden doors, painted red long ago and trying to forget it. I go to number four and knock, hard. No answer. No sound inside. He's out getting drunk.

I walk to the end of the hall, where a dust-caked window looks down on the gravel drive. Now I wait.

———————

He comes up the path at half past two, face flushed with booze. He's cut his hair down to a blond stubble. I move fast, and quiet.

His steps are heavy on the stairs, and he walks right past me: on the cot, shoes off, shirt over me like a blanket. Just another backpacker, sleeping cheap. Then he's at his door, key in the lock. I hear it click and I'm up, behind him, arm around his throat and shoving him into the dark room.

Gasps. Not loud. I realize I've got him dangling, face going crimson. Loosen my grip. "I just want to talk, but I promise if you scream, the conversation will be unpleasant."

A weak nod.

Less than two days back, and it's come to this.

I squeeze until his head will be spinning, then let him drop. Take the key from the lock, ease the door shut. Turn back and he's got a hand in his bag. I drop my knee into his throat, catch the gun as he fumbles it up.

"Here I thought we were friends," I say, and take the gun. Then I hit him with it.

———————

I tie Number Two up with his back against the bed. Rope his hands together with one end of the sheet, his ankles with the other. Not the kind of knots that hold, but he won't make any sudden moves. Stuff a shirt in his mouth. Done, I step out into the hall for my bag. I could use a beer. Then I take a look at the gun. It's a Chinese piece of shit, just like his locks. Bought cheap from some moto—the gangsters carry better kit. I check that it's loaded.

Two stirs, starting to come around. I hold the gun up for him to see.

"You know you couldn't have shot me with this, right?" His eyes are big as headlights: the last few weeks haven't made me any prettier. "You gotta chamber a round first." I do it. "Now you can shoot somebody."

Once I'm sure he's aware of the situation, I set the gun next to me, in reach. "Wanna beer?"

He nods. I take the gag out, slowly, then hold up the can and give him a long swig. He sighs.

I sit back down on the floor. "Sorry about this." He stares. "I guess we're friends, or what passes for it out here, but I've had a hard few weeks. I got broken ribs and broken teeth and I goddamn near lost my eye. I've seen a lotta people killed, and I'm willing to add to the number. But I'm still a hell of a lot nicer than the guys who come next. So talk to me." He nods. "Let's start with why you're carrying that." Point at the gun.

"I was afraid he'd come after me."

"Who?"

Two hesitates. "He'll kill me."

"I can break a knee or something, you want me to prove I'm serious. I can do it quiet." Pick up the shirt again.

"Samnang, his name—is Pisit Samnang! He's, uh . . . he—"

"I know who he is."

The worst cop in Cambo. The one I was afraid to go to, to ask about June's police connections—

You think you own him, then you realize he owns you.

—but he was the connection all along. He's the guy Barry saw arguing with June—the same one she spied on in Number Two's apartment. Her Bad Lieutenant.

"How did you meet him?"

"In the Heart, a few weeks after I came. He . . ." Two chokes up.

I let him stare at the floor and sniffle for a minute before I say anything. "I know what he did. He scored for you. Gave you your walk on the wild side—kept it nice and easy. Let you get in deeper and deeper." Two nods. Wheels clicking in my head. "When did things start to go bad? After Sihanoukville?" Now he looks at me, mouth open. "I know all sorts of things. You just worry about the answers."

"Yeah. Sihanoukville. Things had been weird since that shipment got stopped in Sydney. Sam's supply was in trouble, there was a crack-down and he had no access." In Two's face, shame and fear struggle with a twisted kind of pride. "He thought he was getting cut out of something, so he wanted me to chat up people for him. I have contacts from work, I could find out if they knew anything, without anyone getting suspicious."

"That why you got June involved—to help you get information? Or did you just figure she was an easy lay—"

"No! Fuck, mate, it wasn't like that!"

"She was vulnerable, so you—"

"I was lonely!"

"You, with your dozen girlfriends?"

"Christ, it was a blag, all right? You buy a girl a drink, bit of chat, drive her home, and everyone thinks you've pulled. But it never happens, everyone's too, I dunno, fuckin' scared. This place, right? You don't get close to anyone. Then June . . . I'm not proud, okay? The first few times, I was fucking legless. But . . . in Sihanoukville, it was like Shakespeare or something: we took the piss, but we talked, too. Really talked about stuff, right, not just who's shooting at who? She liked my writing, she cared about the work. It felt good. I didn't realize . . ."

He's trailed off, lost in his thoughts.

"Realize what?"

He snaps back to reality, looking puzzled. Then he laughs—a bitter cackle that sets my teeth on edge. "All that stuff you know . . . but you still don't get it."

"Tell me. Be convincing."

He pauses, gathering himself. "For a while, I thought me and June were really something. . . . Then she started asking questions. Where did I get my stuff, what did I know about drug dealers. I said, 'Bugger all,' obviously. But she knew. She knew about Sam, wanted to meet him. I was meant to set it up, or she'd tell Gus that Sam was dealing to me, and then I'm fucked, back in bloody King's Cross eating shit."

"So what did you do?"

"I told Sam. He went fucking mental on me at first, but June said she knew who was cutting off the heroin, and he couldn't resist." Another pause. I wait it out. "You know the fucked-up thing? Even after all that, I still thought, 'Oh, she's just a kid.' I thought I could handle her. But once she got with Sam . . . she had big ideas. They were gonna move in on this new outfit, get a piece of the action. Sam just wanted to know what was going on, but June wouldn't give him details. I think she started sleeping with him, but I didn't care by then, I just wanted to get away from her. But Sam said I'd brought her in, so I had to keep her close. Keep an eye on her, it was for her own good. . . ." He's running out of breath again.

Cut to the chase: "Why was she doing all this?"

That angry laugh again. "I have no idea."

I put a boot in his ribs, just for emphasis. "You can do better than that. Was it her family?"

"I dunno! Whatever her shit was, I don't—"

Reach out and grab a finger, bend it back. "There has to be a reason."

"I don't know!"

Clap a hand over his mouth: "Softly." He nods. I take my hand away.

"Open my shirt," he says.

"You gonna try something stupid?"

He groans, shakes his head. I slide the gun across the room, well out of reach. Then I undo his top buttons. He smells of whiskey, cologne, and sweat. On his chest: four long, puckered trails of pink skin.

"June gave me those. Her idea of fun. She was always different in bed. Wild, like . . . like a whole other person. At first it was a kick, right? Intense. But then it got . . . just fucking mental. She kept . . . she wanted me to . . ." He can't finish; tries again. "We'd meet up in hotels, different ones. One night, she shows up with some Thai girl who's smacked out of her head, and June wants me to cut her. I fucked off, so the next day she sent the same girl to me at the office. I had to try an' blag it with Gus, and June's just sitting there, watching, not even fussed." He looks up at me, and in his eyes there's nothing at all. "It was the kind of thing you would do." His gaze moves to the beer. "Can I have another sip of that?" It's barely touched. Pour a long swallow down his throat. "June was brilliant at keeping her cool in public, but when she was tripping, things got bad—"

"I thought she didn't do drugs."

"You have no idea. She did more drugs than me, more than you. Smack if she had it, which wasn't much, or a bloody medicine cabinet of other shit. Special K, lots of it, then snorting yaba to go to work and play schoolgirl. She had everyone fooled. But when we were alone, she'd get paranoid and take it out on me."

I have nothing left to say. And he just keeps talking.

"June didn't care about the money. Not at the end . . . maybe never. She didn't care about the story. Or me, or Sam, or even the drugs. June didn't have reasons. She just wanted to see what was in the dark."

I want to say he's wrong, he's lying. I want to hit him again.

"So what happened to her?"

"Sam had enough. He said she was out of control, but he still wanted what she knew. So he came up with this crazy plan, they were going to steal this shipment themselves and take it to Sam's contacts in the army. He never meant to go through with it, it was just to get her to tell him what was up. He figured June would go for it, it was her kind of crazy—but she held out, said the army was too small, they needed the guys behind the army. So Sam gets this other idea, he has some contact coming in from Hong Kong, some big gangster. And he has me talk the guy up to June like he's the power behind the heroin trade. Then he tells June they'll take the stuff to him. It was bullshit, but she went for it. She made up the Siem Reap trip as cover, and they went out to Koh Kong."

"And what was Sam planning to do once he had his information?"

Two sees the danger in my eyes, starts to panic. "Fuck, mate, not that! He said he was gonna put the fear into her—stick her in jail a few days, tell her he was gonna sell her to slavers, whatever it took, then put her on a plane back to LA—"

"Was there a farm, where she could run and play with the other animals?" I realize I'm furious. It's crept up on me as Two talked, and now I feel blood in my eyes. I want to hurt someone. "Sam was never gonna send her home." I say it hard, so he knows how dumb he is. "He got her to show him what she knew, and then he had a nice, shallow grave picked out for her in the swamps. I found it." Two's face crumples. Lie: "I dug up her bones."

"Jesus," he says. "Jesus—"

It takes him a few minutes to get a grip on himself. When he's done sobbing, I go on. "Did you see Sam, after it was done?"

"No. I got a couple texts from him, that it was sorted an' I should lie low. An e-mail—I thought it was from June—saying she'd gone, wasn't coming back. I didn't write to her. I didn't think . . . I thought she was home, and Sam was off trying to use whatever info she'd given him. I thought they'd had enough of me."

My anger has evaporated; now I just feel sick. "If Sam didn't say anything, why did you run?"

"You. I thought that night at the Heart was fucked: I never black out. But I wasn't sure. Then you vanished. Vy was coming round, I heard her having a go at Gus about you and figured you were looking for June. Then these guys start showing up at the office. Cambodian cops, and Americans, guys like, like they think they're in *The Matrix*. Told us you were coming back, and they wanted us to get in touch when you did. I didn't know what you'd say, I knew they'd make me talk, or you would, and then Sam . . ." He can't finish.

Guess I know what I need to know. Two is looking at me again—the same look he gave me back at his place, a million years ago. He wants me to make it go away: to say I've done worse, that it'll all be okay.

I have. It won't.

I don't want to watch anymore. "Why didn't you get the fuck out? Fly home?"

He looks at me like it's a stupid question. "I was going to, but . . . I just . . . I . . ." He breathes deep, trying to summon the words. "I had a life here, man. I had a job, finally. I had mates, I was getting promoted, making contacts with the agencies. I thought, after a year or so, move on to Bangkok or Saigon. For about ten minutes I thought I had a girlfriend. I couldn't just . . . walk away."

"You can now." My voice sounds weak and insincere, even to me. Glance over at the gun in the corner. "When I'm gone, take that and run. Those knots will only hold a minute. Go to another hotel, hide in the fucking tall grass, whatever. Go home."

He stares at me, face blotchy and tear streaked, eyes red and disbelieving.

I stand up.

"I'm sorry," he sniffles. "I didn't mean to hurt anybody. I didn't mean—"

I shut the door gently.

As I step onto the main road, I see a figure in the shadows. Look for an exit, but there's another behind me. Not Cambodian—Japanese.

Friends in high places.

The first moves into the light: Keihatsu. He looks up at the hotel, then at me. I nod and stand there, buying as much time as I can. *Get out,* I think, *run.*

The little interrogator raises his eyebrows: *Is there something I should know?*

I smile, and walk slowly away.

I walk for a long time. In the distance, fireworks; gunshots.

I guess I could pretend Two made it, but I'm not in the mood.

WILL

Night slides past, cold on my face and stinging. Dawn coming soon.

I walked into the center of town until I found some sleeping motos. Gave the last of my cash to a guy with a big two-seater, to take me back by road. I thought the boat docks might be watched.

I don't even know if anyone's after me—I just know everything's burned.

Every part of my body is sore. My ass aches from banging against the seat, my ears ring along with the gas bottles in the saddlebags. I drift in and out of a kind of sleep, June dancing in my head. June the junkie, June the grifter. June who needed something so bad, it drove her off the edge of the world.

Her story should have ended in that swamp—but it didn't. Sam dug her a grave, all right, but he was the one who ended up in it. It's the only thing I can make into sense: If Sam was still around, he'd have come after me, or Kara would have turned him up.

June must have seen it coming. She knew she was being measured for a coffin—but she went anyway. All the way out to Koh Kong, and then—

What? Maybe she did it herself. She had Barry's gun and wild audacity on her side. Even Sam underestimated her. But more likely she had help: She waited until this Hong Kong gangster was in the picture. She wanted an exit, and he was it. No more use for Sam, then.

"She just wanted to see what was in the dark."

If I want to go after her, all I need is a name.

If.

It's pretty likely June doesn't want to come back.

"If you go hunting her, be careful—"

If I were smart, I'd let her go. Let her join my company of ghosts: one more face waiting for me when the lights go out. One more name I can't think.

I already know I won't do it. Not this time. June chose to disappear—so it's still possible she can choose to come back.

I'm starting to understand why I'm following her.

———

It's mid-morning by the time I slide into the old hangar on the lake. We used to fight here, me and Gus. Long, long ago. Up before dawn to grapple barefoot kids with arms like steel: straight out of the trees, hard and fast and hoping for a few minutes in the ring with the champ. A few minutes like as not to kill or cripple them—but it was what they wanted, and they fought for it like Trojans. I see it like it was then, and rub my dust-choked eyes.

A voice. "You should have stayed with us. Or did you get tired of having ninety-pound village boys kick the shit out of you?"

"I never get tired of having the shit kicked out of me."

Gus stands in the shadows, arms crossed. "I see. What kept you?"

"I came the long way."

"I think you're safe, for now." He pulls a pack from his pocket, lights one, and glares at me for watching him. "The suits have got quite a talent for causing trouble. They're taking runs at everyone, trying to bully us into saying you did . . . well, anything, really."

"If they're trying that hard, they got nothing."

He takes another drag, nodding. "That's what I thought. The one I'd worry about is Number Two, but they can't find him."

"I think you're gonna need a new crime writer."

He sighs. "They haven't asked, so I don't think they know you were out of town."

"Good. Then I've got a bit of time. What about the Khmers?"

"Don't know who they are. No sign of anyone after your girl, though." Another drag. "I'm impressed you're still alive."

"Statistics. Everybody spends more time alive than dead, till one day it's the other way round."

He gives me a strange look. "What the hell is going on, Will?"

"It's nothing you'd believe."

He snorts. "I'll believe a lot of things."

"Not this. Only two things matter, anyway. I know how to find her."

"And?"

"The stuff June was mixed up in, it started long before Cambodia. You couldn't have done anything. It's not your fault."

"What makes you think I care?" He says it so badly, I almost smile.

"You still hope you're doing the right thing."

"*Dios mío,* doesn't everyone?"

"No." I meet his eyes.

He holds them a moment before looking away. "What happened up there?"

I say nothing.

"All right, fine. What's your plan?"

Goddamn Gus: he's still with me. "I go find her. Then I'm out. Kara promised me fifty grand if I bring June back alive. That's enough to get me well out of here."

"Where'll you go?"

"Does it matter?"

He looks at me for a long time. "I suppose not. What about your girl, Channi?"

"I don't know." I don't know. "I gotta see her."

"Tell you what—you like the Green Dragon. Meet her there at three. I'll get you a room."

"Gus . . . Thanks."

"*No pasa nada.*" He walks away.

———————

Gabriel's apartment is a dump, but locked up tight. Cinder-block walls, security gates, bars on the windows. Unless you've got a wreck- ing ball, the only way in is through the front door.

So I knock. "I've come to settle up."

"Show me the money."

"Fine, you can come get it." I turn to go.

The inner door opens, and Gabriel squints out through the bars. In daylight, you see every pock and scar on his cratered face. The hand cannon he's pointing at me looks like it fires tennis balls. "Hand it over."

"No. We're gonna sit down and deal like civilized people." I'm hoping he won't just shoot me. It's a pain in the ass to kill people on your own doorstep, no matter how many cops owe you favors. "Any- way, I'm dying for a joint."

That gets a laugh. "There's the Will I know. Come in—slow. And keep, uh, hands where I can see 'em." I do as instructed and he opens the gate, backing slowly into the filthy room. "What's in the bag?"

"Beer." I show him. "Want one?"

He shakes his head, shuts the gate, then the door. The gun never leaves me.

I crack a beer. It's still warm. "About that joint."

He laughs again, points at a table. "You roll." He watches me do it with moist eyes and greedy, twitching fingers. "Will, Will, Will," he coos. "You've been busy, at least if the shit I'm hearing is to be believed—which, well, my sources are all fuckheads, if I believed half what they tell me I'd'a just shot you, but nonetheless your name keeps coming up—"

"I deny everything."

"Even putting my boys in the hospital?"

"Okay, I did that. Consider it the hidden cost of using cheap muscle."

"I shoulda known better." He sighs. "But these days you gotta be careful who you keep close. Loyal's better than smart, if you know what I mean. The whole damn country's like something crawled out of a Cronenberg movie, even the hospitals don't have drugs unless you're sick—what kind of a fuckin' world is that?—and anyhow—"

I finish rolling the joint and light it, and the room gets fuzzy. Pull the memory card from my bag and pass it to him, with the drugs.

"A token. Here's what you paid for. Sorry it's not as useful as you wanted, but the job is done."

His face stays hard as he tokes. "Well, a gesture, okay, sure, but thing is, it's timing, see, all timing: Had I had this weeks ago, I could have made use of the intelligence on it—"

"And ended up like Charlie: in fucking pieces. This is out of our league, trust me."

"I don't, actually." He passes the joint back, looking me up and down. "And a man has to have policies. Y'know, you can't just—fuck, these kids do anything they goddamn like, you talk about standards, they can't fucking spell the word—which is why you beat the shit out of them and now we're here, so, policy"—he hefts the gun—"I can't go paying for late work."

"Put that down," I snap. "We can reach an agreement."

He doesn't put the gun down, but it wavers a bit.

"I'll pass up the money I'm owed because there's something I want more. Information. I want to know everything there is to know about Pisit Samnang. Associates, hideouts—who he's been seeing. I know he's in your orbit."

His eyes narrow. "It doesn't sound like I get much out of this deal."

"Gabriel," I say, echoing his croon. "Gabriel, Gabriel: you're not seeing the big picture. I have. Everything you wanted to know in the first place—just ask. All you have to do is tell me about Sam. And you don't have to worry about him coming back at you, either."

Now he's interested. "Dead? Your work?"

"No more freebies." His eyes flicker. "You get information, so do I. Everyone wins. Like old times." I hold out the joint.

"No deal." He reaches for it. "Times have changed. And I'm the one with the gun."

So I take the gun away from him.

He groans, cradling his arm. The roach smolders on the dirty carpet.

"Probably not broken," I say, as I crack the cylinder. He groans again. "You know, I hate guns. I hate having them pointed at me. Hate pointing them." I'm taking the bullets out one by one, tossing them into the piles of garbage that hold up the walls of heaven.

"Not everybody can kill people with their bare hands."

"I don't kill people," I say.

"Lots of 'em die when you're around."

I finish and look at him. "And I'll be happy to break every bone in your body and leave you lying here." Let that sink in. His eyes burning: fever and fury. "You should have taken my deal."

"You think you can play everything your way," he snarls. "It doesn't work like that. You get me my money or you spend a long time looking over your shoulder, that's how it goes, way of the fucking world—"

"We'll see." I cross the room to the drawer where he keeps his gear: it's well stocked. The red feeling is on me, and my eyes linger on the little white bags. Just one hit—

I start cooking up. Gabriel's eyes brighten, then he looks scared.

"How much should I use?" I ask. "Been a while. Hate to get the dose wrong."

"What do you wanna know?"

"Just one thing, really. Sam had a contact come into town, end of September. Some Hong Kong big shot. I know you keep tabs on the players. I want a name."

"Look, Sam sells everything to everybody, okay? I mean, he connects every dot, and, yeah, true, he's in deep with the Hong Kong crew, but there's a billion of those little fuckers—"

Stalling. I kneel next to him. "Think I can find a vein in your eye?"

"Fuck, fuck, man—you are one sick son of a—all right, look—there's—there was one big shot here, about a month ago, yeah, Chun Song, so, maybe, who knows, he could be your guy—"

"Who is he?"

"He's definitely a big spender, mostly in the sex business. He runs half of Wan Chai, or that's what they say, anyway. Mostly he comes here for girls, the really young ones, you know—and what I hear we're not talking vanilla, that's for sure. I know one guy had a story 'bout how he went to one of Song's places, fucked this girl, cut her up and—"

"I get the picture. How do I find him?"

An ugly light fills the angel's eyes. "Easy. Everyone in Hong Kong knows where he is. Why don't you go looking?" He cackles. "He'll do my work for me."

"Then it's a happy ending for everyone. Now shoot." Hold out the needle and the hose. "It'll ease the pain. And I don't want your scum following me." He smiles again as he takes the gear, tying his arm with the ease of long practice. Looks at me as he finds the vein. Those blasted teeth—blood in the dropper.

"See you round." He grins. "Just look over your shoulder."

A new set of clothes, a hasty shower in a cheap hotel, a string of moto rides I barely remember. I keep seeing Gabriel's face: going slack as he took the shot, eyes rolling up, snot running from his nose. He has the tolerance of a goddamn gorilla, so I put in a lot. Maybe too much. I didn't check, just grabbed the cash from his kitchen—must be ten, fifteen thousand US, neat bundles stashed in a pot in a huge pile of decaying dishes—and split.

Now I'm at the lake again, lost in its maze. The Green Dragon is hidden in the depths and I don't know how I get there, but I walk into the room and there she is, looking out at the water with the sun on her hair.

Channi.

Her feet are bare, shoes next to her chair. Away from her bar she doesn't quite know how to hold herself. She has no map, no good reason for being here: a good girl wouldn't be here at all.

Two mugs on the table, dripping frost. One beer, one Coke. No sign of Gus or Mama T. Channi turns to watch me as I cross the room.

"I have a story for you," I say. She takes my hand, sits me down. I've planned this, but now I don't know where to start. I want to tell her everything. Kabul, Battambang . . . June. There are no words. I want to say something to comfort her, but I've turned to stone.

"Tell me later." She puts a hand to my cheek. Sad eyes. We sit like that for a long time. Maybe she says some stuff. Maybe I do, too. I'm not sure. Clouds fill my head.

"I have to finish something," I tell her. "I have to go away."

She looks up and she's smiling, her face still colored with hope—but her eyes are shining. "I wait for you."

"I want you to come with me."

"Why I don't wait for you here?"

"Channi. I'm going to—to help someone. The girl I told you about. But the things I've done—I can't—" No, not that way. "Come with me."

She takes her hand away, tears shining on her face. They only make her more beautiful. She speaks her own language because it's all she can remember. "Your friend told me you would go. I didn't believe him."

"I'm not leaving you. Come."

She reaches up and I think she's going to hit me, but she just holds on to my face, so I have to look in her eyes. "This is my home."

"Channi—" I try to gather her in my arms, but she twists away, angry. The chair clatters on the deck. She stamps a foot on the boards. "Channi, if I stay, we will never be safe. The people who will come after me—" I can't go on, not against the look on her face. Have to try. "They might—they could try to hurt you. You need to leave. I'm sorry, I didn't mean it to happen, but you're not safe—"

"Safe?" Her voice is hard in a way I've never heard. "Safe? I've never been safe. I've been *here*. I was born in a Khmer Rouge camp. I grew up in the war. Now we have peace, and someone dies every day. But it is always my home." She's screaming at me now, and there's something feral about her, something hurt and ferocious: "I know it's not real to you, I know. It's all a dream, Cambodia's a dream, and you'll go away and you'll wake up. But it's real to me." Sobbing now, and gasping through the sobs—I try to go to her, she steps back, away.

And I am torn apart. I can't move. She picks up her shoes.

"I'm not a dream. I am real. So go, if you want. You get your girl and get your money and go."

"Wait—" Reach for her—

She hits my hand away with the shoes. I grab her then, grab her and kiss her, hard, for all the times I won't get to kiss her. For a second she's with me, and strange flowers grow from the bleached wood of the deck and bloom around us. Then she's pulling away again, running through the room, leaving me alone with the sun and the lake and the two full glasses, and the water runs down their frosty sides and pools on the table.

———————

I meet Gus at a supermarket on Sihanouk Street. He hands me my passport and the journals, I give him a chunk of the cash I took from Gabriel. "For expenses. Look after her if you can."

"Look after yourself."

No more words. Heading for the airport, hoping the Americans haven't found a reason to stop me leaving. No plan. Nothing in my bag but a wad of cash and a history of despair in bad handwriting. The thought that it's done, that the choice has been made, even if I didn't make it, seems to banish June from my head, leaving my mind clearer than it's been in days. A part of me is almost hopeful: I might actually do what I set out to do.

But without June, there's only Channi, and the pain of leaving her fills all the empty spaces. I hear her voice in my head, and I try to go back to the beer or the puppet show or the first night in the Edge, but I'm stuck on those last few seconds:

"I'm real," she screams, over and over.

It isn't even love, just what might have been.

Everything still hurts.

The bike crawls through snarled traffic. This isn't a part of town I visit much: an ugly, commercial street, lined with cheap-built modern things, all glass and plastic. Garish ads for cell phone companies, supermarket signs, boutiques and camera shops and fast food. It could be anywhere.

People in fake Prada and Hilfiger rushing to appointments, heads down, chatting on phones and getting their hair cut. No one is hustling except the sandwich sellers, no one calling out about girls and guns and drugs. No one to call out to. The motodops wait on corners: no big smiles, no childish bowing and cajoling. Just cabbies looking for a fare. Just people, living—hard lives, perhaps, on the edge of an abyss, but living nonetheless.

June never saw this, either. Cambo only existed for her through the lens of those places we created: a world built to reflect us back at ourselves, a world of poverty and deference. She thought she was lost, that she had fallen outside of history—guess that was what she wanted. But history goes on. Even here, where so many have tried so hard to end it.

Kids lounge on the hoods of parked cars, smoking, and don't glance up as I ride past. As the bike turns onto the airport road, I say good-bye.

WILL

Hong Kong: neon city. It's too much. Needles of light piercing the sky—even out the window of the plane I can barely look at it.

Then the airport, a spiderweb of steel and glass. Thronged with people, it still seems empty. Everyone is wearing masks. Voices mumble low and I can never tell where they come from. Sounds muted, suitcases pushed on silent wheels. I keep looking over my shoulder—

Christ, I've been in the woods too long.

I realize I'm frozen in the middle of some silver concourse, head full of echoes and shivering from the air-con. Don't even see a bar. I take a deep breath and go looking for the subway.

The ride to the city isn't long. The car crowded with colors— a Chagall painting of limbs and suitcases and shirts. The silence is frightening: even the train just whispers as it rushes through the tunnels, and I can almost hear the sea pounding over our heads.

I've got to collect myself. Get a plan.

The first thing will be to find Chun Song. That should be the easy part. Getting in front of him: much harder. Got to lie low until I get the lay of the land—hopefully just a couple days. Find some way to make the approach—as a businessman, investor maybe. I still have a few favors left in Bangkok, I could get them to fake a paper trail for me—

Then what?

Depends on what I'm going to find.

A nameless flophouse in a nameless part of town. The cheapest thing I could get, and still far too much, but it's close to where I need to be. This city unsettles me. Cambodia was crowded, but never like this, this endless rush of bodies. Got to walk more, get the rhythm of the place.

Even going to the corner for newspapers is a scrimmage, and I'm aching for a fix the whole time. I can smell the drugs all around me, rolling in waves off the men on the curbs and the sullen barkeeps: uppers and downers and pot and glistening white powders—

Focus.

Back to the lobby, if you can call it that: red light and cheap tourism posters, and a hotel clerk dutifully reading the headlines off the pile of Chinese papers I've brought him. Fighting with the mainland over the Internet, energy policy, local crime—

That's it, I say, give me the metro section. He blinks.

"The city. Business, crime, anything."

He shakes his head, keeps reading. SARS, Christ, and more SARS. Move on. Filipino maid on trial for killing her employer. No. Some foreign mother of three bashes in her husband's skull. Dark stories, but not mine. Then:

"Gangster death house was torture den."

What the hell is that?

Oh, yes, a big criminal, he ran brothels, found dead in his bath, arms and legs slashed open. Suicide? Or not. "Investigating all angles." Now some anonymous police source talking about a room in the house full of shackles, cages, torture implements. Tabloid bullshit? Maybe. But my fingers are itching even before he says the name:

"Chun Song was . . . not arrested, known for being power force in Wan Chai prostitution set . . ."

Chun Song *was*. Now he's a fucking Jackson Pollock.

WILL

November 21

Nineteen days I've been in Hong Kong, and every one of them felt like a year.

When I saw Chun Song was gone, I knew I'd need more time. Found an even grimmer place to stay than the first hotel. After that I found a squat. Hunkered down in the crappiest part of town I could find, living off noodles from street stands, and still I've burned through all my cash—all I can spare if I plan on leaving.

But I know where she is.

I'm in the diner, with Dany, trying to wait. My plate of dumplings cost about thirty bucks but I can't bring myself to eat it. Poke at it with a chopstick. Light another cigarette, order more coffee, watch the lights in the window.

"Boss."

Everything here glows, lit from all sides. It's so bright, it makes the rest of the world seem dim.

"Boss."

I look up.

Dany taps the table with one elaborately painted nail. "Almost time." That low, smoky, Judy Garland voice. "You sure you okay, boss?"

"Fine."

"You gonna eat that?"

"No."

I found Dany outside my second hotel, working in ten-minute increments. We haggled a bit and fixed a salary. She's trying to pay for her operations and hates getting on her knees in alleys, so she gouged me. But she's cute as a button, and can talk the balls off a donkey. She opens doors I need opened. I don't like taking her with me tonight—tried paying her off, but she wouldn't have it. She wants in on the big rescue.

I check the clock again: twenty more minutes.

Song's penthouse was in a building in the financial district, a splinter of glass so tall it makes your eyes hurt. And right across Victoria Harbour: Wan Chai. The red lights always on. I knew June was there, somewhere: lost and invisible in the growling belly of the world.

We've spent two weeks prowling every brothel, strip joint, and street corner. I check the front, Dany the back. I scope out places she won't dare go, she waltzes into ones I can't afford to set foot in. Hasn't been hard to avoid notice—Song's death has introduced a type of chaos into the air. Everyone is on edge, looking for their next paycheck or their next angle. There are so many scouts and spies and independent operators trying to move in, we just vanish into the crowd.

There were days and days of this: phony appointments and bogus tourism and US dollars stuffed in G-strings or hungry pockets, but now we've found her—or think we have—in a highly exclusive hotel for men with a taste for blood and tears. By appointment only: I had to get myself recommended by another client. Dany managed that for me. I was impressed by her stamina. My Bangkok friend worked the background check, and I stiffed him—another city I can't go back to, unless I come into a surprise inheritance.

But I have an appointment. Tonight. It's not much of a plan: Go in, get her, get out. Try not to get seen by the bouncers. If she still has her fake passport, I can bring her back. More likely Song had it hidden somewhere. I won't be able to take her out of the country, but I can get her to the consulate. Fortunately it's right next to the red-light district. I get her there, she'll be safe.

But now it comes to it, and I'm sitting in this stinking noodle shop with cold hands playing piano on my spine. Will she be scared, sobered by what she found in the dark? Will I find her drugged out, ruined, and in pain? Or will she still be looking?

It comes to the same thing: me and her, and a door.

Her photos are spread out in front of me, innocuous on the Formica tabletop. You hardly even see them. She's taken the void inside her and made it real in black and white. Pictures without story: That's the truth. We deceive ourselves with words. Reality is these images, out of focus and unconnected.

I thought learning her trick would help me understand her. Now I want to forget it. If I get her out, maybe I can.

I think of Gabriel: *"Just look over your shoulder."*

I think of Two: *"I couldn't just walk away."*

I think of Channi, the way she held my hand that day in the park.

Put the photos back in their envelope, tape it shut. Stub out my cigarette. No more delays. "Let's go."

We step out into the street.

Hong Kong—so tall it makes my head spin. I spend my days looking at the concrete, afraid to glance up. Dany takes my hand, leans against me like we're on a romantic stroll rather than a march to the scaffold. I try to pretend.

We walk that way to the end of the line.

———————

The hotel is a squat, soot-stained monolith from the eighties. Access is through a bar off an underground mezzanine, and the bar is something out of a nightmare—if your nightmares are directed by the local youth group and involve a lot of Karo syrup. Walls painted like dungeon stone, women chained up dripping fake blood. Women in cages. Women tied up on the floor acting as tables while guys in suits eat off them. Up front, a couple in pleather and rayon doing scenes from *Venus in Furs,* while rapt peepers jizz their pants. Gomorrah on the cheap, packed with folks who don't know the real thing is just behind the curtain.

Here and there, I see guys among the suits who clearly aren't here for jollies. Cropped hair and bulging jackets. They don't have the triad look, they're just security, but tougher than I'd like. Note to self: don't try to walk out the front. I think of Dany, hanging out in the side alley, ready to make a distraction if I take too long—push the thought away. She can handle herself. Probably make a grand while she's waiting.

I try to look like I'm enjoying the scenery as a girl in a chain-mail bra and steel chastity belt comes up to me and says something in Chinese.

I smile at her. "I have an appointment, love." Give her the password.

She answers with a bow and a big smile. "Straight to back door, sir. All the way to back and take elevator to number fourteen. It will be door on the left. Number four door, on left."

———————————

The elevator is small, and it rattles. Silence in the hall upstairs. Mirrored walls stained with handprints, red carpet frayed in the center.

I try not to count the doors: just makes me think of what's behind. Mine is 1482. I stand outside a minute, breathing hard, with the things I've done to get here crowding my head—

Don't act suspicious. Don't think. Go.

I open the door and there she is.

Immediately I realize what a terrible idea this was, but it's about a hundred thousand years too late.

The door clicks shut behind me.

The room is large and dark: the dimness hides the squalor and the stains. Across from me, a huge picture window overlooks the harbor. Walls covered in eggshell foam, plastic-wrapped mattresses on the floor. A tiny, curtained closet. Wide benches against one wall, their tops covered in black vinyl padding. Opposite, a wooden cross, a square wooden chair that makes me think of executions. Leather restraints hang from a board on the wall. Below that, whips. Then knives.

In the center, a low table, and in front of it a wide settee, old wood and red velvet cushions. She's sitting when I come in, staring out at the sea of lights. A thin robe of black-and-red silk, style hinting at a kimono. Her white-blond hair swept back with chopsticks. She turns to me and says something in Mandarin so perfect, I can almost believe I've made a mistake.

But I know her eyes. They are like the photographs that only she could take: utterly empty. She is different. Everything girlish has burned away, replaced by something hard and white and impassive.

"Ju-on." I use her real name for the first and last time. "It's me."

She cocks her head like a bird—like a snake—like anything but a human. I open the briefcase I've brought with me and take out the notebooks. I can't seem to make myself move any closer, so I set them on the floor. "These are yours."

She looks at them with something like curiosity. "Go back." A recorded voice over a long-distance line. "You've got the wrong girl."

"I don't think so."

She stands now, every movement sudden as a knife thrust. "She's gone. It took me seventeen years to get rid of her, but I did it."

I'm struggling to breathe—to quell the fear that's rising around me, like the warm water of the Gulf in my dreams. "Do you remember what you wrote, the night you met me? You said you wanted someone to protect you. I can help. I don't care what you've done. I'll get you out—anywhere you want to go—but you have to trust me and come now." I'm supposed to take her arm, but I can't make my hand move: like trying to pick up a spider.

She looks me up and down, those black eyes burrowing through clothes and skin. "Where's your white hat?"

"It made my head itch."

She laughs, and the sound makes me want to claw my eyes out. "Karasu sent you."

"I don't work for her."

"No. You don't. And it's cost you." She's still smiling as she lets her robe fall open. "I'm the one you really want. You think I'm lost, but you're wrong. You're the one who's lost. You're in pain. I can make it stop." She takes another step forward. "That's why they come to me. The ones too damaged to go on. The ones for whom the only pleasure left is to be hurt. To be devoured. I give them what they need."

I'm backing away, but it's like the whole room shifts and suddenly she's right in front of me, her hands on my chest. They're cold as ice, and for a second I'm covered with ants, flies, crawling centipedes, I feel them writhing up into my hair and down my collar. Pull away, slapping frantically at my skin—

There's nothing there. No bugs, just a pale girl with dead eyes.

"Tell me what happened to you," she says.

For some reason, I tell her. It's so simple. The end of my life in fifty words.

"In Kabul, in the war, I met a girl. She loved me. I told her I was going to get her out, that we would get married. I didn't understand— I was careless. Her family found out and they murdered her, right in the street. I couldn't stop it, I . . . I took a photo of her lying there, and they wanted to give me a fucking prize."

"So you ran." She smiles like it's the sweetest thing she's ever heard. "Ran until you almost forgot."

I'm shaking all over like I'm sixteen hours off the junk, sweat pouring down my collar. Any second my knees are going to buckle. Got to speak, I can't stay here much longer.

"You saw your mother die."

She laughs. "I killed her. She was going to take me away; he found out. He put the knife in her, but I was watching at the door and ran in. And when I grabbed it, it pierced her heart and killed her."

She recites it like a fairy tale—which is what it is, really. A grown man's gambit for a little girl's silence: convince her it's her fault. *"If anyone finds out, they'll come for you."* So she hides what happened in the back of her mind and tells everyone her story about the night Mommy left—tells it until she believes it herself.

Almost believes it: something deep inside refuses to forget.

"Have you ever touched a dead body? Held it in your arms? It's so still it shocks you." I blink and she's in front of me again, inches away, looking up into my eyes. "I still feel it. Every second. I still smell her perfume, and her blood. There is a piece of death inside me, like a seed. I hid it. Until I went to *that place,* and it began to grow."

She touches my chest and now there are no visitations, just a hand cold as iron. She's opening the buttons on my shirt, but I'm looking past her, at the table.

On it, photographs. Her photographs. One I recognize: a flat, gray body of water, dark specks that might be trees in the distance. It's not the same as the one that led me there, not quite: the angle is slightly different, the light another shade of nothing. But it's the same place.

Next to it, a set of wavy lines: a curl of blond hair.

Now, with her icy fingers tracing patterns on my skin, I finally understand. She is a photographer the way the Enigma operators were writers. That day in the mangroves, I broke her code and never knew it.

Those aren't pictures in my pocket: they're trophies.

"How many?" I croak.

She smiles her empty smile. "Stay," she whispers. "Stay."

"Come back. I can get you help." But I know there's no help for this. "You can still go home." There is no home. There is no one to bring back.

I am going to die in this room.

She presses up to me, close, and her robe falls to the floor. She's not naked like a person but like a doll, hard and brittle as porcelain. She's so skinny, a collection of angles and planes.

Her right leg, from the ankle to the hip bone, is covered in scars—some razor thin, others bunched and white, patterned like tiger stripes. The side of the calf twisted by cut after cut into a shapeless mass of tissue. More scars on her belly, her chest. Two long slices nearly bisect her right nipple.

My mind recoils, but as I try to step away I feel my cock come alive, straining against my jeans—

They say you get an erection in the electric chair.

"Stay with me," she says again. Her teeth are sharp against my lips, her tongue small and hard as it pokes its way into my mouth. She tastes like oiled metal. Behind her, I see them all crowding in: Number Two and Gabriel, Charlie and the Aussie, Bunny, Lon, and the whole damned crew. They wouldn't miss this.

I want to run, but I find myself reaching for her, fingers scrabbling at smooth bone. She opens my pants, reaches inside, her cold lips holding mine like she's going to suck all the air out. And I want her, the way I've always wanted her—to disappear inside her, to vanish in her depths. The other dead cheer me on.

June's nails bite my shoulder, draw blood. I'm going numb.

And I hear a voice in my head: Channi's voice, bright and yellow, like the sun coming up in this dark room. *"I am not a dream,"* she says.

Hard white lips on mine. Blood in my mouth.

"I'm not a dream."

Her bare foot, stamping on sun-stained boards. Strange flowers bloom around me, and the ghosts vanish.

"I am real."

I put my arms around June. Find her shoulder, spin and toss her across the room. She weighs nothing.

She comes up screaming, all teeth and nails, and she's on me in a flash. No time for anything fancy, I grab her hands as they reach for my face, and gasp as I'm shoved back against the wall. Pro wrestlers aren't strong like this. Her nails the color of old ivory, aiming at my eyes. The world spins, something cracks against my head—

I'm on the floor, arms up, still trying to hold her off, but those claws are inches away—

From nowhere, I start to laugh, and she recoils like I've slapped her. Then her hand breaks free and she tears my cheek open. The hand goes up again, I can't stop it, she's going to kill me—and then the door bursts open, a pair of crew-cut guards gaping in confusion. Guns drawn, but clearly not prepared for this.

June drops me and goes for them. The first one fires, but I guess he misses, and then she's ripped the gun from his hands and spread his brains across the fan light. The second tries to turn, and she puts a half dozen bullets through his chest. He hits the floor with a wet squelch.

More guards rushing in—the backup station. They come in shooting, and she cuts them down, one by one. Ignore the pain ripping through me as I crawl across the blood-splattered floor. June drops the last one and turns to me. I come up with a fallen guard's gun. She fires.

I die.

I don't die: she's empty.

"Drop it."

The look on her face is something I can't describe—it's so far from anything human. She gives a shriek like razors on slate, like metal torn until it breaks. Then she turns and hurls herself at the window.

She should hit the floor with a concussion, but the plate glass shatters like she's made of steel—maybe it got nicked in the firefight?—and then I'm up, staggering to my feet and across the room, and she's a white shape vanishing down into the lights.

It's so bright down there.

I can't see.

Alarms going off all around me. Footsteps in the hall. Get behind the couch, brace my arm, aim. A last guard runs in, gun out, and I drop him, three shots to body mass, like they say. He coughs some blood, then dies.

My dream was wrong: it's different when you do it yourself.

I head for the fire exit.

———————

So here I am: in a taxi, with the lights of the city vanishing behind me.

Still alive. Still lost.

Dany wasn't waiting in the alley. Maybe she met a rich john and ran off. I don't want to think about the other possibilities. I walked around the front of the building, trying to be casual. Dropped the gun in the alley as I turned onto the main street, eyes watching for the flashing lights, the spattered blood and shattered glass where a body had fallen thirteen stories.

I didn't see anything. Just Hong Kong. Ten million people pressed together, breathing in sync. I kept moving. Got a SARS mask to cover my shredded face. Hailed a cab. Headed for the sky.

It's hard to say I haven't fucked up everything I possibly could. Steve. Vy. Gus. Dany. Gabriel, and Number Two, and Charlie and Phann and Lon and June . . . And Fatima, dear Fatima, always with me. If I live a thousand years, I could never be sorry enough.

Now it's time to disappear. Got a few dollars left in my pocket. There are still dark places in the world. Some South Seas island, maybe: cannibal shamans, kava and ganja and long, white beaches. I can find a way to get by. To forget. It's what I'm best at.

I'm not going.

I've spent my whole life running from the messes I've made. It's time to stop. Maybe I can't fix anything—but I'm tired of it. Cambodia has been through worse than any of us and has endured. We can endure.

And I miss her. I imagine walking her streets again, feeling her all around me: living, changing, dying—still living.

One more airport road. One more trip across the border between earth and sky. And then the wet tarmac, the sullen palms in the distance . . .

Home: The only one I've ever really known. The place that saved me, when by all rights I should have died. Somewhere back there, Channi is wiping down her bar. Laying out the peanuts. Thinking about what she'll do now, when life has offered her so many lies and disappointments. Still waiting for something.

If I'm careful, and lucky, maybe I can convince her it's me.

I have a legion of ghosts behind me, and they can never be appeased; but I will try to show them love and pray that they forgive.

ACKNOWLEDGMENTS

This book is a work of fiction that attempts to capture what it felt like to be an American working in Phnom Penh in late 2003, but it draws inspiration from historical events that were all too real. Hun Sen's Cambodian People's Party did, in fact, fail to secure a two-thirds majority in Parliament in the summer elections, resulting in a year-long standoff with the opposition parties. There really were a number of large drug busts during this period, including one that implicated high-ranking army officials, although the real-life details differ significantly from those described here, and the book's explanation of the machinations behind the drug trade is pure invention. There was also a wave of (presumably) political killings, including that of Ta Prohm radio journalist Chuor Chetharith, who was gunned down outside his office on October 18, 2003. His murder remains unsolved.

The confluence of these events became the skeleton of my fiction, and I dreamed up a rather fantastical backstory to tie them together. In the process, I changed much, and the people and incidents that feature in that story are all products of my imagination, save the few exceptions noted here. Cambodia really has only two English-language newspapers, the *Cambodia Daily* and the *Phnom Penh Post*, which are mentioned briefly; Gus Franco's paper, and the questionable characters who work there, are inventions created to drive along the plot. Cambodian Prime Minister Hun Sen and Chief of Police Hok Lundy are real people, but I have used them in a fictitious way and taken many liberties.

Kevin Doyle and Al Rockoff, who appear briefly in these pages, are also real people and inspiring journalists, and I owe them a debt for what little I understand of Cambodia, along with many others including Matt Reed, William Shaw, Dan Ten Kate, Phann Ana, Van Roen, and Nhem Chea Bunly. Many years after the fact, Iain Philip helped refresh my memory on the details of life in Phnom Penh and Battambang. All the errors and alterations of fact are mine, not theirs.

I am still amazed at the good fortune that led me to my extraordinary agent Noah Ballard, who has read this book nearly as many times as I have, and whose hard work, patience, and great instincts have shaped it into what it is today. John Glynn at Scribner has been a wonderful editor and an endless source of enthusiasm and encouragement.

I am also deeply grateful to the many friends who suffered through my early drafts with grace and kindness. James Luckard, Stewart Schulman, and Hugh Ryan gave close readings and great advice. Pamela Ball, Joy Harris, and Meredith Kaffel offered invaluable notes and guidance when this book was in its infancy. Russ Agdern, Nathan Baca, Bruce Boehrer, Sawyer Cade, Rebecca Dupree, Jibril Hambel, Hisham Kassim, Kevin McCloat, Michael Niederman, Shari Perkins, and Lavie Tidhar all lent me their eyes for a while. Geraldine Chatelard helped me with the French, and Jon Land honed my pitch. To all of them, I owe thanks.

This novel would not exist without the love and support of my partner, Kate Washington, who steered me through years of depression and frustration, and never stopped believing in happy endings.